Belshangles

Belshangles

A NOVEL

Susan Altstatt

2015 · Fithian Press
McKinleyville, California

Printed in the United States of America

Published by Fithian Press
A division of Daniel and Daniel, Publishers, Inc.
Post Office Box 2790
McKinleyville, CA 95519
www.danielpublishing.com

Distributed by SCB Distributors (800) 729-6423

LIBRARY OF CONGRESS CATALOGING-IN-PUBLICATION DATA
Altstatt, Susan.
Belshangles : a novel / by Susan Altstatt.
pages cm
ISBN 978-1-56474-578-1 (pbk. : alk. paper)
1. Teenage girls—Fiction. 2. Rock musicians—Fiction. 3. Kidnapping—Fiction.
I. Title.
PS3601.L8585B47 2015
813'.6—dc23
2015012425

To Bill Graham—

thanks for all the music

Belshangles

Chapter 1

HE THAT DWELLETH in the secret place of the Most High...
["She" in my case, but I never got my kicks re-sexing language]...

Skye says, "Can I put my money in with your money?"

...Shall abide under the shadow of the Almighty;
I will say of the Lord, He is my refuge and my fortress:
My God, in Him will I....

My money. Her money in with my money. Sure.

"Andy?"

"Skye."

"What's the matter?

"We gotta turn around."

"Don't tell me! You forgot your money! I hope to God you got the tickets. Have you got the tickets?"

"Relax. They're in my jacket."

"Where's your jacket? You're talking about my fucking ticket as well as yours! Can you imagine how embarrassing it'd be to get up at two A.M. and drive to Oakland, and wait all day for a place at that concert, and be all the way up to the gates, and *you* have forgot the fucking tickets?"

"My jacket's at home on my bed. Turn around!"

Mama's standing in the front hall, jacket in hand.

"Will you please go back to bed? Skye had to have a book." Maybe she hasn't checked the pockets. Run to my room, grab the first books I see: Armistead Maupin, *Tales of the City*. Carlos Castaneda, *Tales of Power*. Mama's still there, with jacket, a dark shape in the hall. *"All right! I'll take it* if it makes you happy!" Then maybe she did look in the pockets. One never knows. Wonderful thing, diplomacy.

"Also," she says distinctly, "your lunch." (Sounds worried she might have to spell it for me, l-u-n-c-h.)

"I don't want sandwiches. We'll buy food."

"You'll spend your last penny on T-shirts and pins."

"Come on, don't be so—"

"Accurate?"

"Obnoxious."

"Have you got it all?"

"Yes."

"Tickets? Money? Sunscreen? Don't just say 'Yes.' If you haven't got it you'll come home cooked. How many more do you have to pick up?"

None. But it wouldn't do to tell her. Then she'd *know* it wasn't safe.

"Well, be good. Or careful. Whichever comes first."

Escaping down the driveway, now: "Yes!"

"Enjoy yourself. Don't faint when you see him."

"Is she always like that?" Skye cranks the engine.

"Yes."

"Thank God nobody woke up at my house."

Skye's mother's VW bus is notably the same as my mother's VW bus, only rattier, and bright orange. Skye's stepdad is this fringy dude named Noah Avery. He makes art objects out of redwood burls. Skye Milligan is not that priceless person of all people I would have chosen to be a secret-sharer. But she's old enough to drive.

Together in the old VW bus we run the gauntlet of the Stanford campus (for the second time) and fall out into business Palo Alto, unreal at this hour as a toy town on a model railroad. Long vistas of well-lighted expressway, signals all green as far as the eye can see. Far ahead, two low red dots. Somebody's taillights, freeway bound.

> *...Surely He will deliver thee from the snare of the fowler,*
> *and from the noisome pestilence.*
> *He shall cover thee with his feathers,*
> *and under his wings thou shalt trust....*

Mama hooked me on Psalm 90 years ago. I'd started memorizing stuff to keep me company; I was maybe eleven. When you don't much want to deal with other people, a well-stocked memory can be the most inaccessibly private refuge-fortress that there is.

> *...Thou shalt not be afraid for the terror by night;*
> *nor for the arrow that flieth by day;*
> *Nor for the business that goeth about in the dark,*
> *of invasion or the noonday devil....*

She said when she was eleven, they still had prayer in the schools. At homeroom once a day they'd read a psalm out loud. Most kids learned which was the shortest (three lines), and that class heard an awful lot of Psalm 133. But Mama had a thing for Psalm 90. When her turn came, she read it every time. It didn't make her popular.

Always action on the freeway, even at this hour. Noise at its lowest now, fumes at the mildest. People sleeping in the grim apartments just beyond the frontage. The diesel rattle of a semi all the louder for the half-hush around it. Moving North on 101. From here, Dumbarton Bridge approach swerves east through vacant lots and broken glass, black poverty, shut-down industry—to mudflats smelling wild as the sea—open water.

They're building a new bridge out on the left, alongside the funky old one. Tall concrete piers buck the tide, nothing but cormorants perched on their heads. Beyond those, the setting moon lays a royal road of silver up San Francisco Bay.

Somewhere, at the end of that, Tommi Rhymer *is*, not just in my imagination, but for 3D real in some luxury hotel. Real groupies find out where the stars stay. They know when their planes touch down at the airport. Hormone-detecting antennae, maybe, like big moths.

Skye says "Okay, no more brain-drain for a while. Put on the music."

Nothing in Avery's van, you understand, so upscale as a tape deck, just Skye's old radio–tape recorder on the floor: the one with the twisted-off antenna and the buttons you punch five times before they work. I dug in her bag under toll lights at the far end of the bridge, and located the *Sundog* tape: Percussion, finger-bells, the spooky hash-head Arab opening of "The Favorite."

"Come *on*, bitch, *anything* but that."

"This is the stuff they'll do in the concert."

"I *mean*: do we have to *soak* in it the whole day too?"

"Sure. I want to appreciate the differences."

"And how long have you had the fucking album?" she said; "Only six months already. I want *Quadrophenia*."

I love the Who, but a little of good old Roger Daltrey screaming "I wanta drown!" goes a very long way with me.

"Who's driving, huh?" She had a point.

I compromised, and found the side with "Night Train," "Louie Louie," "Green Onions," all those neat old things. We electrified the night with "Louie Louie," all along the northbound Nimitz to the Oakland Coliseum. A forty-five minute run at three in the morning.

You are what you listen to.

My father has this wondrous sound gear, equipment racks full of it: real studio stuff, amps and speakers he designed himself and left with the wires and cables snaking out, a kind of space-age altar. It fills up one end of our living room. Raoul Falconer: professor, Stanford E.E. Department, and archetypal Silicon Valley Whiz. With his morning coffee, he switches on this FM classical station. They power up their day with early music, then go to renaissance and then baroque, and from Bach to Beethoven—Papa goes to the Department, leaving the FM on.

By ten o'clock it's Wagner, and Mama turns it off.

Mary Frances Falconer, née Halloran: sometime writer-historian. Mama has a double Ph.D.: History and English. Her Dis was titled "Soothsaying and Inspiration in the Legendary Ballad Tradition of the British Isles." I got sung to sleep with "Lord Randall," "Minorie," "Sir Patrick Spens," "Fair Eleanor": just a wonderland of sex, violence, and religion: ghosties and ghoulies and long-legged beasties and things that go bump in the night. Mama has her tape library: strange old people singing stranger older poetry in reedy backcountry voices. The FM station doesn't do it for her. She says, "I like the way the air sounds better."

So Papa walks in at night, directly to the switch, and flip, it's Berlioz. The centuries go by on rewind, Mozart to Monteverdi to Palestrina to Josquin des Prez.

If Papa goes to bed first, Mama kills the music with the house lights. If Mama goes to bed first, and I wake at two am., the house is lit up like a ship at sea, and the FM's on white noise; the station quit at midnight. I switch it all off.

Miranda Dolores Falconer: commonly known as Andy.

Mama's bards and soothsayers. Papa's electronics and his Monteverdi, and the Latin psalms we chanted at Saint Ann's every Sunday. Those were the course-markers, judges, turn-marshals, and start-finish of my musical education.

Saint Ann's is the Catholic Chapel to Stanford. It has these three warm-fuzzy-radical folk-guitar Masses each Sunday, *and* one Gregorian-Chant High Mass in Latin, which I've heard every Sunday (when I wasn't at a track meet or in the mountains) since the week I was born. Latin psalms as muscular as snakes, that can grab you by the heart and squeeze you helpless, and swallow you down beyond recall. Chant talks ecstasy, the real old stuff.

First thing I learned at Saint Ann's. Grownups are scared of each other. Not just kids of grownups and grownups of kids, everybody knows that. But those priests were scared stiff. Their whole congregation was hard-ass Stanford Profs and snotty intellectual grad students, and they had to face 'em, with like an A.A. in communications from the local seminary. And the same poor guy would have to preach at all the masses. No priest likes to get lynched, by the right wing or the left, so the stuff they preached was low-fiber content. That's the second thing: what people preach at you is apt to be, as Papa says, "pious garble." It's what they sing that counts.

I learned to sing chant.

My sister Isabel doesn't sing anything. She says she has no voice. (Not exactly true, she just embarrasses easy.) But she listens up a storm. In about fifth grade, she had a really young teacher that she loved a lot. This chick had long, long hair with a blue stripe in it, and she let kids bring their own records and play them during study time.

Boy, what a chance to be disruptive. I know some stuff they wouldn't let me put on twice at study time I guarantee. But Isabel was just faked out. Far as she knew, kids didn't *have* records. *Fathers* had records. Very first girl brought in the Beach Boys—*Surfin' USA*. Izzy thought it was some joke.

She learned, though.

At that time lots of girls had Shaun Cassidy junk and guys were into Kiss. But better things existed. After like a month of rock-by-osmosis, Izzy took her baby-sitting money and the bus to Tower Records, and brought back *Hooligans*, that two-LP retrospective of the Who. When Papa came home, she had it on his turntable, super loud. ("This recording to be played at maximum volume," it says on album jackets, after all.) He walked straight in the door and shouted, *"Turn off that trash!"* You could barely hear him.

"That's not trash!" Izzy screamed back, *"It's the Who!"*

"Who?" He bellowed, and the battle was on.

Nobody kno-ows what it's like—
To be the Bad Man—
To be the Sad Man,
Behind blue eyes—

It was the first rock music I ever really heard. I loved it, every note and every word. It was like the chant somehow, music with teeth. Music that grabs. Rock talks ecstasy: little different *type* maybe, but I understood the language.

Isabel is a lot like Papa in some ways. She kept on buying albums and playing with his gear. After a run of blown-up speakers and ground-down diamond styluses, eventually they declared a truce. He bought her a cassette recorder. She could play her stuff on his equipment once (volume down) to tape it. After that, she was to play her tapes on her own gear in her own room. With the door shut. And she did.

But my room shares a wall with hers.

Isabel and I are a lot unlike in most ways. She never quite commits herself, for fear it won't be fun. I was born a zealot one-track True Believer.

Izzy took the longest time even to learn there is a no man's land between new wave and heavy metal, or which side she belonged on. She bought the weirdest ill-assorted things, listened fervently for two whole weeks, then threw them out or traded them to friends.

At last, like water, she found her own level—English Mod and Ska. The English Beat. The Specials. The Jam. Fun-Boy Three. On and on, with a short detour for radical chic (The Clash), into Madness and Bad Manners. I went quite another route. Among her earlier buys was the Rolling Stones, *Made in the Shade*. When she threw that out—(ditto the Mick-and-Keith posters)—I took them in. I asked for a tape recorder. I was ten.

Papa said "I just bought you one."

"That was Isabel. A year-and-a-half ago."

"Is it broken already?"

"No. It's in her room."

"So?"

"I don't like the music she likes."

"Neither do I," he said, and walked away.

I went to a flea market with Mama, and found a fifty-cent tape recorder in a basket full of junk. "Record" was wasted, but it played back fine. And I played *Made in the Shade*. I played it until Izzy screamed and swore, and her friends all laughed and pointed. She stole it several times. I found her hiding places and got it back. She was not very inventive.

If I could dip
My pen in my heart—
Suicide right on the sta-a-age—
Would it satisfy ya? Would it slide on by ya?
Or would ya think the boy's stra-a-ange?
I know
It's only rock and roll,
But I like it, like it, yes I do!

Isabel bought cassettes in packages of four; I could usually liberate one and not get caught. I got better thrift shop sound gear. Thing I learned early about Papa—he gets no kicks out of helping the helpless. But if he sees you crawling around your bedroom floor with his soldering iron and a bunch of wires trying to set up your own sound system, he's apt to get all interested and crawl around it with you. If for no more than to rescue his tools.

And, borrowing the records of my friends, Izzy's friends, their parents, and their parents' friends, I taped the entire American catalog of the Rolling Stones. Nice people gave me their old records. I had Stones posters and T-shirts and pins. I learned about used-record shops. I had seventeen copies of *High Tide and Green Grass* once. I traded off for an original-cover *Satanic Majesties* and my very first bootleg, *Live-R-Than-You'll-Ever-Be*. That put me into bootlegs. When the action went beyond my price-and-transportation range, I bought an illustrated paperback discography of the Who, and started over.

Venturing out from under my Stones, I slithered happily through the 'sixties (where I was born), into the 'seventies (where I grew up unawares), by way of the 'Oo and Ziggy Stardust. Bowie discographies, posters, and pins.

"Born historian," was what Papa said.

I acted like I didn't hear him.

It was the end of childhood, but I didn't know. My life was an unsinkable ship, built up of watertight compartments. Very little leaked from one to another. September to June was school. No problem. I aced elementary school. When kids voted each other "Class This" or "Class That" at the end of sixth grade, I got "Class Apple-Polisher" and a jumbo can of wax.

September to December and February through July was Track Club. Mama collected Izzy and me from school four days a week and whisked us off to Cupertino. Practices went till dark. Weekends were for track meets, all over Northern California. None of my track friends went to my school. None of my school friends went to track meets. It was like religion. I assumed they wouldn't understand, and didn't talk about it.

Each season, near the end of school, was Northern Pacific Association Championships. And if I'd run as planned, after the P.A.'s was State Meet; a flight to L.A. or Orange County maybe. If after that I was still on top, the Nationals. Summer was for Y-Camp and the mountains. Y-Camp was kickback, let-it-all-hang-out peer-group mayhem. None of my track friends went to Y-Camp. Mountains was for family, and a Sierra cabin inherited from my grandparents.

So imagine July 1981. After the Nationals. (Fourth place, Youth 3000 meters.) After Y-Camp. (Girls' Yosemite Bike-Hike;

strangely unsatisfying, though I hadn't figured why.) It wasn't nearly as much fun. The girls were timid and lazy. All they wanted to do was lie around camp and gossip. Some of them had little breasts.

If the truth were known, so did I. The truth wasn't known much. My hair was short, my legs were long. When I asked for a bathroom key at gas stations, I got the guys' as often as the girls'. Secretly, that hurt a bit. Even if I wore earrings, I got the guys' key.

A lazy, muggy summer evening.

I'd gone with a friend to Tower Records. I meant to buy the Who's *Meaty, Beaty, Big and Bouncy* (which I had on tape already) just for the cover: front—the band sitting on some grubby tenement steps and looking up at themselves as kids leaning out of the windows; back—the band as skinny kids sitting on the same steps, looking up at the windows and themselves grown.

My friend headed for the posters. Together we flipped the big movable racks where grimacing metalheads leered and capered, smarmy new romantics simpered. There were the Stones on tour. There was David Bowie in his Pierrot suit. Last of all, two men. I knew who they were, if I hadn't bought their music: Tommi Rhymer and Harlan Parr of Belshangles.

They had hair enough between them for a metals band, yet that was not the effect at all. Harlan wore evening dress, black tie and tails. He was seated in a chair: small, precise, arrogantly perfect, the Romantic Hero as Musician to the very life. You could gaze at him for ages before it registered: the instrument across his lap wasn't a cello or the like, but a black metalflake Stratocaster.

Leaning out from behind him was the naked apparition of a fevered dream. Oh, his crotch was decent behind Harlan's evening jacket, but you knew quite well that all he wore was a flame-job of body paint and the gold sequins on his eyelids. His hair was the fiery regalia of some mythical tribe. Tommi Rhymer.

What got me was the still white face under the blazing hair

and sequined lids. He didn't show his teeth or wall his eyes after the mode the metalheads consider sexy. His eyes were set too wide for comfort, his mouth was thin and mobile, also a touch too wide. He had a high-bridged beaky nose, and cheekbones to make a *Vogue* model weep.

I actually made it to where the Who albums lived, and found *Meaty, Beaty, Big and Bouncy*, queasily aware of a sudden shift in my priorities. Back to the posters.

It was that look of quizzical intelligence in his wide pale eyes; like he knew something huge about me, I just hadn't noticed yet.

And, standing there, in Tower Posters at eight o'clock on a summer evening, looking Tommi Rhymer in the eye, I noticed. They say that kiddies' "budding sexuality" is a kind of slow awakening. That is bullshit, let me tell you. Desire arrived with all its baggage, like an unexpected guest.

I came home with my poster, and robbed Mama's sewing of four glass-headed pins, all different colors. I unrolled Tommi and Harlan carefully, and fixed them to the wall opposite my bed, between the Apollo moon landing and a Greenpeace harp seal. Only then I noticed Mama standing behind me.

"The dark one," she said, "is a ventriloquist's doll the redhead keeps between him and the world. Or else the redhead is the dark one's thoughts. I almost asked 'Who are they?' But there's only one of them. Who is it?"

"Tommi and Harlan. English band, called Belshangles. You think I could have a *little privacy*?" I shut my door, and locked it in her face. I didn't want Mama's analysis, or even for her to like them. I was in process of discovering my own very personal Icons of Desire.

Belshangles. Tommi Rhymer (vocals, rhythm guitar, violin, etc. etc.), Harlan Parr (guitar, vocals), Nick Cavanaugh (bass), Rollo McInery (drums). First LP album; called (what else?) *Belshangles*. After the first U.S. tour, June '76, the American version wore the following (from a clueless but admiring East-Coast critic) on its backside:

Thought content? Very little. (sic) Social relevance? None at all. (sic, sic, sic) What Belshangles has going for it is sheer insolent seduction set to an English Blues riff.

Tommi Rhymer should be licensed to kill. How does staid old England spawn these creatures? A talented song-writer musician, a very winning singer, and a dancer who defies description. And, stuck to his elbow like Peter Pan's shadow, is one Harlan Parr, a guitar of future-living-legend quality.

What comes on looking glitter-punque (? sic) bizarre, stays on to satisfy, like Jagger and Richards half as old and twice as pretty. If you can resist that combo, there is something wrong with you. All comparisons aside, Belshangles—and especially swivel-hipped scarlet-haired Tommi Rhymer—should be household words themselves before too long. Their New York audience ripped its seats out of the floor. Let's wish them a long, hot future.

Belshangles played San Francisco on that tour.

I was two years too young to realize they existed, four too young to care, and six too young to have been there, belly up against the stage at SF Civic Auditorium.

Born too late, that's all.

1977 LP album: *Retrofit*. Wonderful cover: a towering rack of amplifiers, and Tommi crammed lotus position into the center slot. Back cover: Harlan in a lab coat, holding an enormous screwdriver, a solemn owlish expression on his face as if he intended doing something perverse with it.

And the music was heaven. Oh, the blues may have been at the bottom of it somewhere, filtered through the head of a crazy north-country fiddler, and tricked out in all the whimsy a medieval jongleur could provide. Just this magic *stuff* they'd brewed while they were street musicians.

1978: *More Sore than Sorry*. A gold album.

3/1979: *Steel Tears and Silver Sympathy*. Another. By now they were a witty spangled island between the slough of disco and a rising sea of punk.

11/1979: *Portobello.* Platinum compilation. The cover: Tommi and Harlan in their gaudy rag-tag finery, playing and singing, strutting down the gutter of their old haunts on Portobello Road to the delight of a small crowd.

1981: *Holy War*—

And that's where I came in. Posters, photos, magazine interviews, discographies, T-shirts, and pins. The walls of my room became a viewing gallery of Tommi's face and Harlan's face as childhood mental scenery departed. My ribbons and medals went into a box. Astronauts and Greenpeace beasties migrated down the hall to J.J.'s room. (He was five.) The horse posters simply went away, the dump, Goodwill, I didn't care. Finally the visible section of the back wall of my closet inherited the Stones, David Bowie, and the Who.

Papa said, "I'm not surprised, somehow, at David Bowie going back to the closet, but *Keith Richards*?" I ignored him. Mama suggested I shift my favorites to the ceiling, so I could see them better from the bed. Grudgingly (I hadn't thought of it) I did.

That fall I started middle school, and took promptly, lingeringly sick: too sick to make cross-country practice. I'd always been as healthy as a hog. They tested me for mono; negative. Cross-country season happened without me.

Middle school P.E. was Mickey Mouse beyond endurance. I needed jazz-dance lessons just to keep in shape. Leotards. Leg warmers. Jazz shoes. Simply running a hell of a lot faster than anyone I knew no longer felt so glamorous. I hungered after Tommi's eloquence of body, Tommi's grace.

The whole of middle school was Mickey-Mouse beyond endurance. I'd never seen so many asshole teachers. Honors math was first to go; it crawled with grimly over motivated little geeks. Orchestra followed. Sacred music was all out of bounds and we weren't up to classical; we played a mishmash of movie themes and commercial jingles off TV, hideously out of tune. The director couldn't tell or didn't care. My bullshit tolerance threshold sank lower and lower. My apple-polishing skills were all dried up.

"They flunk her if she hasn't done the work," said Mama,

"not if she's home sick in her room." It's amazing how absent a kid can be, and still make it through middle school.

Spring came. I wasn't too sick to run. I fucking well wouldn't. Mama always *bragged* so to everyone in sight, about how age-group track was part of "a continuum *all* the way up to the Olympics, where a kid can go as *far* as possible in a perfectly adult discipline."

Bullshit. Growing up means learning you can get too old.

The adult world I was prepping for loomed putrid, graceless and unpromising. I wished I could turn and bolt back into childhood, like a horse into the burning barn.

I asked for guitar lessons. Electric bass, really. I could imagine I was graceful when I danced. My ears have no imagination. Electric bass was as close as I could come to Harlan's wizardry and still feel safe.

Papa saw a certain virtue in electric instruments, I believe: beginners can practice with the amp turned off. I practiced along with my Belshangles records, an earphone to the tape deck in one ear, an earphone to my bass stuck in the other, and Tommi gazed down on me from wall and ceiling with a hundred different looks of mischievous indulgence.

I did other things in my room, like read a lot. We've always had this weird enormous library in which I found subversive stuff. I OD'd on *Pilgrim's Progress* shortly, but the very start, where Christian flees his home and runs off down the road yelling, "Life! Life! Eternal life!"—

"Next three exits Oakland Coliseum? Andy! Which one do I go on??"

"The first one. Hegenberger. Turn here."

That was me: exiting the Freeway to Nowhere down a sweet side road I'd almost missed, yelling not "Life!" but "Beauty! Beauty! Beauty Incarnate!" And I wished—

"Here?"

"Here. *Turn off now!"*

"Turn off the fucking music!" (I scrabble on the floor. Ta, Roger, Pete, John and Keith.) "Come on, bitch, *navigate!"*

"Check this side first. See how long the line is."

Pass the near side of the Coliseum, a fortified hill inside its wide domain of parking lots and chain-link fence. I see kids out walking in the dark, arms full of blankets and coolers. So many birds adding themselves to the festive summer rookery of sleeping bags spread on the sidewalk. Police car lights play over the locked gates, the walkie-talkied guards, the hikers back and forth to gas stations and all-night coffee shops. Exactly like I knew it would be.

"You can't sleep on the street in Oakland. People deal drugs on the street in Oakland. People get raped on the street in Oakland!" Good old Papa.

"Not a chance," I said, "I'd just drag 'em under the nearest light, and let 'em get a good look at me."

That didn't make me loved.

"Okay, drive," I said. "The rear's our solitary hope."

Drive back around the stadium, overpass the RR tracks, the BART tracks, hang a big "U", and.... Silently, our headlights intruded on the BART parking lot, bushy, tree-lined, unlighted, and empty. Nothing in it but our own exhaust spilling across black asphalt, a dry-ice stage effect in taillight red.

From here a pedestrian underpass ducks into the station. We got our stuff together in silence. Indian bedspread. Tape recorder. Sandwiches, looking more acceptable already. Sack of tapes. Locked the car. I fantasize the insides of that station: neon lights, vending machines, a bathroom. I will feel very accomplished once inside that station, for, from its upper level where the BART tracks are, a pedestrian overpass leaps the railroad and the street in a single bound, over fences and parking lots, into the stadium itself, a narrow airy ribbon of concrete, magical as the Yellow Brick Road.

The underpass was blocked off roof to pavement with a shiny metal grill. Well, shit! You'd think they *wanted* people getting raped in their dumb parking lot.

"What now?"

Don't panic. What we do now, is crawl through the bushes, (nobody in 'em but us), out onto the street. And stroll north along the backside of the railroad fence through gritty Baja Oakland, ruinous as a war zone. Broken-up pavement. Boarded-up storefronts, spray paint on the walls. People deal drugs on the street here. No one in sight.

...A thousand shall fall at thy side, ten thousand at thy
right hand,
but it shall come not nigh thee;
Only with thine eyes shalt thou behold
and see the reward of the wicked—

Hole-in-the-wall cafes, iron grills on door and window. Paper drifting in the gutters. People get shot on the street here. No one in sight.

...For he hath given his angels charge over thee
to keep thee in all thy ways;
In their hands they shall bear thee up
lest thou dash thy foot against a stone....

Up ahead, a single un-bombed streetlight shows an intersection with an RR-Xing sign. We stroll faster and faster. Hard left. The chain link ends at last; the desolate pavement humps itself across the SP's gravel bed and wooden ties, and slides through the shadow of the BART tracks overhead. No trains, even.

I feel like jogging to keep warm. Skye feels like keeping up. So we do the Survivor's Shuffle, all the way back along the opposite sidewalk. Bleak. A broad divided street to cope with stadium runoff. Better lighted. Let's hear it for urban redevelopment. More chain link beyond that, boundary of vast eerie parking lots. No one in sight.

God. A car. The lights approach, slow, blind us, and turn into retreating taillights. Nobody opens doors to drag us in. Just ahead now is the overpass from the BART station. We abandon all show of jogging, begin to run, then thunder up zigzag metal stairs into the air. Whoa. Brought to a halt on the last step but one. There above, huddled and muffled against the cold, are two black dudes with an enormous radio. The smaller mumbles something. Skye puts her head on one side, which she thinks is irresistible: "You talking to *us*?"

After thought, he takes his mouth out of his muffler.

"Get back. Gates don't open till nine."

Talking to *us*.

"We'll wait."

"Off the stairs."

"We wanna be first in line!"

"Line's on the other side. Walk around."

"There'll be a line at this gate, too!"

"Get back. Gates don't open till nine."

Back down.

So why can't we sit on the overpass by the stadium gate? Not programmed to answer that. It's for sure a whole lot safer than being stuck down on the sleazy street! Not programmed to worry about that. Don't want us raped on their property, that's all. No police cars over here. Can't be *bothered* guarding *us*. They are here to see that we don't trash their stadium.

Another lonely car prowled by. When the taillights faded, we zipped across the street. The main BART station and the tracks were blocked off, floor to roof, with metal grills. There was a dirty dank tile lobby open to the street, and a dirty cold concrete lobby up above, at our end of the overpass. In between, dead escalators. A young guy was asleep on one, near the bottom. He didn't look like much.

"I'm gonna put down this stuff," said Skye. "I am tired of holding all this stuff."

She deployed her Indian bedspread in the middle of the lobby floor, and herself on top of it. Lie on floor and doze. I tried to do it with her.

Cold. *Damn* cold. Dirty. Dull, is the worst part.

I crawled up the unslept-on escalator, hands and feet, till my head came over the top. I could see the guards at the far side of the overpass. They waved. Just below the escalator rim, where the frozen metal steps began to flatten out, was as near as I was going to get. Dude man, if I get raped over here, it's gonna be where *you* have to watch!

Little lights burned in the escalator sides; the metal was warm around them. What a find. I put my back to one. Hey, this is liberated territory! Like the head of the line. I could see a clock on the wall below. Twenty-five to five. The minutes slouched along.

What I'm thinking: none of this exercise in night-crawling gets me really near to Tommi Rhymer. Nearer to the stage, for sure. Nearer to his show. But still your basic street-model consumer's thrill.

There is this wondrous man in Mountain View who holds vast used record sales out of his garage. I don't know what else he does; one is afraid to ask. He has really long hair, and a tuft of long furry chest-hair poking up from the neck of his T-shirt.

We started talking, about how people get to meet the stars. He eyed me in this speculative way. "Well," he said, "you gotta have something to offer. Like. I know this girl. Friend of mine. I got a copy of the first recording Bowie ever made. Real rarity. Sold it to her for two hundred dollars. You expect to spend money doing these things right.

"She took it 'round before the concert. If you're really up on things, see, you find out when they do their sound check. Big tours may do all that the day before. She took it 'round, and hung out at the gate. Showed it to the roadies. They were all laughing at the picture on the thing, how innocent he looked. She just hung out. Finally they said, 'He's gotta see this.'

"So they told her to come back next night, and they fixed her up with a pass. You know, there's all these levels and degrees of passes: there's the ordinary one, which puts you in the backstage audience; the next level gets you in the band-shack, then there's the *next* one, which takes you anywhere. They gave her one of those.

"After the concert she had about a thirty-minute talk with Bowie. He flirted a lot; autographed her record. There was this chick with him, who was really burned at the attention my friend got."

"Guess she thought she had the ultimate level pass herself."

He smiled a slow smile. "Yeah. Well, being pretty doesn't hurt. You shouldn't have much trouble."

"Come on, I'm fourteen years old."

"Depends on who you're talking about. Some of those guys, that might be a positive advantage."

"Tommi Rhymer?"

He chuckled. "You got any good looking boyfriends?"

"Rhymer's not gay!"

"Sure. I know what he says."

"The *S.F. Chronicle* had this 'Who Said What' quote just last week: they tried to get Belshangles to play some gay rights thing, and Tommi Rhymer said—"

"Uh-huh."

"—Tommi Rhymer said, 'I wear my buttons on the right side, and I don't believe in mixing sex with politics.'"

"Right. Well I've got only one real weirdo oddity from Belshangles. Looks like a regular copy of *Holy War*, but it's a Philippine bootleg. Funny enough, but that's not all. Inside, it isn't even vaguely what it says. It's got all the counterfeit *Holy War* labels, and inside, it's Chicago. Different band, for God-sake."

"I can't imagine why Tommi Rhymer'd want to see me holding that."

The used-record man shrugged knowingly. "Well, I got it. If you grow up and want it bad enough, you lemme know."

Still wouldn't work, I could've told him. "Growing up" means learning you can get too old.

· — ·

SUNRISE. Cars on the streets. You can see what color they are now. Cautiously, peer at the guards. They look as cold as I feel. Colder. Then at the sleeping guy on the down escalator. He will have one nasty shock when they turn the escalators on. Skye comes to and drags her bedspread up. The clock's fat hand already points to six and the long hand's nudging twelve. Activity increases. Cars pausing at the curb emit BART workers.

I ease my butt over the rim of my escalator, away from the warm, ready to jump: anyone coming up either stairs will be ahead of us. And there is a couple coming up the street. Up the near stairs, now. They are not BART workers. A leggy beanpole guy in a white suit. He has a white bowler hat, gold glasses, and a gold-headed cane. With him is what looks like a blue-eyed Rastafarian recruit to Sgt. Pepper's Lonely Hearts Club Band. Thomas Dolby and Boy George. Seriously. And Boy George is a chick. At least I think it is.

Thomas Dolby bows from the waist. "Good morning, ladies, my name's—"

Skye says "Thomas Dolby."

"Dimitri, actually, but you can call me Frank."

I see the white outfit was cut for a rounder man. It's taken in at every seam with massive safety pins. I say to the apparition in the Marine's dress jacket, the remains of a black merino skirt, and numerous shredding black lace petticoats, the jack-boots, black bowler, and dreadlocks, "Boy George, I presume."

It is a chick; it squeals in anguish. "*No!* No, *not* Boy George, not Culture Club at all, Kate Garner, Hayzi Fantayzee! Nobody knows. That is *so* exasperating."

Bullshit. I know how Hayzi Fantayzee looks, legs and more legs. Kate Garner wears itsy-bitsy costumes, hardly more than Tommi Rhymer. Whereas this chick is built, well, like Boy George.

"Be thankful. I could have said Cyndi Lauper."

She eyes me thoughtfully, from behind a half-inch mask of makeup. "Well," she says in this husky voice, "My name's Marcella," putting an obnoxious little lilt to the end, "Mar-cel-lah." She plumps down on the other side of Skye, and, fishing from a bottomless bag a rhinestone mirror, makeup brush, blue eye shadow and a tube of base, at once strikes up a conversation. "My makeup," she says, "looks like shit."

It is exactly 6:07. A clacketty roar, the first BART train of the day, invades the station. I stagger up, with Skye and the Indian bedspread, with the sandwiches and the beat-up tape deck, with

Thomas-Frank-Dimitri-Dolby and Boy-Marcella-Garner-George, and stake claim closer to the gates, on an overpass above a dry wash in the urban desert, cut wide and deep to channel sudden floods. Thirty people off the train are settling down behind us. 6:22. Seventy-five people. We are fifteen feet from the gates, and the black guards say, "Get back. Gates open at nine." For them, a losing battle.

Morning winds, damp and merciless off the bay, are scouring concrete and asphalt, skipping trash across the empty parking lots, the gravel and broken glass of the railroad right-of-way. All around the overpass blows a welter of want ads and sports pages from an *Oakland Tribune,* grimly plastering themselves against the suicide fences. I catch a section, spread its papery warmth on the chain link behind me. Another section wraps my knees.

"Old hobo's trick," Marcella says. "You know that?"

I know that. Time blows by in gusts and eddies.

Marcella Garner-George is going on to Skye; a regular motor-mouth, canny and invasive. Old Skye looks stoned and soaks it in. I think she's found a soul mate. Pretty soon she'll be showing her scar. "I've had open-heart surgery, *see?"* Between the biggest pair you ever saw, a scar as long as her breastbone. I used to believe her.

But then, when I was thirteen she had me all convinced that she'd met Tommi Rhymer, that she had his address and letters with her boxes of clothes at her Dad's place in Montana just waiting to be mailed, and that her mom's and stepdad's hippie cottage behind somebody's house was only temporary while they negotiated this six-million dollar spread in Los Altos Hills, complete with swimming pool and covered riding ring. I'm scared of lies, and so I'm gullible.

"So we're *both* in this professional theater company of *Rocky Horror,* you know? We act in front of the screen. Frank is Riffraff and I do Columbia. Actually, I've done *everything* in the *show* at one time or another, except for Brad and Dr. Frankenfurter. But we *both* like to dress for occasions. We've done Harlan Parr and

Tommi Rhymer for the Halloween parade on Castro Street. That worked so damn well, didn't it Frank-o? I got the makeup and the hair just right. Should've come as them today. We had guys begging autographs last Halloween."

For the life of me, I can *not* with my whole mind imagine anything more obnoxious than these two posers gotten up as Tommi and Harlan. Marcella must have done Harlan. Ugh. If I thought for a instant this Marcella person had paraded the Castro in a Tommi outfit, I would put my thumb in her eye. Or some other handy orifice.

"As a matter of fact," she's saying, "I *know* Boy George. I'm an artist by profession, you see. I'm one of the few who's figured out the way to Boy George.

"Vanity. Charming, George. But he's his own Main Man.

"I made him this bisque doll. Of himself. That's what I do, I'm actually a sculptress in ceramics. And it has little jointed arms and legs, all perfect, you know. And real human hair. I used my own. It had a full little trunk of clothes, all from costumes that he's worn.

"I got friendly with his roadies in L.A.; they staked me out in the hotel kitchen where he'd be coming through." (Same, I thought, as how Sirhan Sirhan met Bobby Kennedy.) "He simply *adores* his doll. He's shown it off on television."

· —— ·

SURELY but slowly, a change in the weather, S.F. Bay fog making its accustomed morning exit. I notice I don't need the *Tribune* want ads to survive. Here comes the sun. One of the guards takes off his jacket and hangs it on the fence. He's wearing a D.O.G. T-shirt underneath.

Every Bill Graham Presents Day On the Green has its special T-shirt: the headlining band cartooned as breeds of dogs. They're only issued to Graham's workers, real collector's gems if you can find some guy who'll part with one. Never on the concert day at any price. This one had Tommi and Harlan as Afghan hounds, one red, one black, moonlight and minarets behind them.

Skye said "Oh my *God*. Do you see what I see? That is to *die* for. I won't go *home* without that shirt."

She stood up and shucked out of her black mod trench coat, and for the first time I registered what it was she had on underneath. Her lavender taffeta 'fifties dress. Skin-tight (on her) bodice. Scoop neck. Big silly froufrou skirt. Little silly too-tight sleeves.

"You wore that thing to a concert? You are out of your mind! That dress will self-destruct on you! It's nothing but scotch-tape under the arms already!"

"This is my no-one-can-refuse-me-anything dress," says Skye. "Watch."

The posers seem to find all this hilariously funny.

I say "That dress is *thirty years old!* Do you realize, that dress will be the *oldest single living thing* within fifty yards of the stage?"

"Except for most of the performers," chuckled Marcella. "Translator's the only ones who might be under. Hey. Frank-o. How old are the Translator guys?"

"Search me," said Frank.

"Oingo Boingo are all over thirty for sure, and Parr and Rhymer—God, they must be every day of thirty-five. Pair of incredible old poofs."

More than I can take. "They're both thirty!"

She chuckled. "Well. You know, my favorite is still old Elton John. Talk about well preserved. I've been following him for years. Last time in England, I took a train to Elton's country house. Slick trick how I found out where it was. He wasn't actually *there*, but I met his dear mother. Delightful Grande Dame person. She was very kind." Marcella made another dive into her bottomless bag for the rhinestone mirror, the powder, and the tub of blush. "Oh, my face! *Oh*. My makeup looks like *shit*. Absolutely like *shit*."

And, seeing my opportunity, I said, "Why, I don't know about that. I think I could still tell the difference."

Meanwhile Skye has waded to the front of the crowd in her

lavender taffeta, and the beleaguered little guards have ducked behind the gate. She tries to con the shirt. The guard is very patient. He shakes his head. No deal. Embarrassing. She's started on her *"Money, love, sexual favors!"* routine. *Dumb.* What would she do if he took her up on it?

I feel a sudden longing for the bathroom in the BART station. All black-and-white-checked tile, floor, ceiling, and walls; a Mod-Ska bathroom. Izzy loves that bathroom. She wants to take it home.

Hopscotch back over blankets and warm bodies the whole length of the overpass. It is crammed now with humanity, from chain link side to side. Every style of rock conceivable flows by me as I go, like marching bands at a parade. Belshangles. Oingo Boingo. AC/DC. Van Halen. Culture Club. Duran Duran. The line grows by fifty people as each new train arrives. The end of it is down on the sidewalk now, a block beyond the station. Kids with Belshangles shirts. Oi Boy shirts. David Bowie shirts. The Who. The Eurythmics. The Police.

Wait through another line for the bathroom. It is as ever. I could see Paul Weller doing a video inside that bathroom. Regain place. Skye has given up on the D.O.G. shirt and sat down. A guy with an honest-to-God Tommi Rhymer haircut is trying to con the same poor guards into letting him through the gate. No deal. And he looks so absurd. A grown man with an all-right body and a middling face. He doesn't look much like Tommi; but he *feels* he does. The same red forelock carefully trained into his eyes. The sides quite short enough to be conservative. Then the narrow crown gets long and the narrow back gets longer, and longer, and *longer*, almost to his belt. A mane and tail for a red centaur, not for some poor poser in a business suit. He's too damn old to look anything but pitiful. And he doesn't get in the gate.

Please, God, don't let me get too old to be here. I love it here! I can see Beauty Incarnate from here! Don't make poor Tommi get too old to dance! Don't make me get too old, and have to give up loving him! I can't bear for anything to change. Maybe that's why Frank-o and Marcella look like posers too. They're just trying not to change. And they're too old.

Now there are some people with legit credentials, and they get through. A brusque little Latina in a furry sweater. She elbows up to the guards, shows her pass in laminated plastic. They crack one side of the big gate. She clicks away on businesslike heels, following that curve of empty aerial concrete all the way across the parking lot. The crowd gets up and surges.

Not yet. Hold it there. The guards re-close the gate. What is known as crowd control. Much walkie-talkie. At the far end of those radio waves some controller knows how long the lines are at each gate, the temper of each crowd.

Two small figures on the ramp now, striding from the stadium toward us. Growing larger. They're older than the pair who've held the gate against us since the dead hours, and they're white. No D.O.G. shirts on these guys. Uniforms.

One takes a small electric bullhorn off his belt. He flips the switch. "Okay. *Good* morning, ladies and gentlemen. This is it. Welcome to Bill Graham Presents a Day on the Green. *First* thing. You will have to *back up*. These gates," he continues, unflappable above the chorus of boos and groans, "open outward, that is, *toward you*. They must be securely locked against the sides before anybody gets to move."

Skye juggles her recorder and the tapes. I get the sandwiches. I've got one end of the Indian bedspread and she has the other, so we can't be separated.

"Ladies and gentlemen, could I have your attention *please.* I am telling you what the rules are. The stadium doesn't open until three o'clock; the concert begins at five. You have a *long* wait ahead of you. You can afford to stay cool. You're gonna walk in there *with me*. When I say 'walk,' I mean *walk. That is:* run, or try to cut in this line, and you're *out*."

"Can't throw us out, man, we got *tickets*!"

"I don't care if you got *two* tickets. Run or cut, and you won't see the show." Bullhorn Man sends the other three guards off toward the stadium and sees them get a good long lead. "Okay.

This is it. Nobody passes me until I say." The whole packed column presses forward; the guard backs up ahead of us, arms wide. Can he move out? Like an Indy pace car. They must have hired that guy on his ability to sprint backward. With this stampede against his chest, if he tripped he'd die. And I am eye-to-eye with him. If I tripped I'd die: underneath a human flash flood in a concrete flume.

Cross-country training is a survival skill.

We streamed off the overpass onto the stadium ramps, no more chain link, no more curbs or killer posts in our path, only the curved flank of the stadium, ice-plant-covered banks above and below: a clear way down to the parking lots. There I saw another human wave converging from the north on a chute of ropes and plastic pennants, exactly like the finish of a race.

Bullhorn Man took advantage of a last cross-flight of steps and hopped aside. *"From here, you're on your own! The line forms where the pennants are."*

Forget the scenic route. Two long bounds took me down the ice plant. Skye wiped out in the middle of it; forget her too. Just run like hell. I am neck-and-neck with the first two guys from the north gate, and I've had my winning kick perfected since I was nine.

The bigger guy wastes breath to yell, *"Oh shit!* A girl!" But I can also long jump, and I do. Through the air with my Indian bedspread.

First in line! I would have killed.

Chapter 2

"HEY, MY FRIEND'S UP THERE! She's first in line—I'm not trying to cut, I'm just trying to get with.... Just *ask* her if she's not my friend! Please? Look, I fell down—*Please!"*

A brand new D.O.G.-shirt guard and an old message: "Any more people with friends? Yes? No? Okay, the rest of you. Cut, or try to slide up through this line, and you're *out*."

No place I can slide, man, I be the head of it. Skye arrives beside me, muttering about assholes. And here we are, in between the pennants, next to the garbage Dumpster, down below the stadium, first in line.

Watch the lots fill up with overjoyed people arriving, singing, shouting, laughing, settling close together. Out comes the music, the food, the beer. One group has brought an enormous feast: sacks of deli-delights. Cases of beer. A plastic pail of boiled crayfish, with sauce. They talk and sing and eat the things, and fling the peels toward our Dumpster. Soon there are crawdaddy parts all over.

They have more beer than anyone could drink, for they

intend to sell it. A dollar a can. Run out in no time at that price. Two dollars a can. Still selling briskly. Only a couple of six-packs left. Hurry, hurry, five dollars a can.

The kid behind me buys two cans. Envy. He must be sixteen: the two joints in his wallet are stashed inside the plastic with his driver's license. He can't stop chuckling and bragging over those. Kid brother is about eleven. These are the two who raced me to the finish. Kid Brother thinks Big Brother's sick. Big Brother laughs and swears a lot. Drinks one beer. Breaks down and smokes one precious joint. Now he is flat on his back. His face is turning crawdaddy red. (His mother didn't force the sunscreen on him.) Kid Brother sneers. It's eleven o'clock in the morning.

"Next time," Skye murmurs, "we'll bring beer for sale. You see anybody getting busted?"

"The guys selling beer are in their twenties."

"Guys buying it sure as hell aren't. We'd make enough to pay for everything! Tickets, T-shirts, everything."

I'm first in line at the Belshangles concert. Were I to wish or pray for anything, it might be someone to split a beer with me. Hardly necessary though; I'm on my high already.

Frank-o and Marcella lost ground in the race: what you get for wearing shoes with heels. But I can still hear them back there, behind the Crawdaddies-and-Beer for Brunch Bunch. They're teaching their part of the line to sing "The Time-Warp." And that's not where I am at present. With Saint Peter on the mountaintop, I'm thinking, "Lord it is good for us to be here."

So while I watch, I trot out all the stuff inside my head that I have memorized for company. Like hours worth of legendary ballads, thanks to Mama. All of 'em bloody and most of 'em sexy enough to ace out any externals I might not want to listen to. "Eppie Morrie," "The Gates of Drum," "The Unnatural Mother," "The Unquiet Grave." Yeah.

But my favorite was always "True Thomas":

True Thomas lay on Huntley Bank
A ferlie he spied with his ee
For there he saw a lady bright
Come riding down by the Eildon Tree.

Her skirts were of the grass green silk
Her mantle of the velvet fine,
At ilka tet o' her horse's mane
Hung fifty silver bells and nine.

And he mistakes her for the "Queen of Heaven" anyway, because, he says, "Your peer on earth I never did see."

Oh no, oh no, true Thomas she said
That name does not belong to me,
I am but the Queen of fair Elfland,
Come hither to converse with thee.

Harp and carp—(i.e. play and sing) *True Thomas, she said,*
Harp and carp alang with me,
But if ye dare to kiss my lips,
Sure of your body I will be.

Betide me weal, betide me woe,
That weird shall never daunten me,
And he has kissed her rosy lips
All underneath the Eildon Tree.

Most deliciously sexy thing I know. In so few words, too. So she gets him; he has to serve her seven years.

Do you see yon braid, braid road
That lies along the lily leven?
That is the path of wickedness,
Though some call it the road to heaven.

And do you see yon narrow road
Sae thick beset wi' thorns and briars?
That is the path of righteousness,
Though after it but few enquires.

And do you see yon bonny road
That winds across the ferny brae?
That is the path to fair Elfland,
Where you and I tonight maun gae.

Beauty Incarnate, on a sweet side road. A genuine secret garden. "True Thomas" was a real person in the twelfth century, a local soothsayer, Mama says, a man who "couldn't lie." Which was a gift the Elf-Queen gave him, whether he wanted it or not. (He didn't.)

He was also known as Thomas the Rhymer.

The stoned kid takes up more and more room. An empty beer can's poking me in the leg; I start to roll it away. Hot shit, it's full. I've been blessed with a beer. Wait to see if anybody claims it. Nobody does. I share it discreetly with Skye: a little warm, and very good. Then Skye has to go to the bathroom. Quick, back to the ballads! I can hear Marcella starting on the "Lumberjack Song" from Monty Python.

"Tamlin"! Mustn't forget "Tamlin": ballad of yet another Thomas carried off by an unearthly queen, and the mortal Janet who rescues him from her night revels by grabbing and refusing to let go, while he's changed in her arms from wild beast to burning fire, and finally to a simple naked man. I cherished the sensuousness of it, the haunting bitter grace of the faery queen's goodbye to her lost mortal love:

"But had I known, Tamlin," she says
"A lady wad borrow thee,
I'd ta'en out thy two gray eyes
Put in two eyes of tree!

"Had I but known, Tamlin," she says
"Before ye cam frae home,
I'd ta'en out your heart of flesh
Put in a heart o' stone!

"Had I but the wit yestereen
That I have bought this day,
I'd paid my dues seven times to hell
Ere you'd been won away."

I probably had it all mixed up with *Rocky Horror Picture Show* because of Janet. But I enjoyed myself.

Skye trudges back. "They've got T-shirts over by the toilets."

"They'll have better ones inside."

"They said not."

"They lie. We'll get ours after the show."

"What if they sell out?"

"Never happens. Here. Read a book. I brought you two."

One-thirty P.M.: the heat of the day. Time bakes and shimmers off the asphalt. The Goodyear Blimp is overhead, silver and bulbous, putt-putting laps around a smoggy sky. Behind and beside and in front of it zip two sheriff's helicopters, their rotors going wacka-wacka-wacka, and a biplane with the streamer of a local TV station.

I'm thinking about the cover to *Holy War.*

Aerial photo: an old-style factory chimney, from *the top*. Five hundred feet of blackened brick, and Tommi standing on the lip of it, barefoot and bareheaded, his worn blue work-clothes whipping in the wind. Eyes down, face grave. Red hair flying sideways like some horrific vision out of William Blake.

And on the back, a vandalized deserted factory yard. By the base of—the same chimney maybe? A limousine is waiting. Harlan stands impeccable in morning coat, striped trousers, spats and gloves. He's looking at his watch. Over part of that scene, what appears to be a taped-on newspaper clipping:

A joint solution to bloodshed in Belfast
and the Middle East would be the physical exchange
of Palestinians resident in the refugee camps with
the Protestant population of Northern Ireland—

Critics weren't happy right away with the twelve songs inside: gratuitous sex, gratuitous violence. "Can't see that," said Tommi Rhymer. "It's *about* sex and violence. How can it be gratuitous when that's what it's bloody about?"

Side 1, band 1, "Jihad." The whole rationale of Islamic Holy War, lifted straight from the Koran. ("If you like Tommi Rhymer as a lyricist," said the reviews, "this may not be your album.") The single charted number five in America, and put the Moslem world in a collective snit while it stayed on.

Tommi: "Can't see why. Am I not allowed to quote their scripture? I was taught the devil can quote scripture. Having Iranian death squads after me does sell more records, but I thought those chaps might want it for a battle anthem."

"Hadji": (which is almost Jihad backwards) "A Moslem pilgrim's simple religion getting trashed by commercial interests, western-style."

"Abdullah's Occupation": Terrorist. And Tommi's hand at lyrics sure enough: Abdullah came on as a cross between Mae West and Mehmet Ali Agca.

"Long Black Hair": the killer love-song, best out of Belshangles since "Solace."

"Righteousness": quotes from the Ayatollah: chilling, thoroughly.

Side 2. The "Irish" side. If "Jihad" hadn't suited as a battle anthem, "Make it Hard and Narrow" was quite another trip. The title was from a ballad verse that's turned up in all kinds of songs for centuries:

Oh mother, mother, make my bed,
Make it hard and narrow,
My true love died for me today,
I'll die for him tomorrow.

"Make it Hard" was a screaming dirge over a lover starving to death in the Maze Prison. The IRA took it to their hearts. It was banned off the BBC.

"Gilhooley": Abdullah's counterpart, a wild-eyed, bomb-lobbing Irish Rose. Funny as hell, and just as dangerous.

"Righteousness Version": Reverend Ian Paisley of Northern Ireland, the Ayatollah's blood relation.

Which brings you right up against "The Favorite."

On you—On you, my favor rests
On you—
On you—my favor rests:
Listen to him, listen to him,
Listen to him, listen to him.
Place me—as a seal upon your heart
As a seal upon your arm for love is
As strong as death.

If a man should, a man should offer
All the substance of his house for love
He would be
Utterly despised.
I sleep, my heart watches—
The voice of my beloved knocking.
My beloved—put his hand in through the keyhole
And I was aroused at his touch.

It was the Song of Songs. Except for the hook, "On you my favor rests. Listen to him." That was what the Gospels have the voice of God say above Jesus on the mountain.

They had church-sponsored album burnings in the Bible belt. They said he was playing games with the sexuality of Jesus. I couldn't see that. It was just terminally beautiful, almost too intimate to endure, much too intimate to forget. I loved it so painfully, I wanted to be the only one to hear it. I was twelve years old.

The sleeper was "Angel of Death," another dirge, a ghostly

echo of "Make It Hard and Narrow." The album was out a year before someone suggested "Angel" was a lament for a lover dying of AIDS. AIDS was just beginning to be big news. It hadn't darkened everything yet like a nuclear winter.

"That's a clever one," said Tommi Rhymer. "I quite enjoy that. You may think about it that way, if you like."

Of course, people asked relentlessly if he was gay.

"Know why it is you're laying that on me?" he said. "It sells. Nobody asks if I'm a Moslem. Nobody asks if I'm a terrorist, or a fundamentalist, or Irish or Arabic."

So they asked if he was an IRA sympathizer.

"Harlan is half Arab, and he reads the stuff. He was like, a source for much of this. My stepfamily was Irish. Titillating, what? Now you know all about us."

1981 was the year of Belshangles. Tommi and Harlan had their cover shot and feature article in every magazine this side of *Popular Mechanics*. The T.R. folder on the corner of my desk grew fat to overflowing. Typical was the cover of *Rolling Stone*: the two of them laughing at the world through a Hollywood-harem-girl veil stretched across both their faces.

Harlan: "We simply got tired, very tired if you will, of being slagged as purveyors of soft-porn teeny-bop bubble-gum music."

Tommi: "If you desire to be taken seriously, you have to protest some kind of 'oppression.' That's unreal. Do I look oppressed? Does he? I'll sing about love and sex because they're what I know.

"Life's treated me very well. Make a bitchin' spokesman for Britain's unemployed youth, I would: working for myself when I was fourteen years old. I never took money from the dole. I started poor as any of these yobs. And I could go back to singing on the street. I still know how. Put me out in the clothes I stand up in, I'd make a go. All I'd need is a guitar."

Rolling Stone: "How would you get that?"

Tommi: "Laying the shop-clerk would be my first choice. Stealing runs a close second."

Rolling Stone: "Have you ever stolen a guitar?

Tommi: "Never met a kid in this business who hasn't." (Harlan's hand shoots skyward.) "Well of *course he* hasn't; his family supported him in style before I met him, and I've gone on doing it since."

"*You're* supporting *me*?" says Parr in mild amazement. "I rather thought it was the other way 'round." Tommi, at this point, pokes him in the ribs. Harlan replies with a hard right to the diaphragm.

Rolling Stone (trying to restore order): "Harlan, is he drawing an honest picture of himself?

Harlan: "*Terribly* honest. Never was oppressed."

Rolling Stone: "Tommi, do you have a favorite—I should say—do you have a personal stance among the philosophies visited on *Holy War?* Are you the outsider? What do you believe?"

Tommi (with a lock on both of Harlan's wrists): "'Long Black Hair.' It's from the Sufi mystics somewhere—You cut that out!"

Harlan: "Fakhreddin-al-Iraqi."

Tommi: "Right. That the beauty I see in my lover is the beauty of God, and the eyes I see it with are God's appreciation—is that Moslem? God is love? So what if I choose to take it very literally?"

· — ·

ROUSED from a laughing reverie of colored veils by one of Skye's sudden full-volume verdicts: "*Bored!* I am *so bored*, this concert better make it good. Your books both suck—This one's about nothing but faggots"—lobbing *Tales of the City* into the sack of lunch-garbage—"and *this* one"—*Tales of Power* following the same trajectory—"is nothing but drugs."

I say, "How far did you *get*? Do you realize, that's all you ever find to talk about? Just like a parrot, 'Faggots and drugs! Faggots and drugs!'"

"Not *my* idea. They're your fucking books. Don't you have any *normal* kid books?"

"Like what?"

"I don't know. A good escapist read—Stephen King?"

"Ugh!"

"*See?*" she says. "I'm going to lug our stuff back to the car. We won't want this shit inside the stadium."

"Pitch the trash. Take my fucking books out first." She laughs. I'm not so sure there's anything the matter with Skye's heart. Head, yes. Heart, no. But playing safe can't hurt. "Maybe I should hike instead."

"Bitch, you don't understand. It's sitting in this heat that kills."

"They won't let you out the way we came—"

"My *medicine* is in the car."

"You'll have to walk to the north gate, back down the street, and in on the overpass—"

Skye has joined a flow of people all doing the same thing: trekking to the car: jettisoning the day's support systems, getting ready to run light. It occurs to me, I've never seen her medicine. And meanwhile, I'm still thinking.

1983: *Sundog*. Which critics called a rip-off, the out-takes from *Holy War.* But what about those wild new instrumentals? What about the fifteen-minute extended version of "The Favorite," done for the video that got X-rated and withdrawn? Although Princess Diana is rumored to be wearing out a copy. Rank hath its privileges.

Skye comes back empty handed. Not bored, wasted I'd say, white and damp under the eyes. She has to make it through the concert, that's all. We're almost there. The stadium's massive shadow is crawling out to swallow us. People have been diddling with the sound system inside. All at once, drums! An *incredible* sound-explosion, a force field, a futuristic weapon arcing over from the stadium to the sky!

"It's 'Jihad.' *'Jihad'!* Listen!"

Skye gets her jaw shut. "It's a record."

"It's not *like* that *on the record!* They're on stage; that's the sound-check—" A bright clean scimitar voice lifts up, flashing high above the battle-din. *"That's him!"*

"Easy! God, you don't need to spaz!"

"You don't understand, *I do!"*

Over almost before it began, the music dies. Half the line has levitated to its feet, with little knots of wipeout hysteria around the people hardest hit. Even the stoned kid clambers up scorched and irritable. He never missed his beer.

2:55. The line compresses. All we have to do now when they open the ropes is thunder up wide concrete stairs, past the ticket takers, past the body search and down wide concrete stairs on winged feet, across the green grass to the stage.

I have my jacket tied around my hips. I have my soft much-fingered ticket in one hand. Skye has hers.

3:00 o'clock. They let us go.

All the way up the stairs, I'm still the leader. Arms high for the search. Come *on*, guys, there's nothing in this jacket but me! I'm jigging and dancing with all the despair of a little kid detained on his way to the bathroom.

The middle of three takers takes my ticket. He turns it over and reads the back. He looks at the place where J.J. ripped and I scotch-taped it. He looks me in the eye, and smiling, tears my ticket one-eighth inch at a time.

I don't see any sense in cruelty. Right now I'm seeing everything through tears. Kids stream by to right and left; the stairs below are full of flying people. On the far side of the stadium another wide stair spews kids onto the grass.

Down I go, five steps at a time.

Green grass! Blue sky! Yellow sun!

Giant stage! A looming black steel-pipe-and-plywood Fortress Unvanquishable: its rear sits on the stadium seats behind home plate. Its front invades the grass by fifty feet. Below its edge is a walkway, maybe five more feet, for techs, security, and medics to pass crowd-level, then a plywood barrier four feet high. Plywood covers the grass too for another fifty yards, so massive boogying won't chew their sports turf into pulp.

Now I am racing a hundred kids across the grass. I hit the plywood's edge! Center stage is three rows deep already, it's left side or nothing: *Go for it!* I hit the barrier, grip it with both hands! My own space! *Mine!*

Gloria in Excelsis Deo.

· — ·

TWO models exist on how to live these concerts. You can sit in the stands and listen, smoke pot, boogie on the seats. If you want to see how the stars *look*, check the video screens. *Or*, you can wait all day in line and get down front. You won't hear music; the speakers are beside you and fifty feet above you. But you can almost touch your love.

Men inside the barrier are motioning us down, so the field can't hold as many and we won't get killed. The theory, anyway. Nobody's gotten killed at any show I've been to, but there's always swarms of Haight-Ashbury Free Medical Clinic people and a hospital at the third base dugout.

Skye turns up beside me, looking worse than ever. She snides, "And I thought *you* could *run*." What can I say to that?

The men inside the barrier say, "Get down. Get down." They all wear earplugs and it doesn't help to argue.

Afternoon bores in across the stadium's west rim. Canned music thunders. The biplane tows a different streamer. The sheriff's helicopters circle, wacka-wacka-wacka. No hint of breeze, no breath of cool; time is a motionless oven of battered plywood, rock distortion, and piled bodies of people, victims at the natural disaster of their choice.

I try to rig my jacket as a sunshade over Skye.

Skye says, "Please, I have to have some air."

I begin to see a doubt, not of her lasting *through* the concert, but *to* the concert. I ease up to a crouch and peer over the barrier. Somebody with gray hair and earplugs says, "Get Down."

All right, be that way.

A dark-haired older guy strides by. I see he has no earplugs. He also has a *face*, good cross between a pirate captain and a coach I once was fond of. He has on khaki work pants and a dumb striped T-shirt, green and brown, like grade-school boys wear. It has a hole in it. No generic adult, that one. He sees me too, but he doesn't say get down.

"Sssst." Skye groans; I boost her upright. I have no desire to watch this concert from the third-base dugout. "See that dark man? Next time he comes by, tell him you're sick. He'll let you stand."

She stands there, forlorn and kind of brave. I pat her feet to keep her steady. I know when he comes, because she says, "Hey, I feel so sick, and it's so hot down there—Can't I please stand now?"

He must have nodded yes, because she did. Maybe another hour passes. The rumble of taped rock fails abruptly, a man's voice on a popping microphone says, *"Testing? Hello, test."*

The crowd slams to its feet and up against the barrier. Guys who weren't looking for it swear and try to beg their valuables from underfoot three rows behind. I was waiting for it like salvation. Breeze lifts the canvas at the rear of the stage. Pretty soon the spray-bottled water will appear, and we'll share it around, be as wet with spray and sweat as swimmers in a sea of solid human flesh. All that matters is to keep a good grip on the barrier, push out from it so ribs don't crush. Two rows back is hell.

"Sir? Hello, Sir—will you *know* when Tommi Rhymer gets here?" The pirate chief has paused in front of us again, and good old Skye is trying to get familiar with him.

"When? When does he get here? He's been here since morning, same as you."

She laughs. "But he's a *star!*"

That answer don't sit well with Captain Kidd. "Listen, Rhymer and Parr are two of the hardest working artists in this business; they *live* backstage the day of a show; they eat backstage, sleep backstage. If they sleep. There isn't a piece of masking-tape goes down they haven't seen; and if they don't like it, they'll take it up."

"How do you know all this?"

"Been hiring 'em for seven years, why wouldn't I know?"

"You aren't Bill Graham!"

"Why do you say I'm not Bill Graham?"

"Bill Graham's rich—"

Shit, she's said the wrong thing, said it over and over. And he is getting jut-jawed as a barracuda. "Don't I look rich? How does a rich man dress?" He doesn't wait for her to answer, "Initials on that—" shoving his ring under her nose—"See? What are they?" What one sees, is not so much initials as the diamond, broader than the ring finger it glitters on.

Skye is awed to whispers. "You're Bill Graham."

"Listen. I'm going to tell you something. A rich man dresses to be comfortable at whatever he's doing. Okay? Can you remember that?"

But she recovers herself: "Okay! Can you give Tommi Rhymer a message?"

"Sure, if it's a good one."

Now is the acceptable time, now is the hour of communication! Good God, Tommi Rhymer. I had to think, quick now, what it was I wanted to tell him. I knew I was full of some enormous message which was for Tommi Rhymer, no one else: and here was the messenger, a man who knew him—

"Tell him we love him!" wailed Skye.

Graham snorted sheer disgust. "You don't love him."

"Yes we do! Please tell him for us, please tell him!"

"You don't even know him. You never met him! He might have B.O. For all you know, he might snore! So is that it? Is that the best you got?"

Skye wrings her hands in honest helplessness. She has the wrong answer on a million-dollar quiz show. "What could I have that's *better?"*

"Don't ask me, it's not my message. Been talking to the guy myself all day. So what's your name?"

"Skye Milligan—and my friend is Andy—"

"Skye. Andy. Okay."

"And you'll *tell him* ?"

"What's your ZIP Code?"

"94306! You *will tell him we love him?"*

Six feet and a dozen people to the right of me, a kid cries *"Mr. Graham! Mr. Graham?"*

"Yeah?"

"Mr. Graham, Harlan Parr is my ultimate hero. Do you ever talk to *him?"*

Mr. Graham moves his way. Our audience is over. "Why not? He's human. He likes to talk—"

"Do you just like, call him on the *phone?*"

"He calls *me.*"

"Is he like, really, really bright?"

Bill Graham's back is to us now. What a waste, like the three magic wishes. My only chance to say a non-commercial word to Tommi Rhymer, and Skye had motor-mouthed straight through it. Not that she was *wrong*, exactly. Graham wasn't wrong either: we couldn't know Tommi. Not one percent of the millions who paid to see him glitter could. First name and no last name. ZIP Code and no street. Love and nothing better. Love, an undeliverable package, filed in a cosmic dead letter office with a million other identical packages, all mailed to the same address. And no return address on *any* of 'em.

Consider the crew of girls packed in to my left; they never even saw Bill Graham. Girls with gelled hair sprayed designer colors: department-store punk—you know, *really* expensive dresses artfully ragged at the hems, and skinny metal-stud belts that wrap three times around.

Anyone can tell these chicks come from one school, came in one car: they practically stick together. They all have little crosses on their cheeks in black eyeliner. They're flirting with delirium, egging each other on. Nobody exists in their whole world just now except themselves and Tommi Rhymer. They're going to grab him. Kiss him. Hump him. They're going to climb right on his stage, see if they don't. I wonder how they plan to do it. The place is swarming with security guards all built like Bubba Paris and the stage is seven feet tall.

But how am I so different from them?

Maybe no different, just tongue-tied or something.

Inhibited.

The concert started with no fanfare. One minute it was canned music and electricians on stage, the next, Translator, a middling West Coast band. The girls next to me listened for all of twenty seconds: sharp, painted little faces pointing upward toward the young guys trying to charm them. Then the closest one shut her eyes, drew a breath, and howled *"Go away!"* The giggles of her friends encouraged her. *"Turkeys! We don't want you!"* One by one the others joined: *"You're ugly! Go away! Get a haircut! Get a job!"* They began to stamp the plywood: *"Tom-mi, Har-lan! We want Belshangles!"*

Before God and man, I *still* don't appreciate cruelty. I brought my elbow down across her shoulder: *"Cut it out!"*

"What?" She hadn't even known I was alive, and I am physically jammed in next to her, tighter than any lover.

"Cut it out! Who wants to listen to you?"

"What's your fucking *problem?"*

"*You're my problem!* Being stuck next to *you!* Shut up, so I can hear the band!"

"Who wants to hear *them?* Hey, shit-for-brains," she sneered, "if your *picture's* dead, turn off the *sound!"* They went back to bad-mouthing Translator, but the real juice had gone out of it. Few minutes more, and apathy set in.

All the time I'm still debating, how the fact that I love Tommi could be so almighty crucial to me, and not be worth a shit objectively, or to any other person, Tommi foremost. Except it moves me to spend money on his product.

And all the time, Translator was exposed above my head: vivisected by the sun, trying to make their music work against the will of fifty thousand people, the stage a flapping black cavern at their backs full of Oingo Boingo's drum sets. Little bands who open for their betters in the afternoon don't get full stage and fancy lighting. They get sunstroke.

I couldn't focus anything, eyes or ears or mind, on them. But I felt for them. Up there with their ass and abilities on such a merciless line. The crowd wanted to love. Their love was offered, monstrous, giant, killer love: like in old tales about "The Siege Perilous," that seat of high honor, deadly to all except the rightful occupant. And the only way to tell if you're the rightful occupant? Get up there and perish. Or not.

Translator didn't perish, quite. In their hit song, their only song I knew, "You're Everywhere That I'm Not," at the very end of the long inventory of places the ex-lover is where the dumped singer is not, they stuck in an unexpected "You're in Portobello

Road and I'm not." They acknowledged their audience was with Belshangles and not with them.

People heard. It drew a ripple of laughter; a chance to shorten their set and retreat with ass intact. Before kids started pitching pennies. That's always the worst, the Apocalypse treatment: "Would that you were hot or cold, I say, would that you were hot or cold. As you are neither hot nor cold, I will begin to spit you out of my mouth."

Twenty minutes of stage change: securities and techs with earplugs running around like ants, and canned rock blaring from the speaker towers. We saw Bill Graham stride across the stage. Skye screamed *"Mr. Graham! Remember us!"*

He saw her, pointed a finger and mouthed *"Zip Code?"*

All so ineffectual: my Zip Code, like my love.

But I do like Oingo Boingo. I could look forward to them. I like their frontman, Danny Elfman. I like his brain, where the music comes from. Feisty, burly, little redheaded guy. I must have some very basic thing about red hair.

There wasn't room for Danny posters on my walls, but Izzy had one shot of him tacked up between her Madness calendar and The Psychedelic Furs. I used to sneak in sometimes on the sly, and pay regards to Danny Elfman.

No smart-ass kid is going to shit on Oingo Boingo. They are all grown men, eight of them; they have faces. They play a lot of brass, and weird percussion monsters out of Africa.

And here they came.

They fired up with a bass line like an artillery barrage, a sound so incredibly massive it pulsed the breath inside my lungs and I could feel my diaphragm go thudding in and out. I knew their words. So did the whole front half of the field: we sang, we jumped, a thousand bare arms rose to pump the air.

Hey, neighbor, let me give you some advice
The Russians are out to pulverize us
in our sleep tonight,
That is if the crazy Arabs or the riots

don't get us first,
And the fire will rain down from the sky,
The fire will rain down from the sky,
People will die, people will die—
Well go ahead, sleep tight in your bed,
Remember what the wise man said
There's nothing to fear—
There's nothing to fear but fear itself,
There's nothing to fear—
There's nothing to fear but fear itself—
Temperature's starting to drop now,
Temperature's starting to drop.

Hey, little girl, won't you come this way?
Won't you let me buy you candy.
or perhaps a chocolate shake?
Or perhaps a nice cocaine?
Or perhaps a little kiss?
Or perhaps a ride in my big car,
Perhaps a ride in my big car,
Don't be afraid, don't be afraid—
Won't you make an old man happy?
Won't you make an old man happy?
Won't you let me show you paradise?
Don't ask your mother for advice—
There's nothing to fear—
There's nothing to fear but fear itself—
Temperature's starting to drop now,
Temperature's starting to drop—

They barreled on like that, non-stop through an hour of their best. They couldn't have drawn that crowd, but they knew how not to waste it: they knew how to weld fifty thousand living creatures into one huge living creature, and ride it like a willing spirit-horse.

New stage crew: these wore the orange, numbered badges

of the *Sundog* tour. All extra platforms and electronics went, the stage grew very bare. Ragged awnings pieced out broken walls in a ruined alley in a forgotten town.

They killed the work-lights, powered up the night. There, in a spotlight at one corner of the apron, looking more piratical than ever, diamond ring, green kid-striped shirt and all, stood Bill Graham. "*Ladies and Gentlemen—from London*: head-lining their second Day On the Green: Rollo McInery, Nicky Cavanaugh, *Harlan Parr, Tommi Rhymer!* Welcome Belshangles!" The stadium screamed from one throat. Nothing at all was left between us and the very item that we came to see. When that great voice blew away, a tiny sound persisted:

ting ting ting ting
ting-tic, tic-tic-ting
tic-tic ting-tica tica tica tica tica
ting ting ting ting

A drumbeat joined the finger-bells. All around the edges of the stage, people reclined in shadow. People in robes and baggy coats. The drummer was there. Rollo. The black-robed lap with the stick-bass in it was Nicky's.

Four towering blue-black men entered with a palanquin: in it rode the hooded player of a long-necked instrument. Twice, three times around, to the rhythm of bass and bells and drum they bore the veiled musician shoulder-high, and set him down. One light hand slid up the instrument's neck, caressing out a wail of long-drawn satisfaction. Harlan.

Now the blacks again, shouldering a Persian carpet. Twice, three times around they shuffled, squatted, and unrolled toward the audience their burden's secret core, a slender body shrouded in orange silk. As Harlan played, two clever hands with finger-bells rose obediently snake-like from their silky windings. Awed silence held about that long. Then the stadium screamed again and kept on screaming, while the band went full volume on "Abdullah's Occupation":

I think the serpent
very well designed
for accomplishing the end
he has in mind,
And the vulture's taste
I think is very nice,
He consumes another's problem
for a price:

Think about *sound* so huge, it feels life threatening if you haven't given it prior consent. Tommi undulated to his feet. He wore the long tight shirt and breeches old mosaics show on Persian gods; from his shoulders flew a cosmic fiery train of veils and streamers.

A ten-thousand-body human wave surged to greet him.

There is no salvation
there is no end at all
to conflagration
and iniquity between
nation and nation:
as long as such
remains the situation,
Insh'Allah—
some man will ply Abdullah's occupation!

Inside the barrier, a steel pipe-brace sprung loose and shoved into the dirt. I didn't hear, I felt the squeal of crushing wood and bending metal as the entire barrier began to buckle toward the stage. A passive worshiper at this ceremony, I saw, as the below-stage crew rushed to the break, and with hands and shoulders battled it outward against the weight of the crowd.

The leaders of the world
are moral men,
They uphold their nations'

honor now and then,
And the Men of God
no longer practice war,
for that is what
their followers are for...

If the crew lost, my body would be tomorrow's news, along with the whole front row. No time to be afraid. The noise of the concert and its crowd preempted even thought.

But when some small
obstruction wants removing—
and the balance of
terror needs improving—
They spend their dollars
and their rubles
on a man who has no scruples;
the world is brought to peace
against its will:
And to that end—I kill—
I kill I kill I kill!

But the crew won. The pipe got fastened down again.

The hyena I call
happy in her jaws,
she can laugh at bones
as men do at their laws,
In the rat I see
the future of the race,
the ruin of the old order is his place...

At the same time, Haight-Ashbury Free Clinic people took up duty hauling in the passed-out, the freaked-out, and the injured, reviving them below the stage. Bill Graham worked alongside, two more arms to lift the wasted faithful.

There is no salvation
There is no end at all
to conflagration
and iniquity between
nation and nation:
As long as such
remains the situation—
Insh'Allah—some man must ply Abdullah's occupation!

So Tommi and Harlan sang their songs of worship that became a war, and passion that became a holy worship.

I heard very little of it.

My ears broke. Memory broke. Time broke. But I saw "The Favorite." The two were playing together, Harlan on the oud and Tommi the small fiddle. Tommi spun circles all around him. It was the cover of the *Sundog* album: the sun an incandescent musician, the fiery dancer in orbit.

I saw Harlan lift his guitar-strap—not your ordinary one, but a long solid belt—over Tommi's head. They both leaned back into that hoop of leather and began to spin. Harlan's oud lay high against his shoulder; he never missed a note. Tommi lay on air, his arms in free-fall out behind his head and his draperies rising like a wheel of fire. Their two bodies were the hub of it.

Almost it seemed to be not the kind of thing which should be watched. My eyes kept closing on their own. And what were they? Drowning in a fiery whirlpool? Or rising out of it like phoenixes? Were they the last of the whirling dervishes? Or two kids on a playground? Or all of the above? *God help me: I don't know what the Song of Songs means, either!*

No warning, the girl on my left sagged into me. My first thought was "Stand on your own feet and get off mine," but she was unconscious. It was the foul-mouthed little twit who'd savaged Translator. We had to keep her from sliding down and getting trampled, attract the medics working on the other side, boost her up, get her over the barrier.

All the time one of her hangers-on was wailing "Tiffany!

Tiff! Oh God! I promised Mom I wouldn't let anything *happen* to her!" And when they took her under the stage the other chick went too, still crying "Tiffany—"

On stage, "The Favorite" was over. The whole Arab set was over. There were white backup dancers instead of black ones, blue work clothes and scruffy caps instead of silks and caftans. Tommi had a worn jacket, much too small for him, and jeans. Though I could see from where I was, those jeans had zippers down the sides.

After "Make It Hard and Narrow" the jacket went. He sang his songs of innocence and grief, love and war in jeans, white T-shirt, pulled out tails, with a bump and shuffle and a bit of Irish step dance like a streetwise natural child.

People were fainting everywhere now: all the tiny frail girls, all the fat uneasy girls, all the ones who felt at risk, a steady fall of human leaves. The crowd had sucked Translator's breath, and hardly let them play. Tommi sucked power from the crowd: he was a devastating, light-emitting, one-billion-megawatt device.

And Harlan (as ever) played like the elves had taught him. For the ending on "Gilhooley" the four white backups took Harlan by the shoulders and ankles and launched him onto the hands of the crowd. He lay on his back and played, and got passed around above their heads, not so close that I could touch him, but I saw his face. He was laughing.

Quick, turn back! Tommi. Still on stage, standing very quietly, quite invisible. What a trick. Well, I see him now. His eyes begin, out at the edge of light where Harlan is, and rove the crowd from side to side, moving closer. His eyes pass mine. Return. He sees rows and rows of backs-of-heads and one white face. Oh, he must see all kinds, but he sure as anything sees mine! I'm thinking: I *do* love you. I'm sorry, but I never was taught better—

He looked away, toward Harlan's progress.

"C'mon, give him back," he crowed, "I need him!"

That brought the faces around: Tommi's cue to turn his own back, flip one hip and sail the T-shirt off over his head. Belt and yoke of the jeans were a solid blaze of rhinestones. He was naked to the waist except for a rhinestone diamond netting, a spider-web harness of white fire. Harlan, on stage again, had his own blue jacket inside out: it was harlequin rhinestones on silver lamé.

Tommi slid up to a mike and said in this wonderful soft heavy voice, "You want a guided tour of the Mecca of Love?" Well, all their other stuff is fine, but this was the act that made them famous.

They began their strut across the stage, one behind the other, that mischievous high-stepping gait between a sneak and a swagger. When Castaneda's wizard men spoke of the "Gait of Power," this must have been what they had in mind. The song was "Some in Velvet Gowns." The little fiddle laughed and squealed, the guitar wove sweet warm body-rhythm for it. A snap turn at the wings put Harlan in the lead. Now the fiddle took the low road; the guitar sang.

Now the Hashbury Free Clinic staff had eight or ten unconscious people to haul in. These weren't your fragile little casualties; they were big solid Belshangles fans. Four at least were guys. Merciless lateral waves of shoving and crushing swept the front. I stood welded to the barrier. My arms might kill tomorrow; but for now, I would not be moved.

Skye sagged into me from the right.

"Stand up!"

"I can't—they're pushing—"

"Push back!"

"I can't!" She was crying.

"Hang on! Stand up! Push back!"

"I can't!" Then she whimpered, "I can't feel my arms...."

Arm pains may be heart pains; that's what the coaches told us. I let her slip in front of me. I tried to hold her up. I still had the wooden barrier with both hands, one to either side of Skye. But grip as I might that way, my new hold was not unbreakable. I was getting swept away, and Skye with me. I saw a Free Med Clinic T-shirt.

"Doctor! Help! My friend's about to faint—"

"Do you wanta go out?" He bellowed. Skye whimpered at him. *"Do you wanta go or not?"* Skye was inaudible.

"Yes!" I screamed. *"She wants to go!"*

The Free Clinic guy got her under the arms, but Skye's a big girl and the barrier is four feet high. *"Come on, people, lend a hand, she's going out!"*

Out like a light. She'd even stopped trying to stand up. And I was shouting, *"Help!"* and wrestling around. The Free Clinic man was shouting. You couldn't hear a thing. Two feet over my head Tommi Rhymer and Harlan Parr were blasting through "Your Jeans" like there was no tomorrow.

Some large dude on the other side of Skye linked hands with me underneath her; slowly we worked her feet up through the human jam behind us. People back there caught on when the feet got waist-high, and the medics hauled her in. I remember thinking, now's the time for that sweet 'fifties dress to go. It'll snag the plywood, just watch. One good sliver and it's all over. There were no good slivers. I saw Skye's dress ingested by the dark below the stage, and Skye inside it, limp feet trailing.

I remember mighty-mouth Tiffany and her tearful sister. I never promised anybody not to let things happen to Skye. But what if, after the last encore, Skye's no place to be found? What if she's really having an attack, and the medics rush her—where? What if she's DOA at some strange hospital and I haven't believed in her enough to be there with her?

Byproduct of religious education: I can guilt trip myself faster than you would believe.

"I'm going out!"

"You stay put!" shouted the security guy in front of me, *"Unless you're sick!"*

"My friend is sick, and I don't want to lose her!"

"Once you're out you're out! You can't come back!"

Goodbye Tommi, goodbye Harlan. A little vault put me on the barrier, leg over.

Goodbye, I'll always love you. You know that.

I crawled out of the din and the crowd, the flaring colored glow of the concert, into dark damp earth and bruised grass underfoot instead of wood, and bodies laid out on the grass all over, medics with flashlights working over some. I crawled around hissing "Skye...Skye—" Never realized what a conspicuous name that was, until I had to crawl in and out of metal-pipe framework six feet below the Belshangles concert calling it, while strangers stared at me in the dark.

I didn't want Tommi and Harlan to hear my noise underneath their stage. I could hear them. Not their music, which was overwhelmingly loud, but the rhythmic thump and slither of their feet on the plywood just above my head.

No Skye. Maybe they'd taken her away.

I crawled back, calling "Skye—Skye—"

"Bitch." She was perched in the pipe-work not very far at all from where I'd started, sipping water from a big paper cup.

"Are you all right? Your hands are freezing."

"Ice water," she said, "in the cup."

"Oh yeah?"

"Let's get out of here."

"Are you all right?"

"Uh-huh. I want to go home."

I want to say: look here, you! You'd sure as hell better *not be all right!* Look sick, or else! If you just freaked, and made me miss the end of the Belshangles concert, and made me feel all guilty and concerned, you are a scum and a poser and the lowest of the low. I said, "Hey, don't joke around; what if you pass out on the freeway?"

"I won't. Honest to God."

"Don't you want to tell 'em about your heart?"

"No!"

"There's a hospital at the third-base dugout, they said."

"Please, Andy," she whispered, "I don't want to go there; my medicine's in the car. I'll be all right, really I will."

"I don't like this."

"I'm used to it. Please? Please let me manage?"

A medic crawled through the pipe-maze toward us, a dark shape with a flashlight. He crouched in front of Skye. "How about it?" The light flicked from Skye's white face to mine. "She okay?"

I still had her hand, and it was limp and cold. She dug her nails into my palm. "I'm fine," she said in her best little-girl voice, "Thank you so much for helping me!"

"Think you gals can make it out for the last encore?"

Rhythmic clapping of a hundred thousand hands. Mass despair, the band was gone. Up in the stands, fifty thousand feet stamped in unison; the concrete stadium shell became one monster drum. *"Tom-mi! Har-lan! Tom-mi! Har-lan!"*

"Now that's the side of the stage." The medic pointed with his flash. "Crawl straight toward that light, keep your heads low, so you don't hit anything; wouldn't want to treat you for a cracked skull. You'll be back out front."

A sudden rush of feet across the plywood overhead. Despair gone for the moment, desire was the only god: it was the opening riff of "Anything It Takes." The whole crowd on the green surged forward, compressed, and roared like the first wave of a breaking storm. The metal stage frame trembled. Out front, I saw ranks of faces light up with reflected glory. Dark shapes thrashed against the light. A girl was getting hauled into the pit. Then another. And another. "Alex! Alex get out here! They're coming over this rail like the Normandy Invasion! Jesus! Watch it! Gimme a hand!"

And I was the hurricane's eye.

"Skye. This way."

"What?"

"Look." I yanked her arm. From the back of the stage above our heads, a long flat gangway rested its far end on the concrete ramp of a stadium entrance. "That's how the bands get on. And off. Quick. We're going that way. I want one good look at him, just *one* I haven't paid money for."

"I don't wanta do it! *Please*—They'll throw us out!"

"So what? The show's over."

I crawled steadily. Skye, who didn't like to be alone, crawled with me. We were on the concrete slope now. As we crept up past the stage, the lights washed over us.

There were lots of people backstage. They all stood facing out. Tommi had stripped to nothing but a web of rhinestones—a solid diamond at the crotch was all that kept it legal—an exquisite X-rated harlequin. He turned a complete aerial, a no-hands cartwheel, the fiddle still on his arm, center-stage—at the very edge—faced the crowd, threw both arms, bow and fiddle high above his head, and swept the lowest of bows, almost a salaam, to his fifty thousand screaming lovers.

Skye screamed too. It didn't sound like passion.

I turned around. She was thrashing crazily in the grip of a security whose belt came level with her shoulders. He brought to mind that line on one of Izzy's Specials albums: "—thees one for the bouncers! *Big, Big, Monkey Man!*"

Plain to see what must have happened, his first grab got her dress-front only. The kicky little 'fifties dress was frail as paper. And it shredded. Right down. She was bare-boobed, screaming, squirming, naked down to her Calvin panties. Upstage at the Oakland Coliseum.

House lights were coming up. People ran by us. Somehow it made me furious. She hadn't even wanted to be here! So I grabbed the big ape back. "You let her go! She's my friend! She hasn't done anything!"

He couldn't get me without dropping Skye, and she was really impressively crazy with fear. He was probably very wise not to let go. But I had no effect on him either.

Suddenly something loud and very brightly colored hit his other arm, with a screech of *"Fuck off, asshole!* Don't y'know *who hires you?"* It hit with such impact that even King Kong was staggered, and the whole flailing group of us rotated slowly into the light. I got a good view of the new arrival. It was Tommi Rhymer. *"Look* at her! Oh God." Skye's face still streamed tears but she had given up struggling to cover herself. She just stared at him. He moved in perfect grace as wolves and leopards do.

From down below you couldn't see how stark his makeup was, white as death. His eyes were shadowed in scarlet and rimmed in black. White and red. Blood on snow. An arctic predator. "All I need is a picture of that in the papers with my sweet name underneath!"

More people sprinted by. I saw Rollo McInery's long face. " 'Ere, Tom, if we don't move, we'll not make it out."

Nick Cavanaugh was close behind him. "Come on, love; you had him let her go. She can take care of herself!"

"That ain't easy with your clothes ripped off!"

If anybody knew what going naked in a crowd was like, it must surely be this one. He had a jacket on over his rhinestones, glorious fur, almost as red as his hair. It was a bomber jacket, only way too big: it came down over his butt, and made him look like a kid in his father's coat or a girl in her boyfriend's—coddled and extravagant.

He'd *had* a jacket on. He had it off now, and was putting it on Skye. His shoulders smoked in the cool night air. "Look'ere," he said, cradling Skye swiftly and expertly against his own body, smoothing back her hair, wiping the tears from her face with his hands, "This is Rhymer's show; I don't treat my kids like dirt." In her place, I would have called it a bargain. The best I ever had.

"Mr. Rhymer, I can't take your coat; it's worth a lot of money—"

"Ah, don't worry. Just button up."

"I can't, my stepdad wouldn't let me keep it. He'll think I did something bad to get it."

He turned to me for the first time. "Are you with her?"

"Yes," I said.

"In your own car?"

"Yes." I didn't tell him Skye was driving.

"If she wants to give that back to me, let her give it back. We're in San Francisco."

I said, "You're in Oakland." Look. I've made him laugh.

"We're at the Hotel Montor, top floor. The party's in the

Presidential Suite, I'm in room 3230. Got that? Hop off the lift somewhere; take the service stair."

"Does that work?"

"Should do, s'how we've gotten down."

"When's too late?"

Harlan Parr came out of the dark at a dead run, collected Tommi's arm and dragged him, glittering, half-naked, laughing, up the ramp the way he came. "Oh God," Tommi crowed, "in my business I go down at sunrise!" They'd backed the white limo almost to the stage. Harlan swung Tommi headfirst through an open door. Then he dived in on top. The limo pulled away before they got all arms and legs inside.

"Miss. Hey. Miss?" It was Ape Man talking to me. "I wantcha to know. Mr. Rhymer gets his kicks from being gallant. Like, he enjoys putting on a show. We still just gotta do as we was told. If he wants you guys up to his room now, you'll need a pass to make it through the halls. There is one on his jacket, so your gal-friend's clear. You take mine, or she'll have to go alone."

I thanked him vigorously, and told him he was kind.

"Don't know about that, Miss," he said as he let us out a chain-link gate into the slowly flowing crowd, "You don't know what you're gettin'."

Skye appeared to be in shock.

"We've got passes to his room! Do you know what that *means? We've got passes to Tommi Rhymer's room!"*

"Oh God, Andy, I want to go home."

"We've got his jacket!

"Can't we just leave it somewhere?"

"Where?"

"By the car, in the bushes. I don't know."

"Damn right you don't! We're going to his room."

Chapter 3

STEP ONE IN LOCATING any place: find a gas station. Station's closed for the night. Doesn't matter, find the phone booth. The phone book's been ripped off; the chain dangles empty in midair. Insurmountable problem. Back in the car, drive to the next station.

This one's open twenty-four hours. Ah. The booth still has its books. Ah! It's also being used. Stand around and wait. The guy comes out at last. Check the books. Oakland. No. San Francisco. Yes. Hotel Montor. Gotcha. And I'd half suspected there was no such place. Street address. Now you go over to the station building, and look for the map taped up inside a window. Always is one. Never fails. All it showed was Oakland.

Well shit. Anybody can find San Francisco.

Back up Nimitz freeway to the Bay Bridge plaza in traffic still plugged with concert runoff. I paid the toll. We took the Broadway exit, first one in S.F., and found the big gas station near Broadway and Columbus. There was the right map. Find the index, find the reference numbers, and the street should be—not very far at all from the "Check your location, you are here" arrow pinned to the map.

Slowly we cruised by the lit-up brass-and-glass marquee of the Hotel Montor. What a pile. So drive around once more. Behind the hotel, an alley sliced the block. Skye headed in.

"You can always give me the coat, and take a nap till I get back—"

"Oh, sure," she said.

A dark alley, smelling of sewers. It had some jogs and open spaces in it, and no clear line of sight from end to end. We hopped out of the van on cobblestones.

All the lower part of San Francisco is that way. They landfilled the old waterfront in 1849, Mama says, over the hulls of abandoned ships and used their ballast stones for paving. Wherever there's asphalt now, cobblestones come poking through. History underfoot, right in among the slimy bits of paper, spit, and cigarettes.

Quick, down the alley and around the block. Skye, I notice, shows no signs of napping in the car. We come to the marquee and twirl in through revolving doors behind the whistles of the doormen hailing cabs.

Carpet. Deep, soft, and solid at the same time, maroon and green and gold art-deco architectural flowers. At first all I can see is carpet. And mirrors, mirrors everywhere. It is one enormous place: an indoor public square.

We skulk around edges toward the elevators, past sweet-smelling doors of luxury shops, flowers, jewelry, lingerie: shabby and furtive like runaways and refugees. Except for Tommi's glorious coat. Old Skye is hard to see inside that coat. But look at me. More mirrors. A thief come in to rob the place would need to look more at home.

Lots of people by the elevators. Lots of elevators, in an obnoxious classical brass wall. Lots of people in the lobby. Middle-aged people drinking cocktails at small tables. A dance floor even, and a platform for a band.

A bald man by the elevators has a Belshangles pass on his

coat. He has to know Tommi's jacket. You bet your ass he does. From the corner of my eye I see him check us out, light a cigarette and stroll off toward the main desk. The shit is about to hit the fan. "Look," I hissed, "that guy is going to phone upstairs and tell 'em—"

"Tell 'em what?"

"He had a Belshangles pass on his jacket—"

"What guy?"

Elevator doors ding open. Overdressed people come herding out. So many people, up so late. I shoved Skye in and hit some button fast, before a mob could join us. Inside was mirrors all the way around. We whizzed up silently.

"He said to get out somewhere, didn't he? Andy?"

The door dinged open on the twenty-fifth floor. More heavy carpet, miles of it, red and muted. Nobody in sight. Closed numbered doors. We crept off to the right, hugging the side wall because the middle of that carpet seemed made for giants. I saw a broader door with a lighted EXIT sign, a metal fire door, hard to open and quick to shut.

Now here we go round the vertebrae of the building (dim expanded metal stairs inside a concrete shaft) while a concrete ceiling spirals down to meet us at zero o'clock in the morning. The very last door, by my count is 32.

Fog, cold, and darkness! Bottomless steaming wells and shafts of light! God. We weren't in Hieronymus Bosch's chill hell after all. This was the roof.

So fall back down one round of stairs, through another metal door, and into the middle of another crowd of people opposite a big mirror. Gold carpet on this level, bright and elegant. The music and the party noise was thicker to our left; we went right, as fast as we could without running. "Don't shove," whispered Skye. "C'mon, we've got passes!"

"I don't trust 'em."

"He said we could!"

"Somebody else might say we can't."

"I've got his fucking jacket!"

"Somebody might take it away."

Mostly, I felt guilty somehow. The doors all said 3203, 3205, 3207. It's your standard kid's nightmare; if we could only get around the corner, we'd be out of sight.

So we rounded the corner, straight into the arms of two more little groupie chicks, looking freaky as I felt. One had a see-through blouse. No bra. The other was a light-skinned black girl. Her hair was dyed magenta. They spotted the coat, whispered, and turned to follow us. I knew they recognized it. Now what? March right off to Tommi's room with those two harpies trailing?

"Girl! 'Scuse me! I was just admiring your coat."

Skye still amazes me sometimes. She squealed "Oh my God! Don't you just love it? Isn't it absolutely exactly like Tommi's? My dad had it made up for me last Christmas. You wanta touch it?"

"Fuck you, rich bitch," said Magenta.

They flounced off looking venomous. And when we finally found room 3230, it was the end of a dead-end corridor.

"Did he say 3230?"

"Uh-huh."

"Go ahead," she whispered. "Knock on it."

"You've got his coat. You've got your nerve, too. I couldn't have done what you did back there."

"This is not back there," she said.

So I knocked, and nothing happened for a bit. I knocked again, and could almost imagine soft footsteps on a rug. Tommi Rhymer opened the door himself.

He looked both of us carefully up and down, his head cocked to one side. "Well, well," he said. "My coat. And friends. Come on in. Make yourselves at home."

I'd never seen a hotel room without beds. This was a fancy living room—deep beige rug, beige sofas, heavy glass tables with magazines and flowers. A bar to one side. A hall with mirrors. I guessed the bedrooms were off that. The only thing of interest in the place was Tommi anyway, twenty times more of a shock in that living room than he was on stage.

It wasn't done with lights and makeup. His hair was damp from the shower. He wore a silk shirt, handkerchief-thin, with one of those European fishnet T-shirts under it. His slacks were gold silk, and he was barefoot.

He had the whitest skin I've ever seen, whiter than his shirt, almost silver. At the stadium, running backward up the ramp he shouted, "What? In my business I go down at sunrise!" That's exactly how he looked. Under the white was a web of phantom freckles. In the sun he'd go quite brown with them.

His eyes were the palest blue that human eyes can be, a second eerie shade of silver, outlined in heavy long lashes same color as his hair. Darker than bright copper, much hotter than mahogany. Not quite, but almost, blood red.

The redheaded kids I know have white eyelashes and look like Hereford steers.

He curled himself into the sofa opposite, watching carefully the impression that he made. "Oh, pardon me!" suddenly erupting out of it. "I'm a rotten host. I'll bet you're tired of forced confinement to that coat—"

Somebody knocked at the door.

Tommi froze. Put a finger to his lips. Another knock. You could dimly hear people shifting around in the hall outside. Snatches of annoyed conversation. Tommi's pale eyes glided from the door to us. After a silence, he went on: "I have something for you. I hope you'll think it's special, but your parents shouldn't mind."

He disappeared at a lope down the mirrored hallway.

"It's not real," whispered Skye. "It can't be."

"What?"

"His hair. I've never seen anything that color."

"I have. That girl in the wheelchair."

"What girl?"

"At school. Cissy. Missy. Whatever her name is."

"That gross little fat one that's only three feet tall? She's a freak! She's hideous!"

But her hair's the same color, and her skin also. Poor round puffy little face with the little round goggle eyes that stare up so imploringly through thick round plastic lenses. And the milk-white skin and the bonfire-colored hair are just a bad joke and a mockery: To him who hath much, much shall be given; but from her who hath little, shall be taken away even that which she hath.

Here came Tommi back again. On him it was sheer glory. Like Shakespeare this time—"Beauty too rich for use." His beauty exploded in my head, bombarding me with poetry remembered out of everywhere, which all made perfect new sense hung around his neck.

Even so, I could see he wasn't well. Like a different kid at school, the little guy with allergies and asthma that can kill. The wasted dark hollows around his eyes were just the same. But on Tommi it was only decadent: still gorgeous in a way. Stage makeup had covered that.

Wrong. The black eye-makeup was the dark circles drawn big. Chosen and stylized, flaunted for an audience. He was wearing his scars like decorations. He was the sexiest thing that I had ever seen.

And he was waving around a big orange sweatshirt. "See this? One made up for each body on the tour. Printed with the tour logo. And our names. I'm not much into sweatshirts; you can wear this one for me. You'll know where y'got it from, but your mum can think y'bought it off a stand. Let's see how y'look in it; the loo's down there.

Skye retreated with the sweatshirt. Tommi turned to me. "May I offer you something?" He opened the refrigerator in the bar. Inside was the most dazzling selection of liquor and soft drinks. And it wasn't that I had no wants, but I couldn't recall the names of anything. His presence filled my mind up to exclusion.

"S'all right," he said, quick to pick up my distress, as he always was in dreams. He flipped my choice shut. "I don't force drinks on pretty people."

Skye came back minus jacket. The sweatshirt covered. She plopped into the couch beside me, and the two of us stared up at him. I hoped his social skills were of the greatest; we were going to be hopeless, dumb silly animals in his company.

All at once, an unexpected easy out.

More noises at the door. No knuckles on wood this time, but a key in the lock. Serious business. Somebody was coming in. There was a deadbolt on the door; Tommi took one long stride toward it. Too late. It had opened and closed, and admitted Harlan Parr, a full champagne glass in each hand. He stopped short at the sight of us.

He wore a fur jacket cut the same as Tommi's, but his was a glossy, rusty black to match his hair. As he stood beside the lamp at the end of my sofa, spots showed jet-black in the rust-black fur. Black on black. Oh God, oh God, he has a real black leopard coat!

I couldn't believe Greenpeace, the Audubon Society, Jacques Cousteau, or somebody hadn't strung him up for sacrilege! I could only stare, shocked and amazed and charmed, how the fur of the leopard blended with his hair.

Glorious long black hair. Not punk blue-black, or heavy metal shagged or frizzy white-man's Afro. Just sweet warm dark. He had an ancient tweed cap crammed down over it; the brim met the top of his dark glasses. Wound around his throat was a long, long Chinese red silk scarf.

A hand came up, Champagne and all. Taking his shades with thumb and forefinger, Harlan eased them down from cynical gold-hazel eyes. "Is this a private party? Should I have brought a tray?"

Tommi just groaned.

I perceived a truth. "Handsome" is not the word for Harlan. Nor "cute," nor "pretty," nor anything like that. Not even "megababe." He has a face that makes you want to cry "Oh!" and burst into tears, like all the other faces in the world have some protective membrane over them, and only his is naked.

"Ah," he said, "that time again, I see."

"Don't you press it," said Tommi.

"I'll do more than that to it, if you step a little closer."

They stood and stared holes in each other. Tommi looked really malevolent. "Why don't you stop while you're ahead?"

Harlan set his shades and Champagne glasses on the table. "How many years ago was that?" He flashed this wonderfully bright small smile. It had too many teeth in it. It was coquettish to a scandalous degree and not at all sincere; it looked a little dangerous. It looked very much more than a little dangerous. "Thomas. I need you."

"Good. I'm glad. I need you, too. Now go away."

"Thomas."

"What?"

"Take care of me."

Tommi exploded "God damn! Can't you even wait till we're in private?"

"I am in private: this is my room!"

"Come back in half an hour."

"There is a little gathering down the hall, at which we are the hosts?"

"I have everything I need right here. Do you mind?"

"I mind. God. You know I mind."

"Ah, go stuff yer fucking party! I don't like getting the clap. I don't want herpes. I don't want AIDS. I don't care if y'did slip Sim twenty quid to let the best ones in—"

"Not that kind of party, Thomas. Hors d'oeuvres, Champagne, and half the San Francisco Board of Supervisors—"

"Which half?"

"—and Madame Mayor. You do remember Madame Mayor?"

"Bugger Madame Mayor!"

"I don't consider that an appropriate suggestion. They want to look at you. What am I supposed to do for them? Sing and dance?"

"Try stripping."

Harlan's gold eyes opened very wide. One hip began to flip, the discreetest little echo of a boom-boom beat. He caught a corner of red silk up across his face, and became Salome with the seven veils. The long scarf slid serpent-fashion round his throat; out and out it followed his hand. Until his arm stretched sideways from his shoulder, the red silk flowed along. The end snaked from his collar. The arm dropped. One last flip of hip and wrist laid out a silky Chinese challenge on the carpet.

Tommi flung himself at Harlan bodily. Somebody shrieked. Down the little hall they darted, one on the other's heels. The bedroom door flashed shut between them.

Tommi hit the door full force. "Harlan—God-damn, Harlan! Open, or I'll kick it in!"

The door opened so unexpectedly that Tommi fell inside. It closed behind him quickly as it opened. The two of us sat like birds on a fence, staring down an empty hall.

"Holy shit, Batman, what was that?"

"Harlan Parr," I whispered.

"I know that, but what was it all about?"

"Us, I think."

"What?"

"Not to change the subject or anything, which door is the bathroom?" I suddenly realized, I hadn't been since morning in the Oakland BART Station. Simple discomfort had come and gone. I was squirming. "Skye. Wake up."

"Second to the right."

I didn't want to go any closer to where Tommi and Harlan were. Especially the hall, that gauntlet of mirrors. After looking at those two, the last dumb face I needed to encounter was my own. Eyes locked upside-down to Tommi's silk-screened ones on the chest of my old Belshangles T-shirt, I tiptoed through.

The bathroom was all mirrors too. Beige marble, soft lights, and mirrors. I have to use the toilet! Shut my eyes, that's what I'll do. But now I could hear too well.

Tommi and Harlan were still going at each other in the bedroom. The wording of their quarrel ate right through the wall. Tommi must have his back to me; the voice I heard was Harlan's, cultured, sharp-edged, and intolerable: "Fifteen minutes? Is that all you give them anymore?"

He was cut off by a thud, a sound of breaking glass. I felt

sick. Everybody knows some rock stars trash hotel rooms. I didn't know Tommi and Harlan did it. And I wouldn't have dreamed they'd do it trying to trash each other.

Harlan's voice, bitter and unsilenced: "What could they possibly mean to you? What makes it worth the risk? If you took all night to glory in it, I might grant you my respect—"

Too embarrassing to flush the toilet; they'd know I was still here. All I wanted was to pick up Skye and slink away unnoticed with a damaged heart.

They must have changed places in the skirmish, because the next real howl of anguish was certainly Tommi's: "So what d'y'think I am? What'd you ever think I was? I'm just a street punk after all!"

Tommi and Harlan: my world getting ravaged.

What I'd found to cherish about Belshangles was hardly more than the close sweet fusion of those two in center stage, their music up to maximum revs, orbiting each other like morning and evening of the same giddy blissed-out day. They mustn't quarrel! I mustn't listen.

I opened the bathroom door. At the same instant, the bedroom door flew open and Harlan shot through it. I saw him plainly in the hall mirrors. He got as far as the length of Tommi's arm before he was yanked back.

There was a stone partition just inside the bedroom door, the back of a free-standing fireplace maybe, slate or fieldstone, something elegant, hiding the rest of the room from view. Tommi got both hands on Harlan's jacket collar, and slammed him backward, hard into that wall. And there he pinned him with the whole length of his own body.

I saw Harlan's full face, pleading now in whispers, or threatening, or something in between. So desirable in his distress. He could have seen mine, too, if once he'd glanced into the hall. But for him, there was no hall, nor any possibility of mirrors. There was only Tommi, inches from his eyes. And Tommi bent his head, with a kind of dreadful slow grace, and stopped Harlan's mouth with his own.

I had never seen one man kiss another. I had never seen anybody kiss anybody that way. Real-life kisses are embarrassing fumbles, and movie kisses are all raunched-up plastic hype. This was the kiss of legends: the kind that can kill or bring to life. Or wake the Sleeping Beauty. Or give the gift of prophecy.

It went on almost forever, and I was frozen in the dumb bathroom. I couldn't breathe. My heart was thrashing. Then Harlan's head lay back against the stone. His cap was knocked off, his eyes were closed. He looked unconscious or asleep.

The eyes drifted open. He didn't say a word. He didn't need to. Desire rose up and claimed his face like a warm flood. You could watch it rising and rising, till soon everything that wasn't bolted down in him would float; and there were plenty of such things, every kind of naked fear, loneliness, jealousy, frustration, shame. All headed out now with the tide.

Tommi's right hand slid from Harlan's collar, protectively around his shoulders as if he feared that he might fall. They began to kiss again. He reached back with his left hand, found the bedroom door, and flipped it shut.

And I wept without a sound, bowed almost to the bathroom floor with grief. What I'd seen was not a one-time accident. Oh no. It was how they lived: the rivalries, the differences, the play-acting, a daily ritual between these two. The swift flare of violence. The same sweet mutual meltdown into pleasure.

I had seen into their bedroom, where I never should have seen. I hadn't meant to. I wished I could take it back. I wished I had never come to the concert, or come here. It didn't seem wrong that they were lovers; it was only too right. It was just unbearable. Double-exposed on all my posters and collected photos from now on would float the image of that kiss.

I couldn't hate Harlan. I loved Harlan. If only I could creep inside his skin with him. Talk about Icons of Desire. I would've gladly traded the remainder of my life just then to have that arm around my shoulders, and that mouth pressed close to my mouth, and that door shut smartly in between the two of us and everyone else on earth.

One thing certain. Skye mustn't ever know. In spite of all the rude talk she puts out—maybe because of it—I knew she wouldn't understand. She'd call them fags. She would. Her friends would know in half a day. The nasty jokes, the whispered retellings, I could write the whole scenario.

Like the man said, "Hell is other people."

And it seemed so grossly unfair. This present ache in my chest was no by-product of a religious education. Not of mine, at any rate: this was one guilt trip I never ingested. The only church I knew after all, was Father Malachi and Saint Ann's Chapel.

The entire Saint Ann's High Mass Chant Choir ate Vesper Dinner at our house on Sunday nights, twenty to twenty-five strong. Some were Stanford faculty and some were students. They talked Old Church theology, art, music, wine, medieval history, sports cars, and computer hacking. I talked it with 'em, since none would admit (not in that company at least) to even a tolerance for rock music. But mostly, they talked New Church politics.

It seems the Catholic Church went supernova six years before I was born: huger and brighter, more involved, more relevant, more media-conscious, more, more, more, until the gassy outer shell just blew off into space, and the rest fell back into the Vatican, an ecclesiastical black hole receding inward faster than the speed of light.

American Catholics (like my parents) got told something unheard of: "Form your own consciences." Half the Catholics in the U.S. went up in a radioactive cloud. But the remnant (like my parents) did what they were told.

Ten years after I was born it sank in on the higher-ups that the format of those consciences was not exactly as foreseen. "Okay, folks, this has been a fun experiment. But now, unform your consciences." Meltdown. There go the rest. Descendants of survivors roam the parishes in furtive mutant bands, forming their own consciences.

The Folk-Mass and the High-Mass crews at Saint Ann's don't trust each other very much: your Modern Church in miniature. And the folk contingent runs the Sunday school: power in numbers. I got to be eleven years old and had never had First Communion, just like Saint Bernadette.

Papa looked over the materials the folkies used in their instruction, and at my grade level, when it came to the resurrection of Jesus (one key concept after all), the picture they put in to illustrate it was a two-page full-color glossy spread of—an Easter basket! Green fake grass, dyed eggs, marshmallow eggs, and imitation baby chicks all wrapped up in pastel cellophane; and, get this, outside the cellophane, one solitary chocolate rabbit, free-standing on the table top.

When asked if he's a liberal or conservative Catholic, Papa's been known to say "A survivalist!"

Needless to say, I didn't go to Saint Ann's Sunday school. He tried to take me out to Redwood Priory. They only do boys. But one of the monks is a family friend; he offered to instruct me. Father Malachi is a genuine Hungarian Refugee, and has seen it all. He's also a counselor at Juvy Hall.

He began on me by saying, "The first question in the Baptism you received when you were very small is 'What do you ask of the Church of God?' The answer is 'Faith.' "

I said "Sounds all right to me," which everybody thought was hilarious for some reason.

"That," he said, "is what I try to give you." And he knew what I was like. No chocolate rabbits. He gave me the Saints. All this wondrous stuff from the Desert Fathers, Catherine of Siena, Francis of Assisi, and both the Teresas, right down to Joseph of Cupertino and Margaret Mary Alacoque. People who preached to wolves and were fed by ravens, warriors and wise women and spinners of splendid words, hermits and holy loonies who piped like birds and flew above the heads of the people in church, and the swooning mystical lovers. They were just what I needed: someone to feed on, someone to bleed on, like the song says. I took them off into my blackest privacy and ate them up.

Like I know I was born on the Vigil of Saint Laurence, whom an angry Roman Emperor had broiled on a barbecue.

Laurence's last words were "Turn me over, boys, I'm done on this side." I can appreciate Saint Laurence.

But then, into that select and glorious company, with no real qualm, I'd somehow admitted Tommi Rhymer: better than remembered poetry, a man I recited in my head for company. Is that so strange? I know any number of normal kids surviving much the same way, their whole inner lives hitched happily to different stars.

The Who knew all about it:

I used to wake up in the mornings,
I used to feel so bad
I got so sick of having sleepless nights
I went and told my Dad—
He said "Son, now here's some little something."
And stuck them on my wall—
And now my nights ain't quite so lonely
In fact I don't feel bad at all.

Pictures of Lily made my life so wonderful,
Pictures of Lily helped me sleep at night.
Pictures of Lily solved my childhood problems
Pictures of Lily helped me feel alright.

And then one day things weren't quite so fine
I fell in love with Lily.
I asked my dad where Lily I could find,
He said "Son, now don't be silly,
She's been dead since 1929—"
Oh how I cried that night!
If only I'd been born in Lily's time
It would have been alright—
Pictures of Lily—Lily, oh Lily—

Fantasy Lovers. Icons of Desire.

Consider the gawky, zit-faced, longhaired boys whose every thought revolves around the raunchy doings of Iron Maiden or

Mötley Crüe. And oh, the dear priceless dead ones—not quite saints, but I understood the concept—Elvis, Jim Morrison, John Lennon, Jimi Hendrix. Lily Langtry, dead since 1929.

I'd played with Tommi Rhymer for three years. Slept with him, showered with him, gone to school with him. When I was brave he was brave with me, and when I failed he took my rap. While to parents, teachers, and siblings he was (more or less) invisible. I was twelve, and thirteen, and fourteen: a woman in a child's life with no appropriate place to go, stuck, like a fly in amber. Nobody understood but Tommi. And what was he? Sassy, sexy, witty magician. A child triumphant in a man's life, maybe?

If all the really real I ever got to share with Tommi Rhymer was this one lonely and unwelcome secret, at least it would keep safe with me. Value for value received. I owed him that much anyway.

So I turned myself to face me (as the song says), all damp and blotchy in the bathroom mirror. My eyes looked like they'd just been fried. Skye would know the passage of each tear. Tommi and Harlan too, if they saw me again. They'd know I'd seen them.

I ran hot water, soaked my face, and toweled it pink all over. No makeup on it now, not that much was left after the concert. Mostly dirt. But, almost like magic, on the counter end next to Tommi's jacket sat an elegant little makeup kit. Beautiful expensive makeup. Nobody would see my tears through Tommi's eye shadow. Diving in, I shadowed up my eyes until I looked like a raccoon.

No. Not Tommi's: God help me, wrong colors. Ivory and black and gold, and a wonderful peacock, green as jealousy!

I felt like scrubbing it all off. I didn't want to think about Harlan. He simply had no right to be that beautiful. Or that splendid a musician. Or to be next door in bed with the man I loved. Because that's where he was. I could scream and pound my fists into the floor at the thought of him! Perish the thought of him! There is no Harlan.

Still no sound from the room next door.

I eased into the hall. The bedroom door was shut tight, though I half-expected them to tumble through it locked in a wild embrace. When they didn't, I made it to the living room. Skye was asleep, sunk full-length in the couch and snoring softly. Oh, oh. Well, what am I supposed to do? I looked around the room for hot suggestions. I checked Harlan's Champagne glasses. (There is no Harlan.) Both empty.

Skye Milligan, you are a scuzz.

But that decided what I had to do, sit around and let her sleep it off. Two ritzy little glasses of Champagne shouldn't be enough to waste Skye; there is a lot of Skye. Even so, if some over-zealous CHP should test her under-the-influence, that would put the frosting on the world's worst day. I sprawled on the opposite sofa, my head pillowed on one arm.

Damn Skye. And double damn and perish Harlan. And double, triple damn—No. I couldn't perish Tommi. Not with his milk-white skin and his dark red eyelashes and silver eyes. And his soaring broken-hearted music. I had this awful, awful sense: something like a strong cold wind had forced its way inside my chest, blasting a cavity around my heart, which my heart would have to dilate now to fill.

I surfaced from a cheerless doze—to find two heads resting on my arm instead of one: Tommi Rhymer kneeling by my couch, pure fantasy lover all the way. The lights are turned down low. Shy sly sleepy eyes smile into mine from not six inches distant.

I'm making this up. Have to be. I know that face so well it isn't difficult. I wanted what Harlan got so badly, I'm dreaming for myself the same sweet ticket. He isn't real; this is a fantasy creature of slow luxury.

"And I was just about to pry an eyelid up," he whispered, "to see if y'were home."

He burrowed his nose into the soft warm place on the inside of my elbow, and breathed deep. If this is a dream, it's the hottest one I ever engaged in.

"Please don't," I whispered back. "It isn't very clean—"

He caught my arm gently, so I couldn't pull it away. "Soap was never my greatest turn-on. Let's see what it is you don't want me to find. *Mm-hm.* Crushed grass. 'S'that it, now? Dusty ground. Hot asphalt?"

What a giggle. Really irrepressibly delightful to have him sorting through me and my day like a miser through his gold. "That's parking lot. I spent all day camped in the parking lot." Long hazy pauses. "Any hot plywood?"

He nuzzled my arm with slow interest: "Yes."

"The front of the stage."

"Ah. Spilled soft drink."

"Diet Pepsi."

"No. Orange, I think. Mm. Mustard. Pot smoke?"

"Not mine."

"Not yours. No. Cloves? Not yours either. And sweat, of course."

"That's mine."

"Not all. You smell like a crowd. And a sweet, high-summer night."

"That," I said, "is concert smell."

He laughed. "I love it. One could bottle the scent and make millions instantly, wherever records are sold."

"Not quite. There's one ingredient missing."

"Which is?"

"New T-shirt smell. I never got to buy mine."

He sat back on his heels in mock dismay. "Now how could y'lay that on me? When you saw me give my only item of the kind away?"

"Don't worry, please. I'm glad she got it."

"I guess I'll have to find you something else." He settled his cheek onto my arm again like a caress. "What can I do for you?"

What indeed. He could blow me away with the greatest of ease, that's what. I want to wind my arms around his neck and pull him into the couch, kiss him and be kissed by him, like he kissed Harlan. The thought of Harlan brings with it now a curious little snap of guilt.

"We're all that's left awake, girl," Tommi said. "I think your friend has gone down for the night."

I have to say it. "What about yours?

"Mine?" he pondered drowsily. "My friend? He got what he wanted. Always does, y'know. He'll be good for a bit."

"No, he won't," said someone else.

Abruptly, silently, the lights came up. "I'm sorry, Tom. Forgive me. But it isn't going to work, this time." Harlan stood by the hall, with his hand on the dimmer.

If Tommi looked different to me, Harlan was straight from Oz. All gauzy on the edges, and beginning to dissolve in the light. He wore a green silk dressing gown over his black silk slacks. He was barefoot too. And he had cried. Unlike me, he made no effort to conceal it.

"I like—to play the U.S.," he said, "I like to play the world, in fact. I like to play with you. This is—the life I bargained for, all things considered. I won't stand by, and watch you piss it all away."

I felt like sinking through the couch, but he wasn't looking at me. I was only something wrong with Tommi. Tommi huddled against me, as a really loving dog will when you punish it. "Harlan," he whispered. "Go back to bed."

"No, Tom. I won't." His speech was just as far off as his looks, sad and calm and too precise, with funny gaps erased in it. "Tom. Just because that—person—in Los Angeles was happy to be bought, doesn't mean that these girls don't—belong to someone, who would rather have your hide than have your money—"

"I bought a kid acting lessons."

"You paid blood money."

"I understood those people. You never had nothing. Y'been somebody's treasure all your life. Know that?"

"Oh for God's sake, Tom. I can't bear to see you hurt."

"You're seeing it now."

"Better here than in some American judge's court. And in all the papers. And in prison." He walked to where Skye lay and nudged her gently. She started. "Wake up, dear, the party's over. There's a girl." She sat up, looking guilty. Harlan turned back to Tommi. He had this dizzy little smile. "I called the cops," he said.

Tommi knelt crumpled, motionless; his cheek and hand still rested on my arm. "Y'didn't."

"Yes. I just did. Back there." He directed a vague look and gesture down the hall. "Americans—very practical. Put all the right numbers on the cover—of their phone book. Told them who you are. You have two young—didn't say if they were girls or boys, actually, thought that was a nice touch—up here, and enough good stuff in your room to last the three of you a week. They seemed interested, so—I told them—exactly where you get it, how you got it past their idiotic customs, and exactly where—"

"You fucking bastard, Harlan."

"Now you go pack your pretty children down the stairs."

"Wait a minute," said Skye. "Mr. Parr, just how old do you think I am? Huh?"

"Twelve," he said mildly, "at the outside."

"I am eighteen years old! You wanta see my driver's license?"

Skye had to be getting really shook, she'd started playing poker. Her license said sixteen. Harlan held his hand out for it. All the time he never took his eyes from Tommi.

"I'll help you transfer things, and we'll both be at that party when they come. It was a classic crank-call, really, just some poor chap with a grudge."

"I don't believe you!"

Under cover of his shoulder, Tommi consolidated his grip on my right wrist.

"Why not? I told you in Los Angeles, you clean your act, or I will clean it for you—"

"Is it only my act now?" said Tommi. "I thought we were together." I could feel him tensing.

"Funny," said Harlan, "so did I."

"And if they take a good look at your eyes, what then?"

Harlan retrieved his shades from underneath the wine glasses, and put them on. "They promised they'd be here in fifteen minutes. You have—maybe seven?"

Skye jumped up to confront him. "Look, Mr. Parr, I don't know what you're talking about! All he's done is be kind to us—"

"I know, dear," Harlan said, his black glass eyes turned implacably on Tommi. "He knows how to be so kind. And you can tell them all about it when they come." He checked his watch. "We might still have five minutes, Tom."

Without the slightest warning, Tommi broke across the room like a sprinter off the blocks. I sailed off my couch and straight across the glass-topped coffee table. No way was I prepared for him to be so desperately strong. His other hand found Skye's wrist as we hurtled toward the door.

"Open it!" he screamed at me, "Now! Now! Now!"

I scrabbled futilely, left-handed at the knob for what seemed minutes; then we were racing in the hall. Harlan ran behind us. He shouted at Tommi. I fully expected to mingle with police at any moment, or crowds out of that party. You could hear the party somewhere, loud music and a good sound system, Belshangles tapes. Laughter. Surely we must meet somebody! Anybody! Nobody. There was the heavy fire door, and I had to battle left-handed through it.

Harlan caught the door before it closed. "Them!" he shouted. "Not you!"

But once on the stairway, Tommi had grown wings. "Go fuck yourself!" We were down one flight of stairs.

"Don't be a damn fool, Tom!"

"Do it twice!"

The door slammed up above; no clue which side of it Harlan was on. Down and down we spun, around and around. The metal stairs set up an awful clangor under our feet, which amplified around inside the enclosed well. Tommi's mode of getting down was truly remarkable: each flight of stairs in two big jumps. Take off from the landing, crash somewhere in the middle, ricochet off in the direction of the next landing far below, smash into it, swing wide, staggering and flailing, carom off the metal fire door, a sort of swimmer's racing turn in midair, and repeat.

It was just extravagantly dangerous, a crazy little macho kid trying to be impressive. So damn unnecessary, as if I wasn't impressed already. On every landing he seemed looser in the knees, more like Dorothy's Scarecrow.

Then his heel missed a step and he went airborne, with a firm grip on our wrists, though. I grabbed the rail, and held on for all I was worth. Skye was not prepared at all; she just kept going with him, down half a flight of stairs onto a landing. Broken bones for sure.

But Skye jumped up, scared and furious. It was Tommi who lay on the floor. He made a sound as I bent over him, between a moan and a cry. "Oh, Harlan—Goddamn Harlan—"

My sentiments exactly.

"Are you all right?" He didn't answer. I wanted to say "Please, get up!" I wanted to shake him. I was afraid to touch him. He'd touched me up till this; I hadn't him. A first-class difference somehow. I raised my head. We were the only people on the stairs, no noises above or below. "Listen," I said. "Nobody is after you!"

Tommi rolled languorously onto his back. I stared down at him, and he stared up. There were no bruises visible or bloody places. "Y'got green eyes," he said.

Damn it. Sudden enlightenment.

"Do you know where you are?"

"Heathrow."

Oh damn damn damn. I knew why he'd moved like that, why he'd fallen, why he wasn't getting up. He wasn't damaged; he was just drugged out. Okay. Try to sound firm.

"You were taking me to my car!"

"Right on," he murmured. "Screw Harlan." At least he remembered something. The last thing I wanted to remember.

Tommi floundered up and tried to reinstate his grip. Skye

swore at him; he got her anyway. "Don't! Andy, get him off of me! Can't you make him understand that hurts?"

"Hey!" Try stern, if firm doesn't make it. "We don't need that! We're going with you, but the next time you try to kill yourself, do it on your own."

He gave me this uneasy smile, and shut his eyes. "Right," he whispered.

The going got slower after that. And slower. But at last there was a metal door with EXIT on it. The stairs went on, to basements and sub basements. We came out on a loading dock beside a garbage Dumpster.

Wet night air and distant street roar. Big roll-up metal doors revealed an empty alley, like a stage set. Other lighted doors along the dock fronted for kitchen noises. Two o'clock in the morning. Tommi flung himself down, amiable and slack-jointed, on the edge of the dock. "Sit here for a bit," he said.

Skye pulled me behind the Dumpster.

I said, "What can I do?"

"Let's get away from him! I don't like him!"

"What?"

"I don't even like his looks close up."

"How can you say that?"

"Easy."

So I ignored her, and went to camp with Tommi. He was lying on his back now, knees drawn up. In a way, she was right. What could I do with him? Try to walk him all the way back up the stairs and head him toward his room? And if the cops were really there? As it was, they had no Tommi and no kids. I didn't want to be the evidence come back to ruin him. True, I wasn't drugged. They could test me and prove that. I hadn't had sex with anybody ever. They could probably test for that too; I wasn't looking forward to it.

I could leave him here with Skye, and go tell—no, I couldn't. How about the party? I could go up there and find help. Nicky or Rollo. A roadie. Somebody. A drug bust might have roped in all those guys by now, to give statements or something. Or maybe they all were high. My idea of Narc Squad operations is courtesy of commercial television strictly.

Like my idea how the Church feels about gays. Did anyone ever teach me that? No priest I ever heard preach said shit about that. No, I got the chance to learn it for myself, in all its glory, off the six-o'clock news.

A door behind us belched dishwashing sounds, a trash hamper, and a big-bellied man in a kitchen apron. I looked away fast. Some people will let you alone if you don't make eye contact. This wasn't one of them. He dumped his sweepings. "You kids can't crash in here, you know that."

"Glad you told us," said Skye.

"Don't get smart, it's not my rule. Just move along."

"Okay."

At least he didn't recognize Tommi. Probably a country-western fan himself.

"What's the matter with your redheaded friend?"

Oh God. Here it comes.

"Nothing."

"Sure. If he can walk, get him out of here. If he's still here in five minutes, I call the cops. Fucking punk kids," he said.

Nothing was the matter with Tommi's ears. He reacted promptly to Apron Man's ultimatum by rolling off the dock. I was a little shocked. I hadn't thought he could walk either, but he did. Out into the dark with exaggerated dignity. Never looked back. Neither did we.

"Andy, where are we going? Andy, this is the alley where we left the car! We're going in the wrong direction."

I turned around. Sure enough, there it was. I ran to catch Tommi. "Hey! You were taking me to my car!"

He seemed delighted to see me. "Taking y'straight home," he whispered. "Too many cops. Entirely."

"It's back there," I pointed. "The orange-and-white thing. You can see it."

He got a death grip on my arm, and we tacked back past the lighted kitchen. Apron Man was nowhere in sight. Nobody else was either. Thank God. Tommi was fading fast. What on earth could I do with him? Drive him around to the lobby? Maybe he was used to navigating in this fix; I wasn't used to watching. Even prayer seemed inappropriate. I ached for him.

He leaned more heavily on me at every step. But we made it to the van. A little naked grimy light bulb shone on the wall above, by the name of a Chinese doctor.

Tommi tried to say something. It came out garbled; it even sounded wrong to him. Mild amazement flowed across his face. He tried again. This time the end was plain: "Tell—Harlan—will you?"

So much for mental quarantine. Harlan was where help lay. So they fought. They were lovers, and that was that. Harlan wouldn't want him wasted on the street.

"Tell him what?" No answer. Tommi's forehead rested against the van. "Please, I don't know what to tell him."

He turned to me again, this long, awful look. What was it? Languid terror? Slow-motion panic? "Anything," he whispered. "I'll do it—"

"Come on," I said. "Give me your arm. We'll find him. I'll take you back, and we'll tell him together."

"You better hurry," said Skye. People were coming now, half a dozen of them up the alley, silhouettes against a distant light.

Tommi's eyes drifted, from my face to hers, then back.

"I don't know you," he said.

When he went down on the slimy pavement he did it ever so slowly, a big inflatable toy with the air valve open. He kept on crumpling, curling and curling round into the fetal position before he lay still. We both stared down at him. His head hung over a storm drain. Underneath the alley, water was running.

"Let's go," whispered Skye.

"Are you crazy? You mean leave him on the street?"

"Somebody'll find him."

"Sure they will! They'll kill him for his wallet! Or the police'll run him in for drugs."

"Is that what's the matter with him?"

"They both shot up or snorted or whatever in the bedroom back there. That's why they acted so funny."

"Well I don't know zip about drugs!"

"Don't gimme that!"

"Look, this isn't grass! Only guy I've ever seen pass out is Patrick on his dad's fucking pool table, and that was plain old vodka! They hauled him off by the arms, and he puked down the side-pocket."

"You think I give a shit where Patrick puked?"

"What do you want me to do?"

"Get the car started!"

Unconscious, Tommi looked as thin as agony. Beautiful bones for sure, but every one showed. I could see the sweat standing on his forehead and his upper lip. He looked like a little sick kid. Bet I can lift him.

Bet I'm scared to touch him. I've wanted to hold him for so long, but this is real: no fun at all. The guys up the block are taking a sudden interest in us; one begins to trot. God, they must think we're hookers rolling drunks.

Crouching on the cobbles I got my arms under Tommi, knees and shoulders, said a quick "Have mercy," and he came up easy. He didn't weigh a thing. I hoisted him into the middle seat. But Avery's sliding door won't shut from inside; you have to slam it hard and climb in front.

They were all running at me now, six really tough young Chinese dudes in matching jumpsuits, looking badder than Bruce Lee in hell. I piled in beside Skye, locked my door. They surrounded the car and began to beat their fists on it and shout things in Chinese. I lunged back across the seat and locked the sliding door over Tommi. "Lock your door! Start the car!"

Skye came awake: "Andy, I don't want him in here!"

"Do you want them in here? Is the hatch door locked? I can't even hold that if they start to get it open!"

"Oh, shit!"

She locked her door just as they reached it. They ran down

the alley all around us, pounding on the car sides. One took something hard to a window, but the glass held. We made it to the street. Only then they dropped back in the shadows.

"Where do you want me to take him? To a hospital?"

"Just get me on the freeway."

"I don't know how!"

"Go west, till you hit Van Ness."

"Which is west? Do I have to go up hills?"

"Go like you are! Left on Van Ness, right at the freeway sign. Like you always do."

"Andy, I really mean this. This is my mom's car after all, and I don't want him in here!"

"I'm your friend. I want him." Putting it in words, I know it's true. Gay or straight, sick, well, or bombed out of his mind, I want Tommi Rhymer.

And this means something now, because I've got him.

Chapter 4

A RED LIGHT STOPS HER at the freeway ramp. Green. She drives on. In the dead hours the skyway's almost deserted. One deep breath: "Okay, I've thought of where to take him. We don't want to go toward San Jose."

"That's the way home."

"You think I want to take him home? Try the Bay Bridge."

"What *for?*"

"I'll tell you all about it."

We pass the Embarcadero ramp, and the bridge arches up over the dark bay. Treasure Island off-ramp next. She can still turn around, better stall her. Now the Yerba Buena tunnel: white lights, white tile siding, the middle of the bridge.

"Please tell me what I'm doing. Are we gonna park somewhere till he comes to?"

"Now it's toll-free in this direction, you don't need to worry about that. When we reach the toll plaza, you keep right and follow the signs that say 680, Walnut Creek."

"Who do you know in Walnut Creek?"

"My dad's lawyer lives there." That'll keep her thinking. What's more, it's perfectly true.

Keep right. Another freeway now, through Oakland, through Berkeley, and into the hills. The long grade up to the Caldecott Tunnel: more tile and lights. The long grade down the other side: dark hills and sleeping country houses. Pleasant Hill—Orinda—Walnut Creek—

"Now you take the next right."

"That's back toward San Jose!"

"I know. How's your gas?"

"Okay," she said. She sounded pretty resigned.

Ten minutes went by. "Take the next exit, and go that way," I pointed. "Back across this road."

And she did. Headed east now, traffic thinned in country darkness. It took several minutes for the signs to penetrate. "This can't be right. You don't want to go to Stockton!"

"You got it."

"Andy!"

"Keep driving."

Instead, she stood on the brakes. "I'm pulling over, till you tell me where I'm headed."

No help for it. "I'm taking Tommi to the cabin."

"Your mom and dad's cabin?" she said incredulously. "But that's in the Sierras! That's three hours from here!"

"Two and a half from here. If you keep driving."

"I can't drive all that way!"

"Why not?"

"I'm sick! I feel shitty! I don't want to! My stepdad'll kill me! I don't know how to get there!"

"I do. Drive fast. You'll get home in the morning."

"Why the hell do you want me to drive him to the Sierras and back? Andy Falconer, *what is your fucking trip?*"

"I said *you'll* get back in the morning. I'm staying up there. With him."

She drew a long shuddering breath. "You will be in such deep shit, I don't want to know you! He'll be so pissed when he wakes up! What do you expect him to do? Make love to you?"

"Didn't you ever just wanta be *alone* with somebody?"

"And what the fuck do I tell 'em when they ask me where you are?"

"Tell 'em you lost me at the concert. You looked all over and never found me. Then you just drove around all night 'cause you were too scared to go home."

"Your dad won't believe that!"

"Sure he will. It's a lot more likely than what really happened."

"How will you get home?"

"If I don't show up on my own before next Saturday, you come and get me."

"I'll still be grounded, I swear!"

"Then the weekend after. We've got enough food up there. Don't bring me all the way home. You can drop me off; I'll walk in on my own and make up all the lies."

"What about him? What if he doesn't wake up? If he's really OD'd, he could die in my mom's car! He could be dead now! You haven't looked at him since you put him in."

And I hadn't.

I scrambled back into the middle seat. Tommi had gone in on his side, a pale heap in the shadows. Down on the floor with my ear to his mouth, I listened. If he was breathing, I couldn't hear it. I found his hands; they were limp and cold.

One time I lay in bed with the flu and read the first part of the phone book, the Survival Guide, you know: "Bleeding, Breathing, Broken Bones, Burns, Earthquake, Electric Shock," etc., and I remember "Overdose" was in there all right, under "Poisons." It said, "First, call help." I can't. "Keep the victim warm." I can try. "Watch for breathing. If he isn't, give mouth-to-mouth."

Yesterday, the thought of giving mouth-to-mouth to Tommi Rhymer would have been a long sweet giggle. It's blind dumb terror now. I have to get him up where I can see him.

There was a third seat in the back of this van once; Skye's stepdad ripped it out and carpentered a platform big enough to hold a double mattress on long drives. The ragged old mattress is on it now, with sleeping bags and extra trash.

I got back onto the seat and slid my fingers under Tommi's head. Hair so thick and fine, my hands were full of it. Maybe inside his head was dead already, and he'd soon be getting stiff, misshapen like any dead animal.

You know the little kid's movie-bred horror of dead bodies—decay, green teeth, and empty eye sockets. I'd never seen a real dead person. My grandmother died when I was five. And this was Tommi Rhymer; I still saw him on the edge of the stage, with more sheer life inside him than in the fifty thousand at his feet. The thought of Tommi rotting in a vault or burned to ash and poured into a carton held me paralyzed. The Abomination of Desolation was leering at me from the Holy Place.

Same time, here he was, meek and unresisting in my lap. I wanted to undress him like a doll and see how he was made, run my hands all over him and kiss his closed eyes. Desire playing seesaw with revulsion, terrible speechless war games in my head. Somebody needs help right now; neither revulsion nor desire is going to help him in the least.

I took a deep gasp, locked my arms under his, and boosted myself over onto the mattress, dragging him along clasped to my chest like a drowning swimmer. And maybe it was the pressure on his ribs or the hard flop onto the mattress, but he gave a sudden great gasp of his own. A sob, really. Then another and another. He's still alive.

I wriggle away from him, before the desire part can take over. And we're sitting there alone in the van on the freeway outside Livermore. Occasional cars whiz by us in the night.

I see Skye looking back at me.

"Please, just drive. If you don't, *I'll* die, never mind him. Just drive: I'll take all the blame. I won't let anything happen to you, and I'll look after him. *Please.*"

She doesn't move. Slowly her face goes white. I can see her

wide, scared eyes. The whole inside of the van goes white—the seats, the mattress. My Levi's. Tommi's bright red hair. Two headlights pull along the gravel shoulder close behind us.

"Somebody's stopping!" whispered Skye.

"Yeah. Like to see if we're okay."

"Do you think it's the cops? Oh, Andy!"

"So go on! Go *go, go!* Y'gonna wait'll they knock on your window?"

She turned the key and the wheels shot gravel. We're back on the freeway, gaining speed. Still headed east. Spinning along in the dark.

I ransack my brain for anything at all on drugs. And it seems I remember from somewhere: if a person is drugged, then you should walk him, talk to him, keep him roused and stimulated, not *let* him go down till he sinks. Or maybe that was for a horse with colic. Makes sense anyway.

I think about my brother J.J. My brother is a very freaky kid, tiny and skinny and stubborn as hell. And those are his good points. He's eight, but he still won't eat at the table. When he was really little, maybe three, he wouldn't eat for himself at all, and had to be fork-fed bite by bite in front of the television. If you didn't distract him, nothing went in.

And then he'd go to sleep somewhere, just before dinner. If we let him sleep, he'd come to right at bedtime, hungry for once and ready to go all night. The only way to get him back on schedule was to feed him then and there. Asleep. While he'd still suck a bottle it was simple. Later on you had to get bites in and keep him quasi-conscious, chewing and swallowing so he wouldn't choke. That takes technique.

But thinking of Tommi as J.J.-like, the more I feel encouraged. Sick stubborn kids I am prepared to handle, much better than grown men with drug problems. Or fantasy lovers.

"Tommi," I whispered to him, "what d'ya say we get you warm? Like the book says, 'Keep the victim warm.' Okay? Now here's a sleeping bag...." I unrolled it, making sure to brush and nudge him as I did. Not shake him up; J.J. would have tantrums if you woke him suddenly. Just busy, gentle contact. Never leave him quite alone. Not let him go down all the way. "I could spread this over you, but I think I'd better put you right inside. In you go, feet." His feet were clammy ice. I could warm them in my hands or sit on them. But he was really cold all over.

What does that remind me of? First aid. Ski rescue! I'm sure those people said if a victim has bad hypothermia, someone should climb inside a sleeping bag with him! God help me. I'm getting another attack of fantasy lover.

I shoved his feet in, bent his knees, and worked the whole bag up until his toes touched bottom. Okay, next: get it past his hips. I slid my arms in under him.

Lord God, please help me out. I'm really not trying to play grab-ass with him, just to keep him alive. Have mercy on me. And him.

And when I want something else, I'll ask for it.

I lifted and hauled the bag up to his back. Now this—is my brother J.J.—only bigger—and his name is—Tommi Rhymer. God help me. Resolutely I shoveled his shoulders into my lap. "Hey, Tommi. Come on, you want to know about the place you're going? Sure you do." No sign of life.

"What did you say?" shouted Skye.

"I was talking to him."

"Is he awake?"

"No."

"What are you talking to him for?"

"I want to."

"You better talk to me! I don't know where I'm going!"

"Where are you now?"

"Tracy."

"Do you see a sign that says I-5?"

"What?"

"Highway Interstate 5!"

"No!"

"When you do, go north, toward Sacramento."

"Okay."

"After a mile or so, turn east again on Highway 120. Toward Yosemite. All right?"

"I guess."

"Then twenty miles or so, and north again toward Sacramento, on Highway 99."

"I'm not going to remember this, Andy!"

"Look, there's the I-5 sign: I can see it; I'm not even driving."

Skye muttered something.

"Come on, Tommi. I want to tell you where we're going. It's a place called Pardee Camp."

My words are coming out all hokey-phony, the way I talk to answering machines. You know, "*I'm sorry;* we're not able just now to receive your call in person: you have thirty seconds after the tone to leave your message! *Beep!*"

Message? Faced with one of those I'm lucky to remember my name. Like that now. All I can hope to do is keep on talking. And talking. About the ride, the mountains, my family, friends, fond fantasies, life, the universe, and everything. I talked till my throat was dry and I was drowsing over him. When his breathing got all funny, I'd lift his shoulders, pat, and jiggle. It always came back steady.

"*Hey!*"

"What is it?"

"I'm on this 120 thing."

"Good."

"How long do I stay on it?"

"Till you reach 99. North on 99, for fifteen miles, then east on 88. Waterloo exit. 88'll take you all the way."

· — ·

IF you look at maps of California—I don't mean gas-station maps, but the *real* kind U.S. Geological Survey puts out—they've got the whole state section by section on separate maps. And there are streams and springs, and elevation-lines crowding close on hillsides and spreading wide and placid on the flats. The most remote places you can think of, right down to the dirt roads and the foot-trails, and the little black dots where cabins are.

Anyway, look at those maps of the Sierra Nevada, and what you'll see is like a patchwork, white and green. The green is National Forest, public lands. You can hunt in there or camp and hike, lie around and look up at the trees, whatever. But scattered everywhere inside the green part are the white patches; what's left of the old homesteads, trading posts, mining claims: all kinds of real neat private places you wouldn't know were there, like great-great-granddaughters of the Mexican Land-Grant owners, dispersed invisible through the whole big modern mob of California.

Ours belonged to a rancher in the last century. He used to drive in cattle every spring to graze all summer on the high meadows, and drive them out again before the snow. Stockmen bring cattle up in big-rigs now, and run them in the National Forests by permit. The cows wear bells and nobody stays with them. They wander around dinging and donging all summer. Come fall, the trucks drive back and take them all away. Nothing stays the same. But the old camp where the cowboys lived is still there.

The rancher's widow was my grandmother's aunt.

I can't think of any scene more far-removed from a rocking Day-on-the-Green in Oakland Coliseum than Pardee Camp. The porch leans a little after years of snow. Inside is the old bunkroom, all across the front. It features lumpy sofas now and Mexican rugs. Deer skins on the walls, from Papa's bow hunting. Pot-bellied stove in the corner. Old photos of my grandparents with strings of trout.

The front room reaches to the roof. Behind it, the kitchen and the tiny bedroom and bath my grandfather tacked on are flat-ceilinged at the rafters. Grandmother stored things in the loft on top. But we in our time nailed a ladder up the front-room wall. Izzy and I glued a stack of carpet samples to the loft floor, hauled ten-dollar thrift-shop mattresses up, and made a lair that would sleep us and a dozen school-friends at a pinch, every long summer. Great fun, childhood.

My parents have this bachelor friend named Gavin: some luminary in Geophysics. He eats at our table a lot. He always felt very free around Izzy and me, between Lewis Carroll and a favorite uncle. Took us to Tower Records. Bought us stuff we didn't need. Made rude remarks about our private lives.

When I was twelve and hadn't learned the value of protective coloration, I went around really wailing "I want Tommi Rhymer!" like a Siamese cat. And "Uncle" Gavin made all kinds of sport of me in this *terribly* affected voice: "So what if you *had* Tommi Rhymer, Miranda dear, what *would* you *do* with him?" Until I got so stung I wept. "What do you *think* I'd do with him? I'd take him to the cabin, and take him swimming in Bright's Creek, and walk in the woods, and everything else I'd do with somebody real who was my friend! Why do you want to *know?"* And I went to bed in the middle of Sunday dinner, and cried myself sick and silly.

God Almighty. Tommi Rhymer.

Before my nerve could fail, I bent to kiss his cold damp forehead. And he flinched. And I yelled! He might be out, but not so far out that he didn't know when he was kissed! I might just wake the Sleeping Beauty after all!

"Waterloo? Wake up, Andy, is *this where I turn off?"*

"Highway 88! Waterloo! I'm not asleep!"

Just when freeway speed becomes a way of life, each car a spaceship on its own trajectory, you turn off on the country road. Wake up indeed! Slow down, stop sign, smell of dusty fields and pesticides, music on somebody else's radio. A sudden hustle of gas stations, fast food, freeway motels, coffee shops, all with forty-foot signs. Neon lights at three o'clock in the morning.

"Hey, don't go in here!"

"I'm out of gas."

"We use the cheapo place across the road—"

"I have Mom's Chevron card."

"Well you can't use it! They'll mail her the sales slip with the bill. Pull on through; don't worry. We never got T-shirts. I have lots of money."

"Half of that's still mine, you know."

"Oh, come on."

Skye gets out to pump the gas. I get out too; I have to pay for it. Through the windows of the bus, Tommi is scarcely visible, nestled in his bag.

I made it my job as a kid, when we stopped for gas at night, to check around the station lights and rescue from underfoot all kinds of big bewildered insects. Beetles with internal injuries. Semi-shredded dragonflies. These I carried off piously, so they could mend in the clean air and sweet unlighted nights of Pardee. Some got misplaced and perished in the car. Six thousand feet change in elevation and a total switch from farm to forest probably did the hardiest of them in. But my heart was in the right.

Forget that kind of good works now. I'm into bigger stuff. I climbed back in with Tommi. I'd nearly lost my awe of him (I thought) and could put my ear against his chest quite shamelessly. He rattled a lot (the Darth Vader effect) but his breath was steady in-and-out.

We're off across the dark hinterland, Stockton a mere glow in the sky behind us. Tall corn speeds by, hay fields, vineyards, dozing cows. All the rich lush dusty smells of summer. An occasional light bulb, lonely on the end of a barn. Owls eating mice in the road bank up suddenly from the headlights on wide furry wings.

My job is to see all that for Tommi.

The long drive to the mountains is a different show by day; you can turn out at the farm-stands for white sweet corn and beans straight off the vine. And at the bakery on old Main Street in Jackson (as my grandfather always did) for blueberry turnovers and apple tarts. Bakery girls and farm wives, fast asleep at four in the morning.

Jackson lies beyond the farmland, in the tumbled strip of hills where miners dug their millions a hundred years ago. It's on the far side of Jackson that the mountains really start. The road rares back and heads into the sky. Oaks and digger pines, wild grapes and blackberries keep it company while they can, giving way regretfully to bracken, madrones and cedars. Each climate breathes its own sweet smell. The last to make the scene are firs, puzzle-pines, and aspens, and the pungent scent of a bushy scrub my grandmother called "Mountain Misery." At the first gray dawn we passed six thousand feet and turned down off the highway.

"Oh God! It's gonna break the car!"

"No it isn't; it's just a cattle guard!"

"Do you have any *idea* what the rest of my life will be like if I break this car?"

"About like it'll be if you don't."

"That's with *your* family! That's not with *my* family!"

I talked her down the ridge, on a steep gravel road that pitches through really black forest. At the bottom is a boat launch, gas pump, grubby trailer camp, tiny store. They call it a resort. That's funny.

Past the resort, across the dam: what's left of the gorge dropping grim and stony to the right, and the lake windy silver to the left. Back along the far shore of the lake, past the Boy Scout camp, past the Summer Home Tract. Up the far ridge, up to seven thousand feet this time, where the trees stand thinner and the gray rocks close together, and all roads become pretensions. Down the other side, the next steep empty valley with Bright's Creek at the bottom.

To me, the road was well maintained as far as the Summer Home Tract. It's down the other side, the drop into Bright's Creek, that began to look like something out of Dante. Tommi was abandoned. I had to move up front and nursemaid Skye.

"My father takes this at about thirty miles an hour; it skims over the top that way, and doesn't wallow into every hole—"

"Oh shut up! Your father's God!"

Right along the creek for miles, past the first bridge; and the second is a wooden trestle with two rows of boards across. I thought the panic at the trestle bridge would be the worst. Innocent. It was a mere nothing compared with the struggle up the other side.

"This isn't the road! It's a fucking stream-bed!"

"Straddle the *gullies*, don't straddle the *boulders!* Put one wheel on the boulders!"

"You think you're so smart!" she wailed, waving the wheel around at random, "You don't drive!" She belly-whoppered it onto another rock. "Oh shit! Shit shit shit!"

"Look, don't *do* that. There's just the two of us! I can jump out and stand on the rear bumper if you get stuck, but I've got no shovel; I can't dig you free."

"Oh God, there's a tree down across it! I can't turn! I'll have to back down!"

"Follow the tracks! You can get around...."

It enters my head how fortunate I am: accustomed to thinking cars don't turn over and cars don't break, because Papa's always there to drive and fix them.

We came to the steel-pipe gate. I opened it; it takes the same key as the cabin. Another quarter-mile of rocks and gullies brought us to the end. A long meadow lost in the forest. The road, a sandy track along the north side of it; a chill clear stream and aspen thickets on the south. On this side, lower than the road, a solitary stand of fir trees, and close at the foot of those, a tumble-down log barn and weathered tin-roof shack. The heart of my childhood summers and Sierra Club poster material all the way: Pardee Camp.

"You'll get stuck in the sand if you try to go down closer. We'll have to carry him from here."

I flung the hatch-door open, standing in the cold dawn behind the car. My legs still jiggled to the beat of the long ride. Skye got out looking sulky and white around the mouth. "You carry him," she said. "You lifted him in."

"I'll take the shoulders, you take the feet. Just grab the sleeping bag as it comes out."

"No!"

"What is this?"

"I don't want to touch him."

"All the time I've known you, we've done nothing but listen to Belshangles records and buy posters and buttons and read fan books and tape his videos, and now that he's sick and helpless and here, you don't want to touch him?"

"He scares me to death! This is just unreal!"

"Listen. You get his feet."

I hauled him out the back of the bus, keeping the sleeping bag with him. And when the feet came out, Skye got under them all right. She whimpered a lot and stumbled over bushes. When we reached the steps I had to set him down. I kept him up against me like a sleeping child, while Skye dug in my pocket for the keys.

As long as that pocket's held a ring to put it on, I've carried a key to Pardee. When Mama first gave me keys to the house back home, I wanted one. "What on earth for?" I couldn't tell. It just seemed vital. "Don't give her a hard time," Papa said. Now I know what it was for.

Skye didn't wait to take the key out of the lock. Once the door was open, she hopped down off the porch.

"Help." No answer. Damn. But she was right; I'd lifted him before. It might take more to make her help than to do the job myself. Getting on my feet would be the worst. Then jettison the sleeping bag....

I did a shaky fireman's carry with him through the little house—front room, kitchen, bedroom—the bed was made and ready—pulled down the covers and rolled him into it. Outside, a car started. I ran like hell; she was trying to back it around in the road. Stuck in the sand, *please* God, just this once, stuck in the sand! No such luck.

"*Wait a minute!*" My arms were spread-eagled against her windshield. "Wait, Skye, when are you coming *back?*" I saw she'd started to cry. She popped the clutch as I took to the bushes. "You run me over, and I'll kill you!"

"Andy, I'm *so tired!*" she bellowed through the glass. "Get *away* from me; I don't want to *talk* to you! I haven't slept in *twenty-four hours!* And I have to *drive all that way!*"

"You're driving back next Saturday!"

"I'll be grounded!"

"Then a week from Saturday?"

"After this, why should they ever let me use their car?"

"So rip it off."

"Sure! Goodbye, Andy."

"You picked some time to turn out such a bitch! You've got to promise me: Saturday, or a week from Saturday!"

"Am I the bitch? Am I, Andy?"

"*Please* promise!"

And she really drove away. The noise of a bus bashing in and out of chuckholes faded. I could almost hear it for a minute longer. Then a bird song. Cowbells. Insects buzzed in the early sun, a high sweet tone.

Cue fantasy dream sequence.

The cabin door shuts behind me. I tiptoe to the bedroom. Open shutters, let in the morning, and study my treasure by the light of day. He hasn't turned to dust as vampires do. Doesn't even look too sick, asleep, with his chin tucked over against one slim shoulder. His tousled gaudy hair.

My mind wanders. Can't help worrying about Skye. How far's she gotten? I'm mainly unimpressed by her mysterious ailments, but what if she does put it in a ditch? Or get lost? Or fall asleep? What if the HP stops her?

Twenty-four hours ago, the Oakland BART station had just opened and the first trains rumbled in. We were still camped at the top of the escalators with the dress-up couple, still glowering across at chain-link gates and stadium guards, the long day of the Belshangles concert before us.

Some time later, my head is over on the comforter by Tommi's shoulder. Eyes are shut. This won't do. What if Tommi takes a turn for the worse? With me his only help.

What am I thinking? J.J. Food is sleep. Kitchen. Check out what there is to eat. Coffee, maybe. Pump water. Boil water. That means turning the electrics on. Hey.

First a short walk to the kitchen. There are jars of instant coffee on the shelf. Dried milk. Dried eggs. With those and Mama's jar of bacon-drippings on the counter I can make scrambled eggs. Omelets, even. Then there's Bisquick. *Tons* of that. Have to laugh. Remember every year making cabin shopping-lists with Mama.

"Come on, suggest something."

"Pancake syrup. Instant cocoa."

"Okay."

"Turkey lunchmeat for fish bait."

"Okay."

"Bisquick."

"Is any up there?"

"I don't know."

"Get some anyway."

There is always some up here. We always buy more. Must be half a dozen boxes now. Stale maybe, but here. Kipper snacks. Canned tuna. Canned chicken. Canned beef-stew. Canned ravioli. Japanese instant noodles.

Pardee has electricity; there's a PG&E dam to either side of it. The wires march over the ridge and across the meadow on tall poles. My grandfather put them in himself.

The last pole stands fifty feet from the house, where the line goes underground. The switchbox is on top of a ladder up the pole. Snow pack can be twenty feet at Pardee, over the ridge of the house. My grandparents snowshoed in; we have the snowmobiles. And it's one high-class luxury, being able to power up without first digging up the box.

Deep summer now.

I waded out through long grass to the pole. Waist-high flowers, like bolted cabbage plants with black-eyed yellow daisies on the top. Cow pies. Cows themselves, at the far end of the meadow. Tiny frogs that shut up at my shadow. Grasshoppers that zicked away on yellow wings.

Up the ladder, hand-over-hand. Two big switches in a steel box; no problem there. What took concentration was coming down the ladder, and remembering why I wanted power in the first place. Never been really drunk or stoned; must feel something like that. Hope it's like that: all hazy, lightheaded, forgetful, and warm. Disembodied eyes.

I boiled water, made coffee. Made myself some instant oatmeal (apples and cinnamon), very grown up and resourceful. Not only did I have my man asleep in the family bed, I was a fully capable provider of food, water, and electricity. I remembered how to do it *all.*

I went and listened to his chest again. The rattling was gone. Visions of Bill Graham came to mind: "How can you love him? You don't even know him! What if he snores?" He hadn't snored yet. Then, maybe he wasn't sleeping. Do people snore if they're unconscious? More coffee. My third and final visitation, I edged around the big bed, and on the far side made myself a backrest of spare pillows. I knew the thing to do: keep watch on Tommi till he waked.

You know a fail-safe way to recognize you're sleeping? When you begin to dream. The mind's been jogging round and round, endless laps over the same dumb hurdles and anxieties. Suddenly, bam! It trots right off the parcourse and onto the Magical Mystery Tour: eyeball-to-eyeball with the first bright, wayward, irresponsible dream-face. Well, hello, Love! And I was half afraid that you weren't coming.

Then the alarm clock goes. Two A.M.

Gloria in Excelsis Deo.

First step. *Find* the alarm clock.

If I'm smart, I take precautions, like hiding it before I go to bed. Once I've had to drag it by its cord from down behind the amp, a safe return to sleep is much less likely.

Second step. Sport socks. Newer, non butt-split 501's. My oldest Nikes, with *TommiTommiTommiTommi* closely written in waterproof pen all over every visible inch of the left. My favorite old Belshangles T-shirt, the black *Steel Tears* one: Tommi on the chest, red hair rising like an alien mutant freak. (A very beautiful alien mutant freak.)

Brush hair. Line eyes. No earrings to snag on people's clothes and rip my ears out. No Belshangles-buttons to get lost and mourned. Just basic me. Not so glamorous, but combat-ready.

Dig out my old down jacket, lay it on the pillow. Snap pockets are state-of-the-art for holding onto things, like keys. Money. *Tickets.* My student ID in case some crazy knocks me on the head and nobody knows who I am. Headlights paint a yellow smear across the window. Skye Milligan, turning it around in the dead-end of Salvatierra Street.

Here I go, full gallop down a dark hall, trying to reach my front door before Skye wakes the house with her big thumb on the bell—

The kung-fu kick of a Chinese security guard shocked me from a dream in which Bill Graham figured strongly. Space City. I can appreciate why I've never been a nap-taker. The back of Tommi's hand slid from my eye. More than one of us had queasy dreams. He'd flung his arms wide in his sleep. I picture him cruising up from the darkness where he's been, toward the light surface like a shark.

That surface might not have a lot to recommend it. "Sleep, sleep," it says in fairy tales, "the morning is wiser than the evening." But morning light had drained out of the room. No radio, no clocks, no watch: only way to tell time here is step outside and check the sky.

Check on Tommi first.

His jaw burned red with the beginnings of a really horrifying beard. Unreal. I could not conceive of Tommi Rhymer with a beard. My father has one. That doesn't sound right. I love Papa, but beards are not a turn-on.

Outside, it was evening. Unbelievable. Sleeping away an entire day in bed with Tommi Rhymer was as hard to cope with as his beard. Which reminded me of that dumb jingle to the tune of "The Irish Washerwoman":

Oh, O'Leary is dead and his brother don't know it.
His brother is dead and O'Leary don't know it,
They're both of 'em dead and they're lying in bed—
And neither one knows that the other is dead.

It also reminded me of Harlan.

My feet tapped an idle jig on the porch. Well, neither one of us was dead. I was awake, what's more; and pretty soon, pretty soon—

The bottom porch-step is an excellent place to sit if you like to watch big ants on the path. Top priority would seem to be a thorough shakeout of my attitudes concerning Tommi. Why didn't I let the cops take him? I never thought drugs were a bright idea. Still I hadn't felt ashamed of him. Ashamed *with* him was more the truth. For other people to see him looking witless and disheveled was more than I could bear. It seemed as natural to cover his ass as my own. Because I loved him. But am I prepared to tell him that?

Above in a darkening sky the tiny shape of an airliner sped the eastward route, sun still bright on its wings at thirty thousand feet. Famous people get busted for drugs every day, all the time, and they survive. They even straighten up.

Harlan called the cops. Perhaps he was the wiser lover.

In other words, why the hell am I up here alone with him, when 49,999 other admirers left the concert happy with their pins, programs, and T-shirts and went home?

Beyond the creek, the aspens made their endless shimmying sound. A few last birds winged home across the meadow. The bats would be joining them soon. Invisible cows clanged in the forest. Add to these sounds the whinny of old hinges. I spun around. Tommi Rhymer stood in the doorway.

Wrong word, maybe. He was holding himself up by it. He met my eye bravely but blankly, like something bad in a dream which might change for the better if he stared it down. He tried in turn the twilight meadow, the log barn, the forest.

My heart went out to him. He couldn't know where he was; a grown man in a kid's predicament. I ought to say something, reassure him. Can't think of anything. Keeping my heart inside my ribs is job enough.

The first words to come out were, remarkably, the last he'd managed before he went down over the storm drain in San Francisco: "I don't know you." He looked much better for it. Till the uncertainty took him again. "Do I?"

"Not really."

"You know who I am?"

"Sure."

"Well that's a help." He shut his eyes. "Look..." One long hand waved vaguely. "I just came to in a bed I don't remember, in a house I've never seen, in a place which I...all that..." He gestured around "...looks like the set to some Hollywood spectacular. Am I still in L.A.?"

"No. But you're in California."

"I did play L.A.?"

"Uh-huh. You played Oakland, too."

"Oh Christ. I got to get out of here."

"Don't worry. Your tour's all finished."

He shook his head. "You don't understand. God, how embarrassing. Was that your bed?"

"My parents'."

He winced. "Do they know I'm here?"

"They don't even know I'm here."

"Come on, be kind; twenty questions was never my best game. Don't you live here?"

"This is our summer cabin."

"But I brought you here for the night?"

"I brought you. No. My friend brought both of us."

"What friend?" He looked around dizzily. "Where is he? I want to talk."

"She. My friend is a girl. She drove home."

Tommi suddenly burrowed his face into the doorpost. "Oh, I'm gonna be sick." I jumped up, but he got himself through the door. He lay across the side-rail of the porch trying manfully to be sick, but nothing came. He sank down on the steps with his head in his arms and his arms around his knees. "Would'y'care to tell me about it?" he croaked.

"My friend and I got backstage at Oakland. And the security guy caught her. The friend."

"Yeah. Go on."

"He ripped her clothes up. But you saw it. You gave her your jacket."

"My foxycoat! Hey, it's coming back. The kid with the tits showing. I remember that. Okay. That was Oakland?"

"You said we could bring the jacket back to you at your hotel in San Francisco."

He whistled. "That's a new one."

"What?"

"Never mind. Go on."

"And we did. Then Harlan Parr came in—"

"Whoa." He even managed a giggle. "My knight in shining armor."

"—and you had an awful fight."

"I bet we did. Pardon me."

"So you took him in the bedroom, and we fell asleep on the couch. You came out finally and talked to me, but when he came out, he said he'd reported you for drugs."

"What?" he raised a white drained face.

"He said he'd used the bedroom phone, called the cops, told 'em you had teenage kids in your room and were giving us drugs."

"Did I do that?"

"No way. You only gave my friend your sweatshirt so she could cover her dress."

"But I don't remember any of this. Go on. Did the cops arrive?"

"Not while we were there. Harlan kept insisting you show us out; then he'd help you hide the stuff and you'd both go to some party."

"Well he was lying, that's what. He's got a million tricks like that, all part of the 'Parr Patented Emergency Interrupt System.' Wait till I get my hands on him."

I'd seen him get his hands on Harlan once.

He groaned. "God, I'm wasted. Go on."

"There isn't much to tell. He was doing, like this countdown, ten, nine, eight, seven, until he said the cops would come, when you just grabbed the two of us and bolted."

"Past him?"

I didn't know what to say.

"I got you past him?"

"You were going about warp nine."

"This isn't funny!"

"I'm not laughing."

"So go on: finish your little story."

"We ran downstairs. You really fell once; I was scared you'd killed yourself. But we got to the bottom and sat out by the garbage for a while, until a guy from the kitchen threw us out. Then we walked up and down the alley. And then you.... And then...." I have trouble with this great hard lump of dread.

"Then what?"

"You passed out on the street beside our car."

"That ties it!" he said to the porch step; his head was still between his knees. "You're lying too, that's not my style. I don't believe in accidents."

"I don't think style had much to do with it."

"Somebody put you up to this, I swear."

"No!"

He got his head up, tried to rise, and cringed with pain instead. "God help me, I am so sick." He looked back up to me in helpless faint appeal. He did seem almost feverish, beginning to sweat and shiver. "I'm *sick!*"

"Is there some way I can help you?"

"Lemme use your phone. Call—Harlan."

"There isn't any."

"What?"

"We haven't got a phone."

"We go to the neighbors, then."

"Aren't any."

"What?"

"There *aren't any neighbors!* There isn't *any phone!*"

"What the fucking-hell-kind-of-a-place is this?"

"Remote. No phone *wires* even, for miles and miles."

Slowly he got onto his feet. "He put you up to this."

"Who?"

"You know who! This is the way he thinks; I've seen him working up to it! Slip me something vile to knock me out, bring me someplace I don't recognize, and leave me here until I start to shake! Pay some kids to watch me, trusting I won't get the law on kids, or do you any injury! Well, I don't take to being carried off against my will! I'll get the law on you all right, kid or no kid! I'll see you locked up till you're gray! I'll ruin your parents if you got any!"

We were standing on the porch now, almost nose to nose. "You leave my parents out of this! I picked you out of the street 'cause I felt sorry for you! I don't know what's the matter with you! I gave you a safe bed where you could sleep it off; nobody put me up to anything!"

"You put me in your car and drive! I can't stay here! What time is it, anyway?"

"Eight—nine o'clock, maybe?"

"That's six, seven hours—Why, it can't be so late, there's not light enough!"

"In the evening."

His mouth fell open.

"I haven't *got* a car to put you in." I said quickly. "My friend took it away. She's coming back to get me Saturday, or Saturday after, if I don't turn up at home. I don't know what your problems are, but if you can't stay here, I'll hike out and get somebody in the morning. *I will not* do it in the dark. It's twenty miles to the highway."

Everything I've said is true. For a moment I feel even confident. My good will toward him is endless.

His pale face turned into a mask of violence. He has problems, all right. I don't have the faintest concept what they are.

But I know that look. The look you get when you've tempted an angry animal past endurance, the instant it ditches that last shred of respect and comes for you. Any kid who's owned a biting pony knows that look. What you're supposed to do—like you have one second when you see the eyes blaze and the ears go back—is turn on 'em yourself, with a knockout punch to the jaw. Get the fucker before he gets you. Does wonders for their dispositions.

It might have worked here. But I hadn't been attacked by another human since the third grade. Being slugged by Tommi

Rhymer in particular wasn't even part of my mythology. I see it in slow motion, though it wasn't slow. His whole lean body rises and comes down in a crouch like a shying horse, while his arm is going back and back. He pivots away from me: I freeze. That arm has a fist on the end of it; that fist is coming and coming toward me, and the next thing coming toward me is a clump of blooming weeds about six feet from the porch.

Important things occurred to me as I did my slow arc through the air. He certainly knew how to use his own body. That was a fighter's punch, scientifically delivered: it roared in low and center under my ribs and kept on lifting; we weighed nearly the same, but I'd gone off like a Frisbee.

Second, it wasn't anything a man would do to a woman. He didn't try to slap me around or hurt my breasts. He didn't take advantage. He punched me fair, like one rather decent infuriated guy might do to another. The fact that I was female didn't matter.

That was what hurt the most, worse than the punch and worse than the fall. I had so wanted it to matter.

The sun, impartial, went on setting. I lay on the ground. What became of Tommi wasn't clear; I thought I'd seen him turn back to the house after he sent me flying. Before I could breathe again it was quite dark. I picked myself out of the weeds and came inside.

Only trouble, now I was crying. Ludicrous noises and salty water rolled automatically from me as blood out of a hurt. *Uh-uh-uh-uh.* I went around and clicked off all the lights. Put everything in order. *Uh-uh-uh-uh-uh.* Damn it, tears are more than I can afford. I'm in charge.

A round white tin stood on the kitchen table, cutesy replica of the 1920's canister Campfire marshmallows came in. I happen to know there's a new bag in it. I started popping marshmallows like pills. *Uh-uh-uh.* I locked the front door. *Uh-uh-uh.* More marshmallows. Saw that the stove wasn't on.

I wandered dazed and miserable in the stub of a back hall off the kitchen. And there, with shame for leverage, the tears subsided to an occasional wretched sniff. The bathroom door stood open. The bedroom door was shut.

Tommi Rhymer. Right in there.

My chest still kills. *Ow ow ow.* Broken ribs, maybe. Separated breastbone. Oh God, but he can punch. *Uh-uh-uh.* So stop it, Andy! Hold your stupid breath. Plug your mouth with marshmallows.

My hands go slowly and slowly to the doorknob. Not a sound. Slowly turn. He's locked it on the inside. Well, at least I know where he is. What am I eating these damn things for? I don't even like untoasted marshmallows. Better use the bathroom. Back in the front room, I face the ladder to the loft. With really broken ribs, I couldn't climb it, maybe. I climb it.

I don't need a light to know where all the mattresses are, and which one has my slumber bag on it. That bag has been with me since I was nine. It came from Emporium's kid department: made of fake polyester velour in a phony red-bandana pattern and stuffed with polyester fill.

It's ridden to a hundred track meets in the back of the car, doubled as a ground sheet once we got there. It goes through the washer like a snap. Lucky thing, because the dogs have peed on it. I've peed on it. And barfed on it. And ground my Fritos and bean-dip into it.

Once it got locked in the car with all my crayons on it. The crayons melted in the heat, and the melted wax ate holes right through the cloth. Mama sewed wizardy little blue moons and stars over all the holes. That bag is like the womb. I crawl back into it. *Uh-uh-uh-uh.*

Damn. If I'm going to sob, at least I could try to keep 'em silent. I'm right on top of his ceiling; he must be able to hear me. I'm not crying for his sympathy.

Prayer puts me to sleep like a spell. Lord *(Uh-uh)* Jesus Christ have mercy on me. Lord Jesus Christ *(Uh-uh-uh)* have mercy on me. Lord Jesus Christ have *(hic)* mercy on me. Lord Jesus Christ have mercy on *(hic)* Tommi. Lord Jesus Christ have mercy on me. Half asleep now.

And sobbing again. I could hear myself crying in my sleep. I woke up with a start. Black silence, not a sound. No, there it was all right, only it wasn't me. Somebody else was crying down below. Not the least like me.

I'd never heard a man cry, either.

It was terrible. I couldn't endure it, but I had no choice. It made my chest feel stretched and empty, like when I realized Tommi was Harlan's lover and knew I loved him just the same. Now my heart will have to dilate even wider, to accommodate his awful solitary sorrow.

Other noises downstairs: clash of bedsprings, door flying open, doorknob smashing into wood. Silence. Maybe he needed the bathroom. Scraping sounds. Somebody falling over a kitchen chair. Silence. Bare feet on linoleum. It wasn't the bathroom; he was headed for the front of the house. Oh God, what'll I do if he comes up here?

The front door whinnied open. Silence, silence. I knew what he was seeing. Nothing human. Night impenetrable. No familiar glow from any town, no lights at all on road or building. And the heavens frosted and studded and hung so pendulous-thick with stars, that the slim black tops of trees can scarcely hold them up. The stars at Pardee panicked me, age two or so. I couldn't be dragged out after dinner, when others sat outside. I got over it, and loved the black nights dearly. But once, I knew those stars would fall on me.

Now I listened: rigid fear with two big ears attached. Now for the first time a crucial anxiety raised its head. He might run away. In my mind the fear became a certainty: Tommi *would* run away, I simply had no way of holding him.

I tried to order the possible consequences of his going. It's dead dark now. From the only look he got outside, he might not know which way the road lies. And if he does, would he know which way to follow it? Left is out, but a long way out. Right trails off around the meadow and up the ridge where it divides. Part dead-ends at the edge of Mokulumne Wilderness Area. Get lost in there, he could wander till he died.

The other peters out in willow flats at the back of an overgrown pond called Fiddler's Lake. The real road to Fiddler's Lake comes off the one to Pardee near the Bright's Creek bridge. It has a campground at the end. Pretty primitive, but a Forest Service camp: fire pits, tent sites, porta-potties, men, women, children and dogs. Fiddler's Lake appeals to a certain class of fishermen who wouldn't be caught dead at the "resort," or parking their RVs on the dam, but are still not into backpacking. They like to drink beer and listen to heavy metal.

Bye-bye Tommi Rhymer. Can you imagine this poor beery fisherman waking in his sleeping bag to find a wild-haired, wild-eyed Tommi Rhymer standing over him? Next stop would be the Amador County Sheriff. Then they'd come looking for me. How could I have ever been so dumb?

Below in the eyeless dark, the front door closed. I listened for the porch to creak, the slightest whisper of a breath. When the noise came, it wasn't slight. He'd bashed a kitchen chair on his way to the door; this time he went headfirst over one. And began to cry again, a dreary abandoned sound, like the young of some animal lost and starving.

Oh, quick, in half-a-second I can tumble down that ladder, switch on lights and help him off the floor. I'll say, "Come on, love, this isn't the ends of the earth; I haven't kidnapped you. *Please* let me make you comfortable; I'll make you tea. Tea? How about dinner! No food since yesterday *alone* could have you acting kind of freaky—"

The bedroom door slammed, hard enough to crack the stops. I heard his savage punch of the lock-button, his despairing crash onto the bed. He cried and cried.

Thank God prayer puts me to sleep.

Chapter 5

SCRIPTURE (AS OPPOSED TO FAIRY TALES) says, "Weeping may endure for a night, but joy cometh in the morning." In my case, fairy tales proved more reliable. Tommi's second morning at Pardee brought considerable wisdom. On the joy scale it was so-so.

Thunder passed by in the night, and with it rain. Most wildly luxurious sound I know. If I ever have a real lover, my ultimate would be to make love to him under a tin roof in a driving rain. I slept beautifully after that. Something much quieter woke me.

A breeze sighing through the meadow. Insects buzzing. Bird song. From all the light below, I guessed it was a bright morning.

MONDAY

Good God. Tommi Rhymer. I popped out of that bag like a rabbit. Quick. Shoes on. Laces. Ease down the ladder. I'd made it in silence to the kitchen, when the front door banged. But it was just the wind. *Wait* a minute. Rush to try the bedroom knob. It turned. And opened inward on an unmistakable, unmysterious stench. Oh, shit. Literally. The room was empty, except for the tangled bed and an enormous shit-pile right beside it. Big links.

Could he still be on the floor behind the bed? Look, something funny at the window, a dark swath down the screen. Carefully I edged around. The wet sill stank ammonia. He'd not only shit the floor, he'd peed through the window screen! Scared and angry and distracted I'd gotten used to, but I *did* expect him to be housebroken!

There was a decent bathroom three feet from his door. Did it take some kind of genius to find it? I don't care how long a start he gets, I'm not leaving his shit on my floor. I got two pads of toilet paper in my hands. The pile was still warm. I gagged all the way to the toilet.

With the crazy strength of fear, I ran out after him into the morning. Sand all soft, clean-washed by the rain. Ants all busy clearing out their holes. A single line of slim bare footprints wavering toward the road. I ran.

What happened when he reached the road? Could I tell now, if I didn't know, which way is out? There's not a tire track left. Only the funny, fragile, webby surface a hard rain leaves on dirt. Tommi's prints paused in brief confusion, milled around. Then took off toward the right, and the back of Fiddler's Lake. Oh God, poor Tommi. You are no outdoorsman. *Nobody* I know would have laid down that unsubtle a trail, not even teaching woodcraft skills to Brownie Scouts.

Only one thing to be done; chase him. Head him off before he gets there, reason with him. I'm not in shape for running, not by my standards. But I'm sure as hell in better shape than he is. Bless us, O Lord, and these Thy gifts which we are about to receive from Thy bounty, through Christ Our Lord, Amen. Wrong prayer. Still appropriate. I took off after Tommi using all the gifts I could think of, among which I figured prayer was not the least.

In the assortment of spiritual blocks and pieces Father Malachi provided for my build-a-faith project when I was eleven was a book about the Prayer of the Pilgrim. Lots of saints have prayed it, with more or fewer frills of their own tacked on. Basically: the Kyrie of the Mass, "Lord Jesus Christ have mercy on me."

Words of Power, all right. Simple. Which means you should be able to keep it going underneath your other thoughts, substitute it for the white noise of your mind. The theory, anyway. It also scans. So, as running was my hot obsession, I tried synching my stride and breathing to it. It became the greatest help in winning races:

LORD JEsus CHRIST HAVE
1 2 3 4
MERcy ON ME !
1 2 3 4

Over and over. Not only effective, it was *edifying*. Wonderful concept, also laid on me by Father 'Chi, it means, "that which builds you up" (as opposed to sin, that which "dilapidates," makes rubble out of you). The Prayer of the Pilgrim replaced the good old flag-waver my first track coach suggested:

ARmy ! NAvy !
1 2 3 4
AIR force ! maRINES !
1 2 3 4

And the rock-beat one I'd picked up on my own from Blondie's Deborah Harry:

ONE way—or anOTHer—
1 2 3 4
I'm gonnaGETcha—gonna GETcha getcha GETcha getcha,
1 2 3 4
ONE way—etc.
1 2

So picture me saying it over and over as I shot along, "LORD JEsus CHRIST HAVE MERcy ON ME (4....) LORD JEsus CHRIST HAVE MERcy ON ME (4)."

Trouble was, I didn't need to catch him up; I needed to get ahead of him. Maximum embarrassment: arriving at Fiddler's Campground only to hear him shout, "There she is! Grab the fucker!" Or words to that effect. Like, I needed space for very private conversation.

LORD JEsus CHRIST HAVE MERcy ON TOMmi (4).
LORD JEsus CHRIST HAVE MERcy ON ME (4).

But I also knew the country. Turning left across the ridge, I'd cut off a big loop, and might come out ahead. If he didn't turn right, that is, and wind up in the Wilderness Area. I'd cope with that one if I came to it.

Young trees sprouted thick along the road. The next good gap I saw, I took it: up a long thinning forest slope, then over bald granite, past the occasional monster pine, its base a litter of amber pitch-nuggets and foot-long pine cones, past boulders big as houses and thorny thickets full of deer yards. I spooked a doe and fawn in one of 'em; they pogoed off with an enormous clatter. Fifteen minutes put me on the top.

Fiddler's Valley is a shallow sinkhole overgrown in willows, the lake, a buried mirror fragment at the far end. The Pardee trail's invisible from the ridge, but I knew all I had to do was crash downhill to find it.

It was very dim and secret under the willows, another world. I strained for any sound of Fiddler's Campground. Kids. Dogs. Radios. Nothing. A mosquito whined against my face, I slapped it. I was standing on the trail now, but to either side it vanished under pools of still, brown water. The only footprints on the ground were mine.

I slogged a watery twenty yards toward home. More mud and standing pools. A funny late wet summer, this one. Tattered snow drifts on the Fourth of July. Spring flowers in August. Mosquitoes were singing in both my ears, blackening my arms, biting through my shirt. The only prints I saw belonged to mice and rabbits. But there *was* something, on the far side of a young lake of mud, some torn-up ground and a piece of plastic trash. Check it out.

It was a long slide and a sort of wallow. Looking closer at the wallow part, I saw cloth-pattern printed on the mud. Easing carefully up the slide, I came to footprints. They were bare and graceful. Then a muddy, empty marshmallow sack. So, he'd grabbed it off my kitchen table as he ran. He got this far, and fell down in the mud. Easy. Now his clothes were ruined.

But where was he?

There were footprints going down to where he fell, and yes, I saw some the other way. His wipeout turned him back. The ground was firmer now, so I could jog—begin to make some speed—Whoa.

A muddle of prints, all round a little slimy pool of half-dissolved greasy looking white things. Campfire marshmallows, or the remains of 'em. Sick. Serve him right.

I sped off after him: two sets of his narrow high-arched tracks, one weaving toward the lake and one away. I got to the top of Pardee meadow, where I'd cut across the ridge.

Now there were three sets of tracks to follow; two of his, and one (with shoes) of mine, like that bit in *Winnie the Pooh* where they're going round and round this thicket following their own footprints, imagining they're Wild Woozles, and getting very scared because more of them seem to have joined every lap around.

Thinking too hard to leave my eyes in gear. Longest time before I realize, there are now no tracks at all.

Well, some deer slots. But I mean human tracks, Tommi's tracks. Turn back. Okay. My own, bleakly solitary up half the length of the meadow. Then the path to the cabin. Lots of footprints, messing around. I went a few yards down it. His coming out, mine coming out. His returning. God help me, he's gone back to the house! Maybe he's ready to talk.

First thought. I did a lousy cleaning job.

He wasn't in the front room. I stood and listened. Not a sound. Wasn't in the kitchen, either. But the smell was growing more perverse. And worse.

A different configuration of nauseous smells.

Bedroom door was shut. Bathroom was open. Somebody'd peed the bathroom floor at length, and puked in it. Looked like he might have *tried* to get it in the pot, but his aim was inexcusably bad. Why?

I sat on the edge of the tub, face in grubby hands. Now I didn't need this. I hadn't *bargained* for this.

Or had I?

What came out of his body sick and wretched wasn't so different from my own. I couldn't think of any truer act of love really, than not to be disgusted with his mess.

But why? Was he trying to be repulsive, so I'd let him go? Did he get a concussion off the hotel stairs? Could he still be full of drugs? He'd have had to bring 'em with him in his pockets.

I wasn't even sure those pants had pockets.

My mind wandered off on a detour: seeing guys hiding stuff before the body search at concerts. Tape recorders strapped to the leg. It gives the term "bootleg" a raunchy new reality, but I never saw one get away with it. I saw this dude inside with a tiny camera once. I said, "How'd you make it in with that?" He grinned and answered, "Swallowed it."

Well, the standard place for the little packets of grass etc. is in the jockey shorts. Tommi Rhymer's jockey shorts. Or briefs. Bright red bikini briefs. The whole idea exhaled a faint sweet reverie, an aura of mystery and legend.

Hope to God he hadn't shit in 'em.

I sat up and shook myself. I remembered the progress of events back at the hotel. There'd been no reason for him to hide anything, until it was too late to have done it.

My guess was, he'd had no drugs in thirty-six hours.

He'd had no drugs in thirty-six hours.

My guess was.

My face went back in my hands. Slowly, they felt it twist, grow hot and wet as tears began to roll.

I knew what was the matter with him.

And I'd thought I was all calm and on the level about drugs. I knew all *kinds* of people who took drugs. What they did might be damn silly, or it might be dangerous; they were still just people that I knew. My friends.

Nobody knows an addict. You only hear about them in the newspaper, and in dumb trashy movies on TV.

I decided after a while I was self-indulgent, and made a careful study of that room, picking up on anything I'd missed. There was mud on the floor too, and in the sink. The sink was full of mud. He'd tried to wash. Sick and nasty as he was, he was trying to get clean.

And I didn't know how to help. It made me wish that I'd done drugs myself and straightened up, like lots of people I know. Then I'd have some idea. That's what you get for trying to be virtuous.

Ignorance.

Did I know anything that was similar?

J.J. has, among his other little tricks, a dandy allergy to oats. If he gets into any by mistake, for instance, oatmeal cookies? It is *amazing* how many otherwise helpful adults will come supplied with oatmeal cookies and not pay any attention to a skinny five-year-old who says they'll kill him. To him, they will actually lie. Oatmeal's health food, right?

Two hours later he begins to heave, and heave, and *heave:* every five minutes for the afternoon. First the food comes up. Then after a while clear water comes up. Then yellow bile comes up. And the kid's dehydrated and black around the eyes, half knocked out from exhaustion, and you expect his socks to come up next. Finally it lets go of him, and he can sleep. Sleep he does. For hours.

I sat on the edge of the tub and looked at Tommi's mess. Now the problem, I said to myself, let's say the problem is not heroin. About which I know nothing, and want to know less.

The problem might as well be *oatmeal*. And a kid's pride. And anger.

Fear too, of course.

The first thing needed to cope with the above is baking soda. Good old Arm & Hammer.

Most of my friends' parents are divorced and remarried. This gives 'em two houses, two sets of guilt-tripped parents, pitying grandparents, and an almost endless source of spending money. I've lived all my life on the Stanford Campus, at the dead-end of Salvatierra Street in the white house with the orange-trees out front. My parents have been married twenty years. To each other. Nobody feels sorry for me. I get to do housework at minimum wage. Puke-spots and pee-spots I know about. Go and get the Arm & Hammer.

I've loved that company logo forever. Also the Moon-and-Stars one from Procter and Gamble. Head for the kitchen.

The one I couldn't stand was Old Dutch Cleanser. My Grandmother kept a can under her sink. That big, striding, clog-stamping woman on the label, brandishing her rolling pin, her funny Dutch hat pulled down until it hid her face entirely. Underneath her it said "Chases dirt." When I was really little, she was the very image of a faceless ogress chasing *me*. Funny. I've never seen a can of Old Dutch Cleanser anywhere but under Grandmother's sink.

Maybe that's how Tommi sees me now. Striding down behind him like a juggernaut. No face. Chases dirt.

Blot up as much as possible with toilet paper; send it down the pot. Pour on baking soda and hot water and repeat. At least I'm doing something. Question is, what next? How many days or weeks does it take to throw off heroin? Supposing it was heroin. Is he in any danger? Could he get freaked out enough to starve or kill himself?

Why hadn't I gone to see *Christiane F.*?

Because I thought it was repulsive, that's why. I thought it had nothing to do with me. Damn. Poor Tommi.

Thinking such, I made myself some instant oatmeal. Instant

oatmeal comforts me. When I am sick, that's what I want. And orange juice. Don't have any orange juice. Lots of oatmeal, though. What if we abandon the J.J. analogy, now. Though it's been useful. Say the problem is not oatmeal. (Because it *isn't,* really.) Say the problem's heroin. Maybe instant oatmeal would comfort Tommi too.

Balance the oatmeal bowl and spoon and paper napkin in one hand, imagine a prayer, and with the other—Tap tap tap. Maybe he's asleep. *Tap tap tap.*

"Get the fucking hell away from me!"

Nope.

"I made you some oatmeal."

Wait.

"It's hot."

Nothing.

"Everybody has to eat."

"Get off!"

Smooth move, Andy. Playing the Jewish mother already. You're a nice boy, Tommi, but you should eat. Think of something else. What if I flat out put it in his door; don't make him act polite to get it?

It is so inanely simple. On the outside of most lock-on-the-inside doorknobs, right in the middle, is a slot. They make odd little keys to go in there, but the point of a table knife works just as well. When I got old enough to realize that button in my bedroom knob was for locking other people out, Mama took a knife and came in after me. She never let me see the knife. I didn't know how she did it. She said she knew the magic word. As I outgrew believing that, she said she had very strong fingernails. Isabel told me about the knife.

When J.J. came along and discovered that doors lock, I pulled the same old mossy lies on him. Very satisfying.

Tommi's doorknob was the middle-slot variety. It opened slick as J.J.'s ever did. I reached the oatmeal in and to the right: onto his bedside table. Plop. *Bash!* The door rammed shut in my face. While my ears were still zapped from the noise, while I was still savoring how lucky I was to have gotten my hand out, came another giant crash. Broken glass.

My first thought was his window.

I flung myself out the front door and around the house to see if he was coming through it. What could I do if he was? Window stayed whole. Curtains drawn inside.

So what else is in that room? Not much.

Pine chest of drawers. Somebody'd trashed that out on the Palo Alto dump. Mama hoisted it into the back of the VW van herself. I was still too young to get out at the dump and help; no children or dogs allowed, that kind of thing. No scavenging either. But that never slowed Mama.

She stripped paint, scraped auto-grease out of the drawers, lined 'em with stick-on vinyl. It looks like a backwoods classic now, but it's a tough old thing. It wouldn't make a noise like smashing glass.

Clothes pole. Camp table, a relic of a military grandfather. Bedside lamp. Good God, he's thrown the lamp. I was back outside the bedroom door as quick as quick. Even through the crack I got the reek of fried phenolic.

"Pull out the lamp cord!

"Look! Unplug the damn lamp cord! Do you wanta burn down the house?

"You *think* you've got problems? You don't know *anything* until you *burn down my house!* Unplug the fool lamp!"

I listened carefully between each threat. No sound. He wasn't swearing, crying, or throwing things. Nothing. Maybe he electrocuted himself when he threw the lamp. Table knife. I had it in the knob, when the door jerked out of my hands. I saw no part of him. I saw a wedge of floor, bits of broken lamp and the end of the lamp cord. He had, in fact, unplugged it.

Something flew out past my head and destructed on the wall beside the bathroom door. *Bash. Slam.* Oatmeal bowl. Oatmeal down the wall. Oatmeal on the floor, and chunks of broken glass. Oatmeal in my hair. Well fuck him! Fuck him fuck him fuck him!

Oh God, don't I wish I could.

The truly terrible part was, squatting on the hall floor covered with oatmeal and crying like a baby, I could hear him crying, with just as little adult dignity, there inside the bedroom.

Do I need this? I cleaned up all his oatmeal. *Did I ask for this?* Maybe. Good God. Tommi Rhymer. *Do I have the guts to survive this?* That would seem to be the bottom line. Unless someone or something came to my emotional rescue fairly soon, I was afraid the answer might be *no*. Tommi had stopped crying, and so had I. I went to the front room and sat down on a lumpy sofa.

Lord God Father Almighty, have mercy on me.

Lord Jesus Christ, have mercy on me.

Lord God Holy Spirit have mercy on me.

My eyes made a circuit of the walls. Window. Trout photos. Lumpy sofa. Deerskin. Front door. Lumpy sofa. Wood stove. Other photos. Other window. Chair. Deerskin. Ladder. Kitchen door. The infamous Pardee bookcase. I thought about Skye with her "good escapist read."

Here are the escapist reads I care about, an outgrown childhood too dear to part with. We hauled it to the cabin instead. Makes sense. Mama spent her childhood summers in the country; she still remembers her grandmother's bookcase of funky old nineteenth-century novels, two rows deep on the shelf. When she bought lumber for the Pardee bookcase she got it doublewide. For her, there is an utter mysterious charm about the invisible volumes on the back layer.

Small mystery to me; I know what's back there. Like Izzy's and my entire collection of Walter Farley *Black Stallion* books.

> *The Arabs were crowding toward the center of the landing. Alec heard a whistle—shrill, loud, clear, unlike anything he had ever heard before. He saw a mighty black horse rear on its hind legs, its forelegs striking out into the air—The crowd broke and ran.*
>
> *White lather ran from the horse's body; his mouth was*

open, his teeth bared—His mane was like a crest, mounting, then falling low. His neck was long and slender, and arched to the small, savagely beautiful head. The head was that of the wildest of all wild creatures—a stallion born wild—and it was beautiful, savage, splendid. A stallion with a wonderful physical perfection that matched his savage, ruthless spirit. Once again the black screamed and rose on his hind legs. Alec could not believe his eyes and ears, a stallion, a wild stallion—unbroken, such as he had read and dreamed about!

Black Stallion books are no challenge to a speed-reader. You can breeze through one in an hour. But the whole set? Fifteen hours of total catatonic diversion. If you don't mind eyestrain and a pre-pubescent horse-fantasy OD.

Walter Farley is the merest beginning. Also in that back layer is my complete set of Edgar Rice Burroughs. *Pellucidar, Tarzan, Carson of Venus, John Carter of Mars,* every book of every series. Even if you're normally into William Burroughs, Edgar Rice has moments which can be severely entertaining.

The young Lord Greystoke was indeed a strange and warlike figure, his mass of black hair falling to his shoulders behind and cut with his hunting knife to a rude bang upon his forehead that it might not fall before his eyes.

His straight and perfect figure, muscled as the best of the Roman gladiators must have been muscled, and yet with the soft sinuous curves of a Greek god, told at a glance the wondrous combination of enormous strength with suppleness and speed.

A personification, was Tarzan of the Apes, of the primitive man, the hunter, the warrior. With the noble poise of his handsome head upon those broad shoulders, and the fire of life and intelligence in those fine, clear eyes, he might readily have typified some demigod of a wild and bygone people of this ancient forest....

Grownup fantasy for older children.

What I decided was: skip my least favorite Burroughs series (didn't think I could face *Pellucidar*), start with my next least (*Tarzan*), and dilute them one-to-one with *Black Stallion* books. That reduced my emotional rescue to spreadable consistency. It should last for days.

Something else which had to last for days. Skye might be back on Saturday, or it might be Saturday week. The food should be parceled out to last at least till then.

Once *Tarzan of the Apes* was discovered hiding on the top back shelf of the bookcase, I trotted off to the kitchen for my inventory. Things that would make a meal for one, if Tommi continued to play difficult. Things that would make a meal for two, whenever he changed his mind.

Mid-afternoon already. I boiled more water. Made more coffee. Poured a steamy Styrofoam cup of Japanese instant noodles (shrimp flavor). Thought about it. And poured a second one for Tommi. My natural bent is hospitality. So the oatmeal may have been a fluke. Maybe he was hungry now. Maybe he was sorry.

Maybe hell has frozen.

I was totally silent about it. I had actually table-knifed the door, stuck my arm in with the noodles, shut the door, and tiptoed out of range before the door flew open and the whole thing hit the wall. The spoon caromed into the kitchen.

Shit, what a mess. What a waste. Styrofoam cups don't break, though. Maybe I was getting smarter. This was war! Jihad! Me against him. One I should be able to win, damn it, because his brains were cooked. Think. What was the objective?

Basically, hang tough till he came out of orbit. *If* he came out of orbit. Enough of that. What were my advantages?

Well, isolation, number one. The longer I prevented Tommi *seeing* anybody, or anybody seeing *him*, the better my chances of his being sane when it did happen.

I found a pair of men's rubber-thong sandals under a front-room sofa. A field jacket and a camo hat of Grandfather's were hanging in the broom closet. These items I secreted under a mattress in the loft. Shoeless and thinly dressed, he'd be less inclined to run away.

Number two sure didn't seem to be hunger. How about thirst? I could imagine him starving. I could imagine him relieving himself on the floor. But I could not imagine him going thirsty forever with a functional bathroom three feet from his door. Then he would use the toilet eventually. I had faith. He would want to wash eventually. He would think a shave was nice eventually. At least I hoped he would. Tommi Rhymer with a beard. Ugh.

The bathroom was to be my communication channel. My hotline. I ate my noodles and cleaned up his.

Papa had a stack of white card signs printed up for us, like those posted everywhere in the Summer Home Tract: $100 REWARD for info leading to the arrest of persons responsible for breaking, vandalizing, etc., etc. I turned one of these over, and with a massive black felt-nib on the back wrote:

HERE IS NEW SOAP FOR YOU.
HERE IS A RAZOR, IF YOU WANT TO SHAVE.
DRINKING WATER IS IN THE REFRIGERATOR.
THERE IS ALSO MILK IN THE REFRIGERATOR

Merely *suggest* the existence of the kitchen. Coax him out in the most neutral peaceable manner. On the next card I wrote DANGER. Underneath that I put KEEP OUT: BLASTING. "Blasting" sounds really arcane and vicious to most people, and more believable than "Quarantine" or "Toxic Waste."

Course if any ranger read that, he'd come right in to see what fool was blasting what, and whether we had permits. It wasn't rangers I was mostly worried about. It was dumb redneck hunters and druggy heavy-metal kids on dirt bikes.

When it was half dark, too dark I judged for Tommi to bolt again, I took it down to the pipe-gate. I locked the gate. That way nothing on four wheels could trespass up our road. And I tied my sign to it with baling wire. When I got back, I shook his door to make sure he was in it. He swore volubly at me. I said my prayers and went to sleep.

In the middle of the night, I heard the toilet flush.

TUESDAY

What to do about Tommi.

He fired my instant oatmeal off the wall.

So, some people don't like oatmeal. Some people *really* don't like oatmeal. Maybe he was kin to J.J. more than I supposed, and oatmeal made him sick. Maybe he thought I was trying to poison him, giving him stuff that made him sick.

The Japanese instant noodles fared no better. Almost funny, if it hadn't been so serious. That door flew open, and the stuff shot out and splatted on the wall, like a scene out of old cartoons on early-morning television.

Maybe he didn't like Japanese food either.

Correction. It was cheap-and-dirty thirty-nine-cent instant Oriental junk food in throwaway Styrofoam cups. Who says he has to like it? (Course I was born and raised on the stuff, being a genuine Kalifornia Kid.) This isn't funny. I have to get fluid in him. Whatever ails his insides, dehydration is nasty.

Traditional sick people drink chicken soup.

In among that raft of canned-goods in the kitchen were several of clear chicken broth. Something should be do-able with those. Pry a few dried noodles from a cup of Japanese instant, a very few, so they wouldn't look frightening, and cook 'em in some broth. Right. That's what I did. I took another "$100 REWARD!" card, and on the back wrote, "*Wait!* Look at it first."

Very consoling I thought it looked, on its little tin tray between a folded paper napkin and a spoon. The afternoon had gotten on; but there was time for him to understand, and eat it before dark. If he would. Now the plan was: position the tray on the floor outside his room. Open the door with as little messing around as possible. Slide tray in, shut door, clear out.

I was down on the floor leaning forward, pushing it inside.

A sudden wind, a rush of bare feet, and Tommi hurdled my back invisible as Bilbo Baggins in the goblin mines. The bathroom door slammed shut between us. Nothing to do but stand there and look stupid. He was crying again inside the bathroom. That lost hoarse weary despairing sound. That sound I would be decidedly glad to hear for the very last time.

Then came two crashes. A small tinny crash. Something metal hurled across the room. Instantly identifiable: my razor on the sink. A big soft heavy crash that shook the house. Only one thing in the bathroom could go down that way. *Him*. Quick, outside to the bathroom window. The curtains weren't drawn; I still couldn't see him. Inside again, ear pressed against the door. God, I don't want to keep intruding. And in the *bathroom*, of all places, what am I supposed to do? Back off and let him cut his silly throat? Now he isn't even crying. Maybe he's bled to death already. New philosophy: I cry, therefore I live. Very funny. This must be the life, all right. I'm crying like a hose.

Quietly, the table knife turns in the knob. Getting damn good at this, I am. The door swings in without a sound. There's nobody home. An empty room. What's he done? Cut out and hid while I was racing to the dumb window? Not in the bedroom. That door's open. Out through the kitchen, no one. The front room, no one. He couldn't have made it out the front and into the woods in the short time I was gone. I walked back to the empty bathroom. A little sound came out of it, a stir, and a sigh.

Lord Jesus Christ have mercy on me.
Lord God Father Almighty, have mercy on me.
Lord God, Holy Spirit—

Maybe Tommi was straddled on the bathroom ceiling like James Bond, ready to drop on me if I walked in the door.

I could see the ceiling. He wasn't on it.

Late afternoon shone in the window; the crude small wooden room looked warm, and even cheerful. Something stirred. Be brave. Take a step inside. Take two. Tommi was curled up in the bottom of the bathtub. His arms were wrapped around his knees. He hadn't cut his throat. I saw the razor on the floor, there by the toilet.

He was asleep.

A sunbeam stroked his temple and his cheek. After all that nonsense, still so beautiful. Fine drawn, transparent, breakable. A blown-glass toy. He took my breath away.

His beard must be a quarter-inch long. And it was thick. Who would imagine that he'd have so much? Not the same red as his hair, a virgin stand of thin bright copper filaments.

Study his, and I might learn to find beards sexy.

He still should have the right to be rid of it if he chooses. I put my note and razor back together on the sink. Then I made another note:

DO NOT DRINK THE WATER.
IT COMES OUT OF THE CREEK.
THE COWS SHIT IN THE CREEK, AND IT MIGHT BE BAD FOR YOU.
WE BOIL IT FIRST.
THE WATER IN THE GREEN PLASTIC PITCHER IS FOR YOU.

My chicken soup still graced the bedroom floor among the fragments of dead lamp, undrunk but unspilled too. I refrigerated it. I swept the lamp into a sack. Last of all I brought his comforter, laid it feather light around his legs, and shut the bathroom door.

WEDNESDAY

Tommi vacated the bathroom in the night, taking his comforter with him. The green plastic pitcher and a glass went also. My notes were in the trash. In the sink with the razor was a red snowfall. His beard-shavings. Part of him. Maybe I shouldn't try to wash it up. Save it in a crystal vial or something. They did look just like copper glitter; they clung to everything.

THURSDAY

I learned that Bisquick with dried eggs added instead of real ones makes appallingly horrible pancakes, and Bisquick with no eggs added doesn't make pancakes at all. A person with dried eggs can make scrambled eggs and omelets. Out of all those cutesy recipes covering the Bisquick box, the only thing a person with dried eggs can make is biscuits.

I seem to remember from Mama and a long bygone Saint Patrick's Day that Irish soda bread is only a recipe of biscuits baked in one big loaf. Nothing to lose, I'd rather have bread than biscuits. I made it round, and cut a cross into the top. It came out doughy in places and black on the bottom, but trimmable after it cooled, and sliceable.

Tommi had left his empty pitcher in the bathroom. I refilled it. I also left a mug of milk and a plate with three slices of bread all covered in plastic wrap.

FRIDAY

Pitcher and plate and mug all empty. I think he rinsed the mug. I said the Latin Gloria in thanks for my progress. More boiled water, more bread, more milk. With any luck, Skye would come tomorrow. And Tommi might be well and civil enough to accept a ride in peace.

SATURDAY

Cold and nasty. It had rained two days that week. I thought of unlocking the pipe gate, and decided against it. Skye could walk the last half-mile: I didn't want drop-in visitors. Though the weather was so dismal and un-summery, I wondered if there was anyone in all the forest beside me.

> *The Island Stallion*
>
> *It had come to him with the suddenness of the stallion's shifting gait as he had half-turned across the valley. Now there was nothing fearful about the ever-lengthening strides or the wind that tore at his tear-filled eyes.*

Leaning forward, Steve moved with his horse, glorying in the surge of powerful muscles beneath his legs. No longer did he feel that the stallion was separate from him, that he was riding Flame. It was entirely different now: it was as though he and the horse were one. He WAS Flame! He thought the same, felt the same! They were running because they loved to run, because this was the way it was meant to be....

Make instant coffee; drink instant coffee. Spending a week at Pardee as a couch potato is an abomination before God and man. I wanta get out and run around!

Tarzan the Invincible.

For some time they had sat in silence, the beautiful eyes of the high-priestess resting on the profile of the forest-god. "Tarzan!" she said.

The man looked up. "What is it, La?" he asked.

"I still love you, Tarzan," she said in a low voice.

A troubled expression came into the eyes of the ape-man. "Let us not speak of that."

"I like to speak of it," she murmured, "It gives me sorrow. But it is a sweet sorrow—the only sweetness that has ever come into my life.

Tarzan extended a bronzed hand and laid it upon her slender, tapering fingers. "You have always possessed my heart, La," he said, "up to the point of love. If my affection goes no further than this, it is through no fault of mine or yours."

La laughed. "It is certainly through no fault of mine, Tarzan," she said, "but I know that such things are not ordered by ourselves. Love is a gift of the gods. Sometimes it is awarded as a recompense, sometimes as a punishment. For me it has been a punishment, perhaps, but I would not have it otherwise.

I have nurtured it in my breast since first I met you;

and without that love, however hopeless it may be, I should not care to live....

Half a can of hot tamales. Heat and eat. How the hell can I give hot food to Tommi if he won't come and get it? Cold Dinty Moore beef stew should be a grease-ball gut bomb. Cold canned tamales and ravioli even worse.

The Island Stallion Races. OD time. More instant coffee. Drowse off into it.

Tarzan the Triumphant. Twilight. Guess who isn't going to show up today.

Get yet another $100 REWARD card and a ballpoint from the kitchen table drawer. This note promises to be much more wordy than a big felt-nib allows.

Dear Tommi: I don't mean to sound familiar, but I've been your fan forever, and "Dear Mr. Rhymer" doesn't sound right either.

Here is my problem. (Yours too.) We are 200 miles from where I live. My friend drove us here. I made her do it. No one paid me. No one put me up to it. I made her promise to say she lost me at your Oakland concert. She either did it, or she got wiped out on her way home, because no one seems to know where I am. And obviously, no one knows where you are.

I tried to make her promise she would drive back here today (Saturday) or at least next Saturday, and get us. Maybe she never agreed to either one. Or maybe something's happened to her.

But I apologize for everything. Please forgive me. And please, can we help each other?

Signed—

I consider the implications of "Andy." "Miranda." "Miranda Dolores Falconer." An alias. I signed it "M.D.F." and left it on the bathroom sink.

That evening was a red sunset. Then a cold wind got up, trying all the doors and windows, rattling the tin above my head. It was indescribably lonely. Not even prayer put me to sleep till almost dawn.

SUNDAY

A day for sleeping in. Tommi was, by my observation, fully nocturnal. He woke around noon, and didn't go down (as he'd originally said) till sunrise. That's why busting his only bedroom light was a less-than-fortunate gesture. That's why he was spending nearly whole nights in the bathroom now. No telling how he occupied himself, but I could see cracks of light coming up through the floor.

One would think he might unbend enough to check out the kitchen. Nope. If he'd come as far as the front room he'd have escapist reading. Nope. I should leave a good book in his bathroom. Not the stuff I was ingesting. I wondered if he'd consider *The Wind in the Willows*. Its characters use each other with such healing kindness. Half its chapters end "So they all went to sleep that night in great joy and contentment." Which was all I wanted for him. Me, too.

I'd like to feed him something beside bread.

· — ·

THE first thunder woke me. I sat on the front porch for a while. I could see clouds building around the edges of the sky. More rain coming. Lots more rain.

My note was still in the bathroom. It had a peculiar chewed look to it. He'd taken something sharp, a nail, no, a piece of broken lamp I'd missed (there it was in the sink): and across the middle of my lame-brained apology had gouged "GO—" (followed by a deep hole where he'd put a letter "F" then tried to scrape it out) "—TO HELL."

I understood perfectly. Do it twice. The bedroom wasn't locked: there was nothing in it but an unmade bed.

I grabbed the pair of rubber thongs and my down jacket from the loft. Now who was the dummy who'd wanted to get out and run around?

His tracks went left, down the roadway toward the creek.

And from the depth, the stride, the gouts of sand where his toes dug in, he was going flat-out, too. This man hadn't wandered off; he was running to lose me.

Spring melt takes a shortcut down our road; in June the ruts are two feet deep. I went bounding along. It was a beautiful place to break an ankle. Miles from help, I wondered what I'd do. What would Tommi do if it happened to him? Maybe I'll find him sprawled out in a gully, damaged. God help me God help me. Maybe I won't, too.

Gray muttering piles of cloud have towered up behind the trees. Like strands of floating wool, their thin outriders snare the sun. Surely I have to catch him up before the rain does. Around each bend I expect a sight of flying heels. He's an addict. He's all wiped out on dope and booze, God only knows what else! Kinky sex! He's spent the whole week sick and starving, how can he cope with this? Guess what I'm *really* boggled at: how can he outrun me?

Behind the trees is blue-black now. Behind the high peaks the thunder's walking. With a lovely wet-dust smell the first fat raindrops spatter down. Speed up.

C'mon, c'mon! I've seen worse cross-country courses where the only incentive was a stupid ribbon! To be sure, there were also doctors and coaches and doting parents to scrape you up and mend you if you killed yourself.

Raining hard, now. And after the bridge? What then? On Bright's Creek Road there'll be no tracks to follow. Right goes to the reservoir, the resort, the highway. Left veers from the downhill plunge of the creek, and dead-ends miles away on a logged-out ferny hillside in a Federal Game Preserve. I can't see him taking off across the trackless ridges. So I'll still be between him and the world if he goes that way. Unless he finds some fisherman etc. to take him in. Oh God oh God.

Then he could be headed the right way.

What if he truly does come back with the sheriff? What if he does sue? I'm a minor, but I'm not sure what that means. Could he ruin my parents? That isn't fair! Lugging him off to the mountains wasn't their idea; they knew nothing about it! They still think I'm the kidnapped person! They'll be worried sick about *me*. Could he get me *taken away from them and put in Juvy Hall?* Can Father 'Chi get in to see me, or do they only let him counsel the damn boys?

Fear and fury burned a hole in my throat and trickled unchecked down into my lungs. What could I do to stop him? Threaten to tell the whole world he was gay, that's what! What kind of audience of screaming teen-age sweethearts would he have then? I could *fill their ears!* Hit him first! Get the fucker before he gets me!

I could see my scorching exposé in *Rolling Stone*: I could say he had sex with me. Maybe Harlan too. They *both* had sex with me, and gave me drugs! Never mind that they could test and tell I haven't had sex with anybody; nothing is as trendy as a molested kid! People'll eat up every scuzzy tall tale I invent! Besides, I could imagine things he might have made me do that wouldn't show on any test....

The pain inside my chest was almost intolerable. I wailed out loud as I ran. Heartburn of the soul. Terminal spiritual dilapidation. Like I'd torn all my pictures of Tommi and shit and spat on them, then stepped back in a kind of horrid dream to gloat at what I'd done.

Look out, Tommi Rhymer—you unforgivably fleet-footed fucking sleaze—Look out—I'm gonna *expose the shit* out of you—I'm *gonna expose you all over the mass media!*

Oh, damn, oh damn ohdamnohdamnohdamn. I made it all sound like some really tatty perversion, like him exposing himself! God help me, what am I trying to think, he never exposed anybody—just—kissed somebody he loved on the mouth—kissed somebody's—pretty mouth when he thought he was in private. And there I simply had to be—*voyeuring* away in the fucking bathroom.

Extra! Extra! See Tommi Rhymer have a dumb, miserable fight with his lover.... *See* the great Tommi Rhymer get screwed, bewildered, and wasted by mistake.... See Tommi Rhymer wipe out like a poor stoned idiot in the filthy alley and the curious gaze of strangers....

I don't wanta expose you!

I want to go to bed with you!

All I ever wanted, all I *ever, ever* wanted, all I ever ever ever wanted.

Stop!

I stopped by myself in the middle of the forest in the middle of the road, bawling tears. Rain thrashed down. Rain all over me. Rain inside me and out. I didn't *care* if he and Harlan slept with each other. It only showed they had good taste.

I hadn't meant to hurt him or to scare him.

If only I could find him.

I began to run again, mechanically at first, more intent on my own mental ruts, my muddy gullies of the heart—a whole lot trickier to steer between, it seemed, than the ones in the road. The Desert Fathers had this neat analysis of the failure modes in human behavior, and how you could go about reversing the effects of each. Unfortunately, like most people, I could remember the names of their seven failure modes with ease, but their handy-dandy, sure-fire self-help remedies escaped me:

PRIDE ! ENvy !
1 2 3 4

ANger ! dePRESsion !
1 2 3 4

LUST ! GREED !
1 2 3 4

GLUT-TON-Y !
1 2 3 4

They had a certain loggy, dogged sound. And, *sudden enlightenment*, I knew them all firsthand: I had *wallowed* in them all with a vengeance the last few days.

Except for Gluttony. I didn't seem to have much of a feel

for gluttony. Be thankful for small favors. Then I remembered Campfire marshmallows. Oh God, if they were to let Father 'Chi see me in Juvy Hall, the first thing I'd ask him was the remedies!

And so, indulging, I took my first good fall. Downhill on my face. I had mud in my mouth and the wind knocked out of me; gravel embedded in my hands, knees torn. Funny numb anesthetized feeling to new torn skin. Stiff, like it doesn't belong to you.

Grounded.

In the nitty-gritty of reality.

In every way.

I had an ant's-eye view of the weather. Flat on my front in the road, never so alone in all my life, surrounded by the overwhelming, pouring, roaring white noise of rain in the forest. The hard drops slapping the nylon shell of my old down jacket. The ruts and ditches beginning to run. Clothes beginning to soak through.

Big fat drops rebounded off the dirt, so high and hard it seemed like raining up as well as down. And when they hit a second time, they rolled. That wasn't water; it was ice! Hailstones. No wonder it felt cold. No wonder my breath is smoking! Have to run in earnest now, or else I'll stiffen up. *Ow ow ow.* Bloody torn Levi's. Ruined knees. I hopped and hobbled the final downhill slither onto Bright's Creek bridge. Here trees gave way to open sky. I saw black, wet bridge boards pebbled in ice. Below, the water lay prickly green, the hail dimpling and popping off its opaque surface like goose bumps and scared fur. I crept across on feet and hands, shuffling through the ice.

The road along the creek runs north and south, an avenue of trees. Mist and hail swept across it from the west in hissing curtains. Hail battered out all hope of footprints. It began to whiten the road: first the depressions, then all over like a fall of snow, slippery as ice ball bearings.

Bright's Creek Road. Nothing but good associations. A fragrant summer place. Deep fir-needled banks. Trees and trees of every kind: great huge gnarly standers, tall symmetrical young cones with silver trunks, fuzzy green seedlings. Lots of happy traffic. Families in campers. Kids on dirt bikes. In winter it was a crystal chute of sparkling sky and snowmobiles. Recreational wilderness. Not now. Even this sweet place I trusted returned a verdict of no sympathy.

Hail drove sideways at me, flayed my cheek. Hair turned to sopping string. My right eye froze blind, so I shut it, and pelted on and on. My right ear was going to freeze for real; the wind hurt like a spike poked in it. I put my soggy chilly coat sleeve up to cover ear and eye.

All I could think about was Tommi and Tommi. Tommi lost in this. Tommi gotten up all sexy for the Midnight Bop in a luxury hotel. No coat at all. He has no *shoes*, for God's sake. I *found* a coat and shoes for him, and hid the damn things, so he wouldn't get away.

And didn't anybody ever try to teach me about sin? Me, who's gone around mouthing off for years about how much I *loved* him. And morals, what about those?

A USDA Grade A bitch is what I've been, like Skye suggested, caring only for myself from the moment I first laid hands on him till now. Worse than that, much worse! I haven't even cared intelligently for myself: If he should die out here, there'd be nothing left of me. All he wanted was his liberty; I hope not bad enough to die for it.

Then again, if I've been dumb, maybe he was smarter. He could be sitting dry under a log someplace. I could have passed him. Maybe he watched me flounder by weeping in the hail with my arm over my eyes, and laughed. It would certainly serve me right.

Lord Jesus Christ, have mercy on me!

I don't wanta be served right!

I reached the place where the road bends left from a boulder- and willow-crowded creek, and starts the first of its long switchbacks up the ridge, the first of the loggers' clear-cut places. The storm roared and the hail slashed at the hillside. Newspaper sensations came to mind: hail the size of baseballs and weighty enough to brain cows.

There'd be nothing to block the wind above for half a mile I guessed; only boulders, grass, wildflowers, stumps, and stocky bright green Christmas trees. Could a really desperate person shove his way in under one of those and find a stickery, scratchy shelter? A determined little boy, maybe, not a grown man with long legs. And bonfire hair. And skin as white as milk.

The grade was slippery; I fell, and fell, until my hands were ruined. In a kind of fury I squinted up at last into the very origin of the hail, and saw it tumbling toward me through the sky from God knows where, an unimaginable swarm of small gray missiles. Also something else.

Above, in the middle of a hillside green and gray and white, there was a flash of red I thought I knew. It didn't matter how slick the road was after that.

He hadn't been smart at all.

He sat on a stump beside the road. His arms were kind of wrapped around himself. His shirt was thin and wet. Everything showed through it. The mesh of his net T-shirt. The color of his skin. His trousers clung soaking on his legs. His poor feet, where they showed, were mottled orange and gray. His lips were dead gray. Little hailstones frosted his hair and melted in his eyelashes. Only his eyes were still his own. Those held mine with an all-out, last-stand, trapped-animal defiance. You could tell he'd seen me coming, the whole way up the hill.

Lord Jesus Christ, have mercy on Tommi.
Lord Jesus Christ, have mercy on Tommi.
Lord Jesus Christ, have mercy on me.
Lord Jesus Christ, have mercy on Tommi.

Frankly, finding him was as far ahead as I'd imagined. There I stood, stupid in the road, while hail pelted my back. Whizzed and hopped around my feet. Skittered off downhill and into the gushing ditch that lay between us.

"Well?" he cried, against the soft roar of it. "What are y'going to do?" His nose was streaming down his face. Mine too, probably. I didn't give a damn. All I wanted was to get between him and the cold. Shelter him. "Y'like the way I look?"

I still did, in fact.

"Y'satisfied? Look at you! Picture of fucking health! I bet you could deck me—with one hand now—if I tried to cross you! Didn't do just what you wanted."

I guessed his strength was pretty far gone to exposure, and shouting took the last of it. His speech was getting slurred, like when he had OD'd in San Francisco. But I underestimated him. Rage is a first-class motivator. Shouting didn't satisfy; Tommi lurched to his feet shaking a mini-avalanche of hail out of his clothes.

The wind doubled itself with a stinging roar. "So what do I have to do?" he positively screamed against it. "What d'y'want from me?"

I yelled, "I wanta take you home!"

"In a pig's arse, you will!" Down the bank he inched unsteadily... "I'm free of you! On my own ground, now." ...and gathered himself for the final bound that would take him to the roadway. "I'm free out of your house forever!"

Funny, I thought, but if you're beautiful it doesn't much matter if your nose is running. He jumped, and would have made it too, if the bank hadn't been all mud and hailstones. Back into the ditch he slid, knee-deep in icy runoff.

"Please lemme give you a hand!"

"Shove it," he said distinctly.

The bank where he was offered no footholds; downstream there was a boulder in it. He got onto the road without my help at last, smeared and disheveled from head to foot. Then he bit his lip and, heading up the grade, hobbled a wide elaborate detour around me. His feet were bruised and bleeding through their crust of mud.

"Please let me help you. Any way at all!"

If his set face softened, it wasn't much. But his chin came

around a little in my direction as he passed. "You can tell me...," he mumbled proudly, head high, condescending, "...only tell me, how much farther have I got to go—to some place with a phone?"

"Eight—ten miles, maybe." The truth, if not the whole truth. The Summer Home Tract is over the ridge. Even in the middle of the week he'd find somebody at the summer homes to give him dry clothes and a lift to the resort.

"Eight *miles?*" There was no hiding the anguish in his voice. "How far did I come?"

"About six."

"Six miles? Ten kilometers? I can run ten K in half an hour when I'm *well!*"

"But that's five-minute miles!"

"Goddamn right it is. Only thing they liked me for in school."

"Wait!" Still he plodded slowly forward. "Please wait!" I sprinted up to get in front of him, slipping crazily in the hail, tugging at the cheap rubber thongs wedged inside my pockets. "Here. Take these at least. Come on, I brought 'em for you! Take my jacket, too. It's soaked, but it's warm inside. You won't make it *anywhere* if you don't! I can still run to keep warm." God, the look on his face. Quick, dance back out of reach. I'm not going to get punched again.

"So why don't you run off home?"

"No."

"Go away!"

"No!"

"Fuck off!"

"No, God damn it!"

"I don't want you!"

"I don't care if you want me or not!"

"I can't stand the *sight* of you!"

"Then don't look!"

He had ground to a halt, shivering and crying with frustration.

"If you're really going on," I shouted, "I'll go along behind you till you meet someone. If you sit down again, you won't get up! You only got up this time to run away from me!"

"I was resting."

"Resting, my foot! You were passing out! You'll be out here tonight, if you go down. It must be forty degrees; this stuff's not melting! People die of exposure at forty degrees! Especially sick people!"

"So what if I go down in the road; what could you do?"

"Carry you!"

"Bet you couldn't carry me six miles!"

"I bet I could! If it meant your life I'd try!"

He shut his eyes abruptly

"On the other hand," I yelled, "maybe I couldn't carry you six miles. Do we wanta find out the hard way? What if the best I had to offer was just to sit down and die of cold with you? Come on; let's turn around! Please, while you can still walk, and we don't have to prove how strong I am!"

The eyes did not reopen. He looked dazed, bewildered, and very sick. Don't know if he's giving up or merely passing out, but I mean to take advantage of it. I skinnied out of my body-warm soaking jacket. At once the cold was on me. This is summertime? How had he stood it at all?

"Here." I chattered. "Left hand!"

He tried half-heartedly to jerk it away.

I held on and shoved it down the sleeve. Like J.J. all over. "Good boy. Won-derful. Now the other one."

The free arm swung a futile punch at my head.

"Oh ho! Try that on me again, I'll punch you back, you big bully. See if I don't! I will punch you out."

His blue lips formed the words "Fuck you."

"Oh yes!" I said. "Do it! Come on, I really wish you would! Is that your only answer to everything?"

His face crumpled like paper. It *was* his answer to everything. Poor brave, cheeky, inappropriate answer to everything.

I managed to corral his arm and funnel it down the coat. Now for the thongs. Squatting and shivering at his feet, I made him slip them on. If he really was a little kid he'd have his bloody places kissed; but I value my teeth. I got him turned around.

"Okay," I bellowed. "This is it! Six miles! Your bed's turned down! There's lots of hot water, hot coffee, and funny food! The road is even downhill for a bit!"

We walked. The hail was rising to a grand finale, straight in the face now, even worse than in the ear or down the collar. If I don't go faster in my wet T-shirt, I'll soon be in as sorry shape as he is. I begin to jog big slippery circles round him.

"You cut that out!"

"Then move! C'mon, please! It's death to go slow!"

He rouses to a shuffling trot. Not up to coping with the Prayer of the Pilgrim, I would judge. Some pity.

"One, two, three, four, who are *we* for—"

"Ah, shut up, do!"

ARmy! NAvy! AIRforce! maRINES!
Army—Navy—AIRforce—marines—
Army—Navy—

It was almost evening when I cajoled and bullied Tommi up the steps at Pardee. Hail had melted into the ground. Most of the clouds had hurried away eastward on their own business and left behind a raw, red, windy sunset. He made at once for the bedroom, tilting forward and staggering to catch up. I shouldered by him.

"No you don't. Get in the bathroom. Don't argue, I'm going to warm you up. Now, listen," I said. "Look at me. Look right at me. Okay. Our water heater's small; you won't get a full hot tub from it. I'm starting it on warm." I plugged the drain. "Get your feet in. As soon as you can stand it, start turning down the cold. When the hot runs out, turn it off. I'll boil more water in a pot."

I jogged into the kitchen. Fastest way I know to warm the place: turn on the oven with the door flopped open. There is a massive black enamel canning pot with ears. I put it on to boil. No change of nice dry clothes for either of us. Too bad. My waterlogged Nikes and socks went in the sink. I jogged in front of the oven till the pot simmered. Now, the challenge is to lug it to the bath without boiling myself.

Damn. Tommi's shut the door. I've no free hand for the knob. "Open it!" No answer. I gave the door some thundering kicks, as well as I could with bare feet. "Come on, please? I *know* you need hot water." The door turned out to be locked. Okay. Set down my pot and go for the table knife. Too late I realized why he hadn't opened. Oh, for heaven's sake. "So wrap a towel around yourself! I'm not looking at you! I don't care what you look like." (Not true, of course.)

He already had a towel, or maybe several. He perched on one end of the tub, untidy and furious, like an enormous owl. His legs were perfectly blue; even the orange spots were gone.

"Not looking, okay?" With my back to him I tipped the pot, a slow steamy stream into the foot of his tub. "Come on. Stir it or boil."

He stirred it.

Now to warm the inside of him. Back in the kitchen. Greater love hath no man than to give up his last packet of instant oatmeal for his friend. Back in the bathroom. He had made it all the way into the tub. One towel draped his shoulders. Another floated in the water across his lap. So much modesty. Wow. Can I stand it?

"Here." I offered him the bowl and spoon. "It's hot. It's easy on the stomach. Eat it."

"You know damn well I don't like slops."

Regaining his rebellion capabilities. What a pain. "Look," I said, "I'm not *asking* you to *like* it: just to *eat* it." A logical distinction J.J. understood perfectly.

It caught Tommi off guard. He shot me this funny shy lingering glance, and whispered, "Gotcha." God what a look. Sexy, sexy. The sensuality of distress. That look was worth the whole price of admission. It was just almost a smile.

I haunted the hall while my pulse came down in the acceptable range, and listened to the squeaky noises a bare butt makes sliding around a bathtub. It's only now I have him off my hands (if never too far off my mind), that I feel free to realize how very cold I am myself.

There is the solitary can of hot green chili and beans in my inventory of things that wouldn't make a meal for two. Put in some dried onions and three or four good wollops of Tabasco sauce. My hands shook so, I beat a tattoo on the pan as I stirred it. No sense messing up a bowl, the hot pan went to the front room with me. Tommi ought to have a chance to reach his bed in private.

Finished, I brought the pan back to the sink. Bathroom door and bedroom door stand open; the bedroom's dark. Look in the bathroom. Nobody home. The oatmeal bowl is empty, almost clean. He's eaten it too, not dumped it down the pot, because the pot isn't flushed.

I used it myself and flushed it.

Then there's his water, still in the tub. Still warm. Warmer than I am. And he didn't use any soap. You have to *hand* J.J. the soap and stand over him for use verification. What the hell. I shut the door and washed myself before I washed the ring out of the tub. Tommi Rhymer's and my bath water. Tommi's and my bathtub ring. I oughta frame it. Poor proud battered lover.

I put on my damp gritty clothes, mopped the floor. He must be in the bedroom. No place else he could be. Sure enough. A big lump under the comforter, a shock of red hair barely visible on the pillow. Score a first; he's gone to sleep with the door open. I gave myself up to compulsive voluptuous shivering.

It had been a Sunday. Sunday all day long.

I made it through the Latin Gloria before I went to sleep.

Chapter 6

NEXT DAY, HE NEVER came out of the bed.

I crawled down my ladder early, stiff and sore. My knee killed. My hands had real live bruises on the palms. But I made a pot of tea, and did it right. I cut the little bags and took the tea out so the paper wouldn't taste. In the back of a drawer I found a metal tea ball on a chain. My loose tea went in that. I even warmed the pot, and remembered to fish the ball out while the tea was mellow amber and hadn't gotten hostile.

One cup for myself. The pot went on a cookie-sheet with a little thing of sugar and another of reconstituted milk. Oh, and a cup and saucer. Paper napkin. Spoon. Should have had some lemon. Well, he's English. I'm not certain what he'd want.

I walked right back and set it on his bedside table. Afraid to look in the bed. Maybe he'd died in the night. He hadn't. Up came this incredibly startled face.

I didn't stick around. His clothes needed me, a gritty soaking pile on the bathroom floor. Silk slacks. Silk shirt. (Anxiety:

what if they shrink too much to wear? That'd *really* give him cause to hate me. Funny, though.) Fishnet T-shirt. And the tiniest bikini briefs on earth. Plain white. I survived the urge to try them on.

They all got tub-washed in detergent and cold water, with at least five rinses, until the mud was gone. I hung them on a fir tree and gathered a fistful of flowers from the meadow, tiny hardy weedy stars. The hailstorm never touched them.

The last of my soda bread became hot toast. Cut in neat triangles it filled a plate around a little pile of jam. Flowers in a glass of water. All on his table to replace the empty teapot. He'd drunk it. Milk *and* sugar. He was sitting wrapped in the comforter so that no skin showed, and he gave me the most curious look.

"I haven't swiped your stuff; it's drying." He nodded. I shut his door.

My own clothes were next for the wash. I covered up with my grandfather's ancient camo field jacket out of the broom closet, and went back to Edgar Rice Burroughs for the day. The Tarzan series is all read up. I'm onto John Carter of Mars. My favorites.

All clothes were dry by evening. He got his, folded, with his dinner: hot tamales; he ate four out of his six. I went to sleep that night in the closest I'd come yet to the desired great-joy-and-contentment, and was waked in the morning by a series of noises. Whumpity-bumpity noises.

When I got down the ladder they were still going on. Curious. Curious enough to sneak outside and take a swift spy in his window. He was doing exercises, push-ups, sit-ups, knee-bends, crammed between the bedstead and the wall. His clothes still fit.

I trotted back in and pounded on his door. "Hey!" The noises stopped. When I knocked again, he actually opened. Shock. Wonder if I ever could come face-to-face with him without that little loss of breath? "Say, you don't have to do that in here. Go outside and do it in the grass where you've got room." His own breath came quickly from the exercise. He studied my shoes. "I won't even watch you."

"Do you trust me?"

"No," I said.

Mischievous bright eyes flicked up to tag mine and flicked down again. He blushed like a rose. I got out fast.

That blush was quite the trick, though. Shy with full knowledge. Bold and yielding. Modesty that's almost an assault. I feel like such a gawk beside him. But he did his exercises outside the next morning. And I didn't watch. At least not much.

His little workout ended in a brisk half-mile around the meadow. He has the flattest straightest walk. No switches or jiggles. Everything he's got just clean, strong, and in forward-gear, like the dancer he is or some top athlete. I bet he could run like the wind.

· — ·

WE'D come to Wednesday evening, every day ticked off on a wall-calendar. Basic weirdness would have me think days were forgotten or marked down twice. Almost for certain: it's Wednesday. Trying to invent some new camouflage for Dinty Moore beef stew. I'd made more soda bread, a fair success. The winning entry involved toasting bread, fishing all the chunks of beef out of two cans of stew, and making a genuine roast-beef sandwich. The remaining vegetable soup stuff could get spiced up for me.

I was doing that, when a noise came behind me.

Turn head, very slowly: don't want to frighten anybody. Tommi's sitting at the table. He's pulled his chair back from the light. (The noise). But score another first. I think I said, "Hello." He nodded. I set his sandwich in front of him with his napkin and glass of milk. Got my soup, said a silent grace. For both of us, if he was willing. He ate it all without a word and I started to clear away.

"You do much cooking where you live?"

"No." I thought about that a bit. "Shows, huh."

"Maybe." Long silence. "Wasn't trying to complain."

I went on clearing.

"Thank you for the sandwich," he said. Got up from his chair. Went back to his room. Shut the door.

Well. This is a whole new ballgame. So why aren't I a gourmet cook? Didn't it ever occur to me as a survival skill? No, the problem is *something to cook*. I've done as well as any with the cans and stuff. I want some wonderful fresh food for him. I go to sleep thinking about it. Venison seems out of the question, but what about trout?

Fiddler's Lake. Trout are *planted* there, dumber and easier to lay hands on than the real ones in the creek.

Gray dawn sees me quietly bound for Fiddler's Lake with thirty feet of monofilament wrapped around a stick, a tiny hook and split-shot on the end. I have no great thing for fancy poles. Papa takes those home with him anyway; not much insurance against theft at Pardee. Halfway there I kick a rotten log apart and get a bunch of winged ants in a bottle.

The campground is across the water. Either nobody's home or nobody's stirring. The trout are stirring: feeding and flipping themselves into the early sunlight over the whole face of the lake. Bless us, O Lord, and these Thy gifts, which we are about to receive from Thy bounty, through Christ Our Lord, Amen. *Gloria in Excelsis Deo, et in terra pax hominibus bonae voluptatis.*

I had four gorgeous ones before the first radio turned on in the campground. Unseen, unknown, and in triumph, my fish flapping safe on a stringer, I headed home. And I ran all the way. So witlessly unsuspecting. I only wanted Tommi to admire my trout while they were still iridescent, no anticipations of *anything else*, all the way to his room. The door's standing open. The bed's made up, sort of. There's a sheet of paper on the pillow, a note in a funny spikey spidery hand, legible but super strange. I recognize it from his album notes.

GIRL. (Not being rude; I never knew your name.) One last word to clear the air: I do not intend to sue. I hit you. Called

you names. Broke up your stuff. Gave you hell, in fact. The way I see things, we stand even. Hope you feel the same.
T.P.R.

That's him all over. Sly, beguiling, and gone.

Just when he'd begun to look a little friendly. He knows the way now. The weather's turned mild and pleasant. He's rested and well fed. I don't stand a chance in the world.

I put my wretched trout in the refrigerator, why bother to clean 'em? Washed the fish smell off my hands. Why couldn't he have stayed and been nice? Locked the front door after me. Now I have to waste a whole day chasing his tracks.

I try to match my stride to his, down the middle of the road. *No way*. He's inches taller, and it's all legs. Damn his five-minute miles! There I go again. I couldn't damn a thing on him, not for half a breath. Why did he have to go be so desirable? Pretty, pretty, long straight legs.

Such a beautiful morning to run on, too. I bet he's enjoying himself. Nya-nya! Can't catch me, I'm the Gingerbread Man. Well what am I supposed to do? I have to see him safe somewhere.

Brown and yellow butterflies sipping from damp places flushed up at my feet and bopped off down the road ahead of me. I almost ran into a four-point buck. Hey. Papa should be here to check out that one.

Guilt. Papa would be checking all of them, if only I hadn't been so damn self-directed, and had let poor Tommi stay a fantasy lover. Next week must be the opener of bow-season. Papa would be here by choice, certainly. Now here is the place of places he can't come, as long as I play missing person. I had that figured before I started the game, back in Skye's van in San Francisco. My family will sit tied to the phone as long as people scour the countryside for me. Guilt inconsolable. I can picture Papa's office at the Department, stacked knee-deep in computer paper and proceedings of the IEEE. On one wall, Hieronymus Bosch's *Garden of Earthly Delights*. On the other, a poster of three printed slogans. Both items have hung tacked there all my life. The slogans say

YOU GET WHAT YOU PAY FOR.
THERE IS NO FREE LUNCH.
NOTHING'S GOING TO COME IN THE MAIL.

What, of all the stuff that Papa's ever done *for, to,* or *about* me, was pay for the dirty deal he's getting?

I remember this colleague of his, distinguished technical attaché to somebody, mountainous and intolerant as hell, leaning back from Sunday dinner once, at a re-hash of my religious ed., and saying, "How could you, in all seriousness, Falconer? All that myth and ancient history? Drop her into some university Newman Chapel or Prep for Catholic Marriage Group, as will surely *happen*, they'll think she comes from Mars and she won't know what in blazes is going on. You're doing the child an injustice not to raise her in the Real Church. What communion do you expect her to take part in?"

"The Communion of Saints," said Papa.

And when the guy harrumphed at him, he said "*Well?* Anybody looking forward to eternity across the Table of the Lamb from Augustine of Hippo, Ignatius Loyola, or the like, needs all the myth and ancient history she can cram, if she means to stand her ground and speak her own mind!"

I will never make the Communion of Saints at this rate.

Ka-bam!

A rifle shot. Not near; not very far, either. The echo rackets off between the ridges. *Kabakabakabakabakak.*

Dumb fool hunters. Rifle season isn't for another month! Deer aren't that stupid you know; once the practice beer-can-blasting starts every legal buck in earshot tiptoes off grinning toward the Game Preserve.

Ka-bama bakabakabakabak.

That's what they're doing: shootin' cans. Drink 'em first and shoot 'em second.

I remember sitting in the edge of the woods one evening, casing Hamm's Spring meadow with Papa. There was this distant roar and it kept getting louder. Here came two dumb-ass guys on dirt bikes, churning and thrashing up the whole long meadow. They had their green makeup and their camo clothes, their compound bows and quivers, the total outfit. They were so faked out when we stood up in front of them.

"Howdy!" they shouted. "You folks seen any *deer?*"

Some people never seem to learn what things are all about. Then, some people suffer from the Sin of Pride a lot, like me. I sped across the Bright's Creek bridge.

PRIDE ! ENvy !
1 2 3 4

ANger ! dePRESsion !
1 2 3 4

LUST ! GREED !
1 2 3 4

GLUT-TON-Y !
1 2 3 4

Look how Tommi made the turn, his stride growing even longer. Oh God, but he is one sweet mover. I bet he has a kick left, too. The search for me must be *puny* beside the one for him. With his own special someone keeping anguished vigil by a phone.

"But had I known, Tamlin," he said
"A lady wad borrow thee
I'd ta'en out thy two gray eyes
Put in two eyes of tree!
Had I but the wit yestereen
That I have bought this day—"

Wow. What if the two sets of searchers compared notes? What if they gave old Skye the third degree? If all the searches were *one search*, what a great search that would be. Picture Harlan and Papa arriving in the same squad car.

Ka-bam! Ka-bam! Ka-bam! Bakabakabak.

I've heard shooting more than once during the last few days. Tommi must have heard it also. Tommi must be hearing it now, wherever he is.

Oh, I *know* very well why he's running away from me this time: pride, pure and simple. Stroking his own ego. He just had to escape. Just had to outrun me. Just couldn't bear to lie around until I let him go. So maybe he'll run into some blind-drunk hunter and get pot-shotted for his pains.

Ka-bam!

Second thought, that isn't funny. Those bangs are up ahead: guys are probably shooting beer cans off the side of the road.

Tommi. Run like hell. All along the creek it kept on getting louder. Normally about this time I would have turned around and gone the other way.

Bam-ka-bam! Bakabakabakabak.

Rattling like mad around the rocks of Bright's Creek Canyon. So I came to the bend and the beginning of the grade. The shots were still ahead. No sign of Tommi. For the first time his prints were mixed with others.

I ran. Up and up, past the place where I'd found him in the hail. Even that seemed like a happy memory. I kept close to the bank, so I wouldn't be seen from above and reached the end of the clear-cut section. Woods ahead. Then the road switches back across the open.

Ka-bam!

Good God. Shooting right over my head. Sounds of laughter and loud talk. Guys messing around. I crept quietly across to the far side of the turn where I could see. A flash of yellow paint. A dumb Toyota Jeep, to be exact. Four or five young guys with guns, bows, green faces. A big black hyperactive dog.

Suddenly I feel like wild game. I can picture getting raped. May be silly, but I can't force my legs on up that road. No man's ever said "Boo" to me. It *is* silly. I don't *know* they're all drunk and horrible, I'm *imagining* they are.

And Tommi's somewhere on the other side of them. He must have passed before they came. Dear Tommi has made his escape. Intolerable. But what's left? Crawl straight uphill and strike another bend of the road? What if they hear me in the brush and start shooting? Stranger things have happened.

Just above me is a steep sandy bank. And just above that a windfall tree, its great flat pad of broken roots heaved high into the air. I've been around woods enough to know there's a hole below it where the roots pulled out.

Maybe I can sit in there until the Jeepsters waste their ammo. Only fifty yards and a fringe of bushes in between us. They could see me if they looked my way. Their damn enthusiastic dog is sure to see me any moment.

All I can think about is Tommi, getting the better of me. All I can think, to my exquisite aggravation, is *Run! Run! Run!* Catch me if you can! You can't get *me*, I'm the Gingerbread Man, I am I am! I've run away from a hotel full of groupies, I've run away from my guitar-wizard lover, I've run away from a Jeep full of hunters, and I can run away from *you*, I can I can! And *the girl couldn't catch him—*

Quick! Up the bank on hands and feet, over the lip of the hole: a silent wriggling scurry like a lizard.

Then I must have dropped a good six feet, into the lap of Tommi Rhymer, who was sitting at the bottom of the hole. I never was the kind who could faint. There are times when it'd sure be useful.

Diplomatic, even.

But he was up to the occasion. He clapped one hand over my mouth, the other around my waist, and there we sat. He was great fun to sit on, too. Warm and lean under his thin clothes. I thought, I've got to be imagining this. He let his hand off my mouth when he was satisfied I wouldn't scream, and tucked it with the other one. His cheek was next to mine. My body rose and fell a little with his every breath.

For one bad moment, the hunters' black Lab appeared

against the sky and bayed down frantically at us. The guys in the road threw beer-cans at it. The cans went in the hole between my feet and Tommi's. Some were almost full. The beer gurgled out. The dog went off embarrassed. After what seemed hours, the Jeep fired up and drove away.

And the breeze blew and the sun shone. A yellow jacket buzzed around the beer cans. I sat in Tommi Rhymer's lap at the bottom of a tree-stump hole.

He made this little chirping sound against my ear. "Hey. Y'wanna hear my true confessions?"

"Uh-huh."

"First off. Hard to admit it, but I think I'm almost well. I don't feel half bad just now. I've done some heavy thinking while I hid down here. About me. About you."

I waited for more confessions; none surfaced. "How long did they have you cornered?" (Treed? Stumped? Holed?)

"Don't have a watch. What were those people anyway?"

"Bow-hunters."

"Painted green?"

"Sure. So the deer won't notice their faces. What did you think they were?"

"I couldn't tell. I thought they might be Indians."

"Oh no! That's so silly."

"Not to me! I'm English."

"I'm sorry."

"What? That I'm English?"

"No! That I said you were silly."

"Well I am. Worse than that, I've been a fucking fool. You trusted your friend would come back for us before now."

"Uh-huh."

"You never meant to shut me up against my will?"

"All I wanted was to help you out."

"Think I can see that. So. Where do we go from here? Do y'suppose she's coming back at all? Your friend? I really don't want to hike out of here alone if I have any choice. I'm not fond of playing hide-and-seek with drunks and crazies."

"I'll hike out with you, if she doesn't come this Saturday."

"Hey, you're on. You know the way?"

"I've spent every summer here since I was born."

"What day did y'say this is?"

"Didn't. I think it's Thursday."

"So would'y'take me home again? For one more go?"

"When can I start?"

He snickered. "Y'get off me, we could help each other up out of this hole."

"Sorry."

"Not required. Come on. Give us a hand." Warm hard hands placed in mine with kindness.

Halfway along Bright's Creek we met the Jeepsters. "Whoa," said Tommi. He whipped the camo hat off my head onto his own. When they got close, he put his arm around my waist and waved. They waved back. "Am I learning?" He held the pose until they disappeared.

And then we walked. When we reached the bridge, I lay on the warm slivery wood and watched the bottle-shaped bottle-green shadows of trout in the pool underneath. The trout under the bridge always grow biggest, big and streetwise as hell. Nobody catches *them*.

Tommi lay on his front and watched them too. So damn splendidly polite. Steal a glance at him from time to time. At the lowering of his eyes, the sweet availability of his cheek. He's slick and wary as a trout himself.

Sense the balance of terror shifting. I'm afraid of him. Why?

He's only being kind, like back in the hotel. When he was sick and crazy and knocked me off the porch, I knew he was out of shape and maybe dangerous, but I didn't feel like this. How can I be afraid, and *desire* him as I do? What if he suddenly took his barriers down? Then I'd get what I wanted.

What if I got everything I wanted, and didn't want it?

What if I had sex with him and didn't like it?

Not to change the subject, but I saw a newborn mouse once with no mouth. Izzy kept a colony of spotted mice for years, and peddled 'em to local pet-shops. Good money. As with everything else, some were born defective. This one was blind and pink, warm and hungry as its littermates. They were all nursing, and it had no mouth. No sign of one. For it, there was no possibility of milk. Hunger to the death. No chance of fulfillment. Next day it was gone.

Now I've known *all there is to know* about desire, all the ins and outs of it. Anyone at all can know that, by him/herself in his/her room. I know nothing whatever about fulfillment. Not even whether it exists. Could be I don't want to learn.

So wound up in myself, I might as well be alone. No wonder I was frightened; I was having a vision of hell.

Slowly we climbed the ridge, and came to Pardee Meadow. Neither of us spoke. I let us in. There was the dumb refrigerator with those trout inside. I opened it and looked. Four little stale gray withered bodies. Between the desire and the fulfillment falls the shadow. Fulfillment might be standing there behind me, so close he warmed my shoulder.

"What's the matter?"

I suppose I was crying. "I caught these nice trout, and you ran off, and I didn't get to clean 'em, and they're not going to be too good, because I've got no lemons, and you need lemons to go on trout."

He thought, and I messed around.

"You got vinegar? Vinegar goes on fish."

I did.

"C'mon. Get to work, girl."

"Why?"

"'Cause you can't do your good job on those fish and cry all at the same time; it's infuckingpossible."

"Who says I do good jobs?"

"See there? You're laughing. Clean the fish."

"You're funny."

"I," he said gravely, "am a professional clown. That's what Belshangles means, a fool with bells on."

"No you're not; you're...."

I found I couldn't tell him what I thought he was.

Maybe I had my metaphors all wrong. I fixed the fish and thought about it. Finding no mouth to one's hunger is not the same as finding milk to be illusory. I was born a zealot one-track true believer. Cry as I would, I still believed the milk was real. And he looked like the very warm white essence of it. Whether I had a mouth was quite another matter.

The trout got cleaned, scaled, sprinkled with vinegar, and rolled in flour and black pepper. The longer they sit in the flour, the better they hold it in the pan.

They looked much better with the heads off.

Then I made instant mashed potatoes with lots of milk, soaked the last of the instant onions, fried 'em up in bacon drippings, and stirred 'em into the potatoes with parsley flakes and fresh ground pepper. The trout fried brown in the oniony skillet. After all that agonizing, it was backwoods heaven. They tasted just like trout.

Tommi absorbed his quota, with multiple cups of instant coffee, and slid down on the back of his neck in the chair. "What do you do around here?" he asked.

"Kick back and enjoy it, mostly."

He looked thoughtful. Outside was dark already. And when everything got quiet, you could hear the thin, sharp, tingly cries of bats hunting the air above the meadow. "Enjoy what?" he said.

"The *place*. The woods, the creek, the lake, you know."

"If I did, I wouldn't ask."

"Would you really like to know?"

He thought for a very long time. "I might."

"Would you like to go walking with me? Oh, I don't mean now! But in the morning? And I don't mean another mad dash down the road and back."

"I think I would."

"Boy," I said, "you are in for something *won*-derful."

Tommi grinned at me quite unexpectedly, and his hair fell in his eyes.

· — ·

SO it was next to the last day. Maybe.

I jogged down and unlocked the pipe-gate after sunup; sailed my DANGER: BLASTING! sign off into the bushes.

The last dried eggs were scrambled up for breakfast. The last canned tamales turned into their pan for dinner. Close to noon we set out. Neither right nor left along the sandy road, but across it into the woods, past the old dump where the cowboys buried their garbage.

Underneath the scratchy brush the ground's still full of rusty tins and bits of crockery. Neat things in there. I used to dig in it with high hopes every summer and catalog all the antique junk I found. That's where I put the lamp that Tommi broke. He stopped, and turned the pieces with his foot. I hurried on pretending not to notice.

The trees thin out at last on a barren granite hogback, one end of the same that borders Fiddler's Valley a mile or two east. Here the other side falls away steeply to the Fiddler's Lake road, and across it is an open space where loggers piled a hill of stumps and burned them once. Over the edge of the old loggers' landing goes our secret way: around brush thickets and rock turrets, along a green trickle in a vertical braided fringe of trees.

Push through those, and you see the little water leave its moss and launch itself into the sun to join a company of thousands.

Gray cliffs! Hot sun! Down below, a glitter and smother of bright water; shouting, playing, jubilating little river. Smooth warm granite thighs and shoulders with the ice-green, ice-cold water sliding all between them. Green pools strung like a necklace on a granite breast.

Tommi had come out behind me.

"What do you think?"

"In-fucking-credible." He looked suddenly thin and embarrassed. " 'Scuse me."

"What for?"

"Oh, I don't know. The language, I guess."

"You think I never heard the word? I go to school."

We squatted on the rocks. He looked and looked.

"I feel such a prat, y'know? I said it before, but it bears saying. And this has been out here—like this—all the time I was sick. Even that's a fool thing to say."

"Been here a lot longer than that. At least ten thousand years, since the glaciers left it."

"There were glaciers here?" His face wore the sweet amazement of a really little kid, before they get all into cool and macho and other brands of derision.

"Sure. What do you think polished off the granite so?"

"Guess I thought the water did it." He gazed a while longer. "What d'y'call this place?"

"It's just Bright's Creek. After a pioneer named J.C. Bright. There's a Bright's Station up on the highway. Old stagecoach stop. You've been over this creek half-a-dozen times already, but where the road goes through, it's all flat and full of fishermen. You look at the bottom in those places, it's a solid red carpet of salmon eggs."

"What?"

"Where the dumb weekenders lose their bait. Nobody hardly comes here. I found it when I was nine. I could start to hike around without people thinking I'd get lost."

"Did'y'get lost?"

"Never."

"Like to go down there."

"We are. It isn't tricky, watch how I do it."

Ten thousand winters have split the cliff into enormous slabs and shingles. Forest litter washes down the cracks, and bushes grow there. You slide off to the left, waist-deep down one of those cracks, keeping a sharp eye out for rattlesnakes. (It doesn't do to put your hand on one.) The crack dumps you out on a steep granite slide you can still skid down on your butt, or climb up on your hands and feet; a kind of terrace, with a four-foot drop at the end. Then another steep terrace and another drop. I'd know where every hand and foot goes in the dark.

You come down on a flat-top boulder twenty feet across, between one green pool and another. Part of the water slides a shallow slippery race across the stone, but part darts underneath. The whole slab pulses with the life of the river as the water drums its underside.

I checked the approved descent route for my man.

Wild seconds passed when I felt sure he'd run away or fallen into something. But Tommi was already at the bottom, below the place we started. He lounged full-length on sunny granite, slim arms behind his head, ankles crossed, watching me with lazy half-closed eyes.

He must be really agile. Well, I *knew* he was. I thought about the man on stage. The man on the hotel stairs in San Francisco. So he'd gone off a couple of fifteen-foot drops. A subtle little slap at me for having nerve to offer him my greasy-kid assistance getting down. A man proud of his own body. Not in the bad sense, but a man delighting in himself. How it must have burned him, these two weeks, to be so awkward and dependent on me.

Almost unwillingly I went to him, and he smiled up.

"May I sit here and enjoy it?"

"It's yours as much as mine," I said.

"Oh." He shut his eyes. "I didn't know."

I did so want him to enjoy it. I wanted him to find peace and get well again. I wanted and I wanted. It didn't seem to matter what I wanted.

"Hey," I said, "I'm going to climb down there." His left eye opened, and I pointed to the next green pool downstream. "If you want me, I'll be that way."

He nodded. The eye shut.

He wasn't interested in my company.

Like that Marcella person said before the concert: "You have to come up with something that they *want*." I had no bisque dolls or rare original albums. I had nothing whatever he might want. One more warm body doesn't count.

But he liked the creek. No wonder, so do I. *Holy, Holy, Holy*. A place where the glory in heaven and earth gets tangible. I mean, were I to picture going out on vision quests, this is, right off, the place I'd come. It didn't stand or fall on my merits.

I climbed down a stone face six or eight feet high, beside a pouring, shouting fall. The pool at the bottom is a large one. The water swirls around a green bowl full of trout. Warm, smooth granite places cradle it; I could sit on any one of them for hours.

And there are potholes in the granite ledges, round as barrels and as deep, filled with clear water, but cut off from the stream. Three in a row. The farthest downstream has a sandy bottom. The sand glints and flashes where the sun hits it; I fantasize it full of gold. The next has a bottom of stones, round as eggs, orderly and splendid in a Japanese-formal-garden sort of way. The uppermost is clean and scoured bare, a smooth round cask of polished granite. In the granite are boat-shapes of a darker stone; at the bottom they appear like fish. Stone fish swimming in champagne stone, perfect mimics of the flesh-and-blood fish suspended in the champagne water of the large pool. Joy and sorrow go off in opposite directions, but when they've come full circle, each resembles the other so, that tears become the only right response.

> *Agnus Dei, qui tollis peccata mundi:* Warm stone, cool breeze bright water,
> (Lamb of God, you've taken on the sins of the world, have mercy on us.)
> Green moss, and trickling springs, *Miserere nobis:*
> (Lamb of God, you've taken up the sins of the world)
> *Agnus Dei, qui tollis peccata mundi*: Clouds of gnats and feeding trout:
> *Miserere nobis:* (please, please, your mercy on us)
> (Lamb of God, you've taken away the sins of the world, why do they look so much like they're still here?)
> Green trees, blue sky, silver driftwood:
> *Agnus Dei, qui tollis peccata mundi*
> Give us peace

· —— ·

I ROCKED through this again and again, and other things much like it. Peace and the Mercy of God. I couldn't even imagine what the Mercy of God might look like in my case. I had a horrible foreboding that I knew what Father 'Chi would say: certainly what the damn Desert Fathers and people of their stripe would say. That is: the proper gift to ask, and true solution to my pain, was to *stop wanting*.

I didn't *want* to *stop wanting* him!

I wanted *him*.

Cessation from want was not the trick at all. No *way* could I picture that as God's good gift; it looked like loss irreparable. Like I was starving and praying to be fed, and God in reply would take away my hunger pains, and leave me satisfied to starve.

Pretty cheesy mercy, I would call it.

No matter how I prayed, my pain kept growing: huge as mountains streams have washed, and glaciers worn smooth.

Lord Jesus Christ, who was once a human child,
have mercy on me.
Lord God the Father Almighty, who made me as I am,
have mercy on me.
Lord God the Holy Spirit, who teaches me to pray,
have mercy on me.
TAKE aWAY my PAIN .
1 2 3 4

I'm watching a small dark bird bob and strut along the margin of the water, so sleek and trim and self-assured. So very much the gentleman. That bird reminds me of—I can't remember who. It vanishes into the pool. A water ouzel! Hurrying to the edge, I can see it promenade the bottom, bobbing and feeding, just like in the air. Then it takes off and flies across the pool. Underwater. In privileged delight I watch until it flies away downstream. Through the air, this time. One of the world's better performers.

Further down, below a slippery granite shoulder, is the

string of potholes with the different bottoms. I like to study them, and see what other differences I can find.

The one with the sandy bottom is full of caddis fly larvae, all trundling slowly about the sand in their protective worm cases. They show no interest in each other whatsoever. When two happen to meet, they bob away in opposite directions.

In the middle pothole with the stones, there are no caddis worms. One water strider rows the surface in solitary splendor, like a Roman galley.

Try the top one. Smooth, scoured stone. Several water striders here; I count three. No. One of the three has twice too many legs. A mating couple. Whenever a single encounters the lovers, it hops on top of them. And hops as quickly off when it realizes the job is taken. Whenever the singles meet each other, the same little song and dance occurs. On. Off. Gone.

What are they? Wrong sex? Wrong politics? Wrong religion? Don't they turn each other on? I wondered what would happen if I scooped one (or both) of them in with the solitary of the pothole below. Do water striders bite? Not knowing, I left them where they were.

At about this moment, I noticed something else. Something unprecedented.

Inexplicably strange.

All the prayers had stopped while I wasn't looking. An enormous silence rested where the words had been.

I had forgotten all about my pain. It simply wasn't.

I was nine years old.

Ridiculous.

No, the world was the same. Tommi was still there. I groped around inside my mental baggage, and yes, I was still very much in love with him. Thank God. I wasn't nine years old.

Maybe instead I was a wholly preposterous romantic poser, and a little decent, solid distraction was all it took to prick my bubble.

It didn't feel quite like that.

I should go back where Tommi was. He'd been abandoned

far too long. Wasn't sure how long, it might be hours. I edged and crawled around a smooth rock shoulder which cut me off from everything upstream. The green race churned precariously close below my heels, so I didn't look up till I gained the flat rim of the pool.

Tommi stood at the top of the falls, a naked ivory statue. He had stripped to the skin. White against leaves and stone and water he shone, perilously potent, a grave-faced power out of myths and dreams.

Now here I was, no warning, like I'd been at his hotel. He hadn't meant to flash me. He'd stripped to swim while I was nowhere visible.

And there he was, too simple-proud to cringe and clutch his crotch. And he wasn't too thin anywhere. He wore about him a terrible naked human dignity, like Adam before the fall. Like people were designed to look, and never do.

The tears crept down my cheeks. One moment longer, and I would have bowed to him.

"How deep is that?" he motioned to the pool below.

I couldn't tell him. My eyes clung to his eyes in despair, away from the rest of him.

"Come on, come on."

"Not very," I faltered. "About five feet."

The harm was done. I couldn't look away from him. He was a white-hot image like a burning iron, charring slowly deeper through my mind.

He snickered. "So much for my Olympic form." He went in with a whoop feet-first and spent the next few minutes swirling around the pool with the ice-green current and yelling, "Cold! Cold!" In the water he didn't look much older than me. One of Izzy's mod friends, maybe. His hair was slicked down in his eyes: wet red satin.

"Hey, y'come in with me?"

It wouldn't make much sense to say I didn't have a suit. What did he care? I still felt stricken and tearful at the sight of him naked. Wounded, somehow.

"Come on, you!

And I couldn't strip myself. Not in front of all that beauty. He lunged half out of the water like a laughing crocodile. He had my ankles; I couldn't get away from him. Well, it wouldn't be the first time I've gone in Bright's Creek fully dressed. Somebody always falls in, accidentally on purpose. Then of course that person has to soak the rest. Once everybody's in, nothing matters. Like that now.

So we both swirled around the pool, him in his milk-white skin and me in my Belshangles T-shirt and Levi's. I showed him where the trout hid under the rocks, and he ducked down to see. He splashed me; I splashed him back. He did a lot of laughing. It was good, very good; as good as anything can be. I felt uncommonly, tearfully grateful, and tried to pray the Latin Gloria in time to the chattering of my teeth.

Bright's Creek is much too cold to have fun in for long. My clothes and shoes acted as a kind of wetsuit; he had *nothing*. I couldn't afford to be reminded. Happy as he looked, he was turning blue on the ends.

But getting out posed problems. "Hey," I said, "I'm getting out." (The direct approach.) "Want to check on something, two-or-three pools upstream beyond your *clothes*." (How's that for tactful?) "I'll be back in a while."

"After I've got them on?"

Not tactful enough. "Yeah."

I did what I said. I lay facedown on the hot stone while the sun dried my back, then moved out of my wet silhouette and did the same face up. I wasn't afraid he'd run away. I may have slept, because in dreams I lost all fear of him whatever. I gave him time.

When I scrambled back to collect him he was sitting by the waterfall, singing a high wandering harmony to the sweet rush of water. A new kind of knowledge had opened up between us; bond or chasm, it was hard to tell.

We climbed out of Bright's Creek in the late afternoon. We crossed the Fiddler's Lake road in the dusty wake of an RV full of fishermen. Tommi stared with open curiosity.

I had to look down when I talked, now. Avoid his frank pale

eyes. I'd seen him practically naked on the stage, so I thought. Untrue, untrue. His web of rhinestones obscured the truth of him as thoroughly as a crowd of 50,000 obscured me.

Tomorrow was the last day. If Skye didn't come back, Tommi and I would hike on Sunday. Very much as we were doing now, through the forest side by side. Almost like friends.

He was most concerned that nobody should know he'd been here. That suited me. Of course I meant to tell my parents where I'd been. No chance of concealing it, with the food we'd eaten. But I thought, if I played it right, they might not realize the missing groceries were enough for two.

We should wash his sheets and put them clean on the bed tomorrow. He could use a sleeping bag for one night. Bury the garbage. Scrub out the sink and bathtub super well. Check everything, especially for long red hairs.

So we came to the cabin.

"From that highway, can we hitch to San Francisco?"

"Probably."

"One thing though," he said. "If it comes to that, can you cut hair?"

"I do my brother's."

"Would'y'do mine?"

I have to look at him. "I don't want to cut your hair! I adore your hair!"

"Then I won't try hitching rides! Nobody that'd pick me up looking the way I do would mean me any good. I might take chances on my own, but if it's between butching my hair and getting us both raped, I think I know where my choice lies! Besides," he said, almost apologetically, "can't go around looking like Alice in Wonderland all my life."

"Can we put it off till last?"

"Fair enough."

"Let's get the sheets off your bed."

"Wait," he said, "I'll do it." He disappeared into the little bedroom and shut the door. He stayed for the longest time. This is ridiculous. Even a rock and roll star can get sheets off a bed in less than that. But he came out with the sheets in a bundle.

"Toss 'em in the bathtub."

He looked embarrassed. There was another small bundle in one hand. "Could you do these with the rest?" It was the shorts and T-shirt again. "You don't have to, now; I can do it myself."

"Come on, give it."

"Thought you might not want to."

"I've seen underwear."

He grinned and dropped his eyes. My God, what a look. I could just jump him. "Well," he said, "I've had underwear shredded off my body a couple of times for souvenirs, and more normal times it gets to a laundry somehow and somebody pays to have it done. But there's nothing in between, no volunteers to wash it for me. You know, I don't even know your name."

"It's Andy. Miranda, really."

"I like Andy. Never had a girl named Andy. That's a bit of fun. Can I call you that?"

"Sure. If I can call you Tommi."

"Name's Tom."

"Who's Tommi?"

He shrugged. "I don't know. The man on stage, I guess. You call me Tom."

"Underwear."

"Right," he said, and handed it to me.

So I washed the things. (B.O. indeed. Bill Graham is a scuzz.) When I opened the bathroom, Tom wasn't in the house. I had a moment's dire panic thinking he'd split on me again, and went flying out the door with the damp sheets clutched to my chest.

He was over by the barn, standing in the yellow flowers. I walked toward the meadow as if I hadn't seen.

On the south side of the little clump of firs I hung the sheets and underwear out neatly. When I turned back toward the buildings, he was gone. But from the barn I heard the sound of someone singing.

It was dark already inside the barn. It took me a while to see him, sitting on the straw-bale in the loft and watching me.

"Sorry," I whispered. "I don't mean to follow you."

"No offense. Come join me." He stretched out on his back in

the loose straw, motioning me to the bale. How funny. All I can feel is dread. "Tell me about this place."

So I tell him all I know about Pardee Camp and the cowboys, and all my days here. Again. Because the first time he was in the car and he doesn't remember.

"We had a barn like this where I was born."

"Like this? You did?"

"I was a farm lad, you must know that. What kind of fan are you? I talked about that in the *Playboy* interview. Well, it wasn't exactly like; it was tumbledown stone, set into a hillside, with a sod roof on it. But inside it was quite like this, with the earth floor and the mangers and a loft. I wanted so to sleep out in that loft, and my grandmother would never hear of it. She said only tinkers' bastards slept in barns. I left there when I was eight." He twisted around and smiled up at me. "Would you let me sleep out in the barn tonight? Promise I'll be good. I won't run off."

"Sure," I said. "We've slept out every summer with our friends. That's what the straw bed's for. Could I fix it for you?"

"What did you have in mind?" He made it sound so sexy, I ignored him.

"Oh, I could turn the other bale loose. It'd be twice as soft then." So I undid the baling wires, and Tommi helped. We laughed and threw the straw around. "Wait," I panted. "Be right back." Clean straw feels fantastic at the first, but in the middle of the night, it itches.

I ran into the house. The sun was down behind the trees, no twilight in the mountains. I found Mama's and Papa's sleeping bags. Quick, untie, unroll, zip 'em up together. Run. I couldn't imagine him sleeping in a narrow bed.

He was still on his back in the straw, singing something private, looking out the chinks in the old roof at the last of the sky. He transferred his body to the bag with what I feared was a little amusement.

"You need anything more?"

"Oh," he said, "friends to sleep out with, I guess."

I can't say anything.

"Would'y'stay with me?"

And this is what I've wanted, after all. For years. Laid out unexpectedly, like new clothes for me. If I only have the nerve to put it on. What the hell am I going to do? Run and get another sleeping bag? Say no? Say yes? Yes thank you please, Sir? Say nothing at all?

Slowly, I slip off my shoes, and climb in beside him. Just as far from him as the bags will allow. There is a real, thick silence.

The nylon sleeping bags make whispery silky sounds. I can hear my pulse against the nylon. This is not to be believed. I can hear his, too. Slower than mine. In phase, out of phase. In phase. Out. In fact, he's going to sleep. He puts off body-heat like a stove from his side of the bag. I know what I'm going to do, too. Lie here all icy hands and icy feet and rigid wide-eyed dread until the morning. Anything, I decide, would outclass that.

"Why did you leave the farm?"

"Say what?"

"Your farm. Why did you leave it?"

"My father died."

"Oh." I've chosen the wrong diversion.

"My uncles bought what would've been my share. Mother took me off to London. Well, she wasn't any country girl. She married a bloke she'd known in school, didn't wait a year. They had two daughters right off. Why am I telling you this?"

"I wanted to know."

"My stepdad wasn't a bad sort, I guess. Never had money, but he still bought me guitar lessons. Only to get on with me, too. He didn't see that he was giving me a trade. I always hated school. Mother died when I was fourteen. After her funeral, I packed up my guitar and ran away. Didn't run, really; I just walked. Well, I had nothing whatever in common with those people."

"Where did you go?"

"On the street. I played and sang for my supper. Most of four years. Greatest way to learn all kinds of things."

"You supported yourself?"

"Oh, God, yes. In London you can do that. I ate very well. See, I am a born musician. I was singing before I could talk. Making up my own little songs. I'd play any instrument I got my hands on. Grandfather's fiddle was under the bed. I had it out when I was three. Whip me, and I'd have it out again before the welts went down. Take that away, and I drummed on things: pots and pans, what have you. Make me quit that, and I danced. If you bound and gagged me, I'd have songs inside my head.

"When I was four or five, my folks drove up to town and left me in the car. When they came back, there was a crowd around, and I was singing and dancing on the car top. I can remember that. I was a natural on the street."

"Where did you sleep?"

He gave a silent little laugh. "That was never any problem either. Look. I can't say that I care much for this conversation. I'm going to change it, if I may. When you had me in your friend's car on the way here, you kissed me then, didn't you? You see, I wasn't as far out of it as you thought I was. You did kiss me?"

I make some kind of noise. A lump has grown in my throat the size of a young tennis ball. I'm discovering that I can't lie to him.

"I want to pay you back."

God help me God help me God help me, here it comes.

"I've never let a boy really kiss me."

The laugh again. "So you can start right now, with world class." He slid forward and kissed me softly, neatly, and precisely on the mouth, like a little child.

Of all the game plans I hadn't expected! I gasped and wriggled. "Why did you do that?"

"To see what you're so scared of. I don't think that was it." The next kiss was all different. Long and slow. No great passion to it, even yet. But what do I know about passion? I would have called it more like comfort. Just deep pure animal comfort.

When he was through, he drew a little breath, and ran the

tip of his tongue lightly across my upper lip. I squealed. It was no fair at all! He was a master! He was a scoundrel and a joker, that's what he was. He was just enormous insufferable fun. My hands and feet pulsed warm, down to the end of every toe and finger.

"You're virgin, aren't you? Don't need to answer that."

"I won't. And you can't know it, either."

"Yes I can."

"How?"

"T.P. Rhymer's highly educated guess. Like what I said about your kissing me in the car. I might have been a corpse for all that ride. I knew nothing till I woke up here. But I'll still say you kissed me. Am I wrong?

"So you're shaking scared I'm going to fuck you, and you'll be shaking disappointed when I don't. It's not my answer to everything, I'm sorry if y'been misled. I only asked you for a kiss. I do know how to tell the two apart."

"But, they teach kids that the one thing leads to the other, and people do things that they don't intend—"

"Perhaps," he said stiffly, "my education has been, a slight bit *different* from yours? I may not be the most disciplined creature in this world: but there are *two* matters where I've got excellent self-control; and if I do anything there, you can be sure it was bloody intended and no accident. And one of 'em is making music. Okay?"

After that pronouncement, both of us were laughing hard, and the next kiss was a very strange affair indeed, where all the air I breathed came warm from his mouth, and his from mine. Every breath we drew was a sweet game.

I was suddenly overcome with something, like a kind of dire need to eliminate all cold air remaining between my body and his. Which I did,

"Whoa," he said, "let's have a bargain here. I won't put my hands in your clothes, and you don't hump me, and we'll get along all right."

"Sorry." I whispered. Mortified.

" 'S all right. It's perfectly natural. I'm just suggesting, if you act a little less natural, you can keep it up for a whole lot longer."

That set me laughing again. I felt like saying, "What if *you* humped me, and I put my hands in *your* clothes?"

I didn't. Other gentler things were going on. And he was right, they all seemed very much like music: rhythm games between the entertainer and the entertained. Only music is confined to hearing among the senses, while this played all of mine like a marimba.

Except sight. Everything was pure deep dark. But he probably could keep it going till the dawn's early light—no doubt he could. And never repeat the same moves twice.

And funniest of all. I was grateful to him for not giving me the whole show. I had as much of him as I could handle. I fell asleep in laughter, in comfort, and in gentleness.

Chapter 7

MOST MATTRESSES DON'T mellow out with age.

Mine must be some exception. My antique slumber bag feels twice as large and sweet on top of it this morning, marvelously renewed. The loft at Pardee can get stuffy when the sun beats on the tin. The tin appears in unexpected tatters. Have to be fixed before the snow of course, but it lets in breeze and light in a most splendid satisfactory way.

The reality of these improvements took the slow route through my mind. Clean straw, goose-down bags, and the rich simple ease of Tommi's body pressed close to my back. I'd woken up in the barn

My head was on his arm. His other curved around my shoulder. His hands lay clasped in front of me, in the middle of a sunbeam. Fine, long, steel-hard musician's hands. The soft hairs on his wrist blazed incandescent, bright enough to scorch his skin.

I dozed and woke in a still shared pool of body warmth, nuzzling the inside of his arm discreetly. Paradise: definition thereof. I didn't want to wake him. Nothing in the world smells quite as sweet as somebody you love.

His sunbeam crawled away across the straw. I thought I'd have a go at turning over quietly inside his silk-sleeved arms where there'd be more to nuzzle and to look at. I got too much. His eyes were open wide. "Hello," he said.

"Hello."

"You know, if your friend should turn up early, we'd give her a bitching show crawling out of this barn with our mutual sleeping bag."

"I don't care."

"I do."

"I don't want to leave."

"Now, let's not fuss about it. We've had one good time together finally; hope you're not too disappointed with me. If y'only knew, the kissing and the cuddling are the best part of it anyway."

"I don't believe you."

"Didn't think y'would. C'mon now."

He walked beside me through the long grass to the cabin. He looked so young and well. He was beautiful. By day I knew a different reason why he hadn't broken down and made hot love to me. Not much to do with kindness. He's gay. And covering up. Mercilessly, heartlessly beautiful. Beautiful like Harlan's beautiful.

There, couldn't help it; he's gotten in my mind again. My Icons of Desire have turned on me. They're beautiful only for each other. I am a wretched dumb consumer-person; I spend money on them.

The sheets came off the fir tree nearly dry. I rolled the sleeping bags. Now every time I see those blue nylon homely-familiar rolls, I'll have this memory of Tommi in the barn. He didn't fuck me; it isn't his answer to everything. He held me close as close. What sweet question did I ask to finally win that answer? I might not ever figure out. My parents' sleeping bags are transubstantiated into shrines.

He sat at the kitchen table while I busied myself with coffee. Everywhere I moved, he watched me steadily. Unnerving. Now I can't even look at him; I'll only meet his eyes. Think how it must be to live as he does: wherever he is, some hungry person staring. I couldn't stand it long. "What are you looking at?"

"You," he said.

"Have I got straw in my hair or something?"

"No more than me. I was thinking about something else."

"Breakfast."

"No."

"Sex."

He laughed. "Not hardly. Thinking about myself, as usual. I'm quite scandalously well off, y'know. I'm on the top of my pile. I've got the whip hand now in everything I do, while I'm still young enough to relish it. Nobody would suppose I need much mercy to get by. Surprise, nobody thinks to show me any. It's what I call the 'Tommi, you are God' syndrome. And I'm not, y'know. Sure. You know.

"On the flip-side, is my image as a 'Public Sinner.' "

"Don't say that!"

"Well? It's true. I worked hard for it: 'T.P. Rhymer: by appointment, purveyor of vicarious debauchery to a society largely incapable of providing its own cheap thrills.' Everybody *knows* what I deserve: to be ragged on and lusted after all at the same time, by the same people, even. Mercy is not the currency my kind are paid in.

"Which brings me around to you. What have you imagined you were doing?"

"Oh. Rolling with the punches, mostly."

"I guess. Y'know, I hit you? Funny, considering the walk I come from, but I never hit a woman in my life before. I've not been a very charming guest. I've sworn at you. Threatened you. Run out on you. I've been ugly and terrified and sick. Really wonderful person, y'know.

"I shit and puked your floor. You cleaned up after me like

you—like I was your—I don't know what. You've spread mercy over me at every turn; when I wanted no part of it, you made it stick. And I'm touched. This doesn't happen to me every day. I don't usually cry. Oh, I'm used to following Harlan around with a towel. But I got the tables turned on me now, don't I? Tell me, what am I supposed to do?"

"I don't know."

"I don't like being in debt. You do understand what's been the matter with me?"

"Uh-huh."

"What?"

"Drugs, I guess."

"Nice antiseptic way of putting it. You can go look up 'withdrawal' sometime when you're home. Might look up 'cold turkey' while you're at it. Do you have any concept of the cost of checking oneself into some exclusive clinic, to be what they call 'detoxified'? Not to mention 'rehabilitated'?"

"Look, I don't want your money."

"Not the point, girl. Would you know how much it costs if your name is Tommi Rhymer?"

"They shouldn't charge you more because you're famous!"

"Still not my point. First there's the cost in public ridicule. I don't like to hang my head. But much more than that, is the fear that I'd not live through it. Not just my body, but myself. I don't know if you understand, but I still value myself. I may be over the top, someway, but I'm fond of my own company. I'll stand up before God the way I am.

"Not to say that there aren't things in me that need to be put right. There are *years* of things that need to be put right. But it's *me* that has to do the putting right, if you get my meaning. I'll have no shrinks and moralists and jailers fucking with the inside of my head. When they got done sweeping out all my antisocial tendencies, might be there wasn't any music left."

He studied his own long hands. "Then there's Harlan. I would do most anything, before I see him get subjected to such outrage of his privacy. His privacy means much. Harlan's very—chaste in his way."

I can only stare at him. I want to cry: the two of you are *lovers!* My friends have fifty-seven different filthy names for what you *are* and what you *do*. And here you sit, defending his *chastity*, for heaven's sake, you make me want to scream at you, I want you so!

"So I won't lock myself in any hospital. And Harlan couldn't. What's more, I couldn't quit all on my own. I've tried. I don't have the balls to hurt like that, not when there's easy means at hand to turn it off. Comes a time, you realize you're headed full throttle into the ground. The two of us have been locked in on that last joyride for some while now.

"But I didn't plan on you. How could I? You've gone and cleaned me out against my will. And if my conduct wasn't always very admirable or dignified, it's a pure secret between you and me. I know of no handy tables of monetary equivalents for personal benefits of that kind. How old are you?"

I want my mouth to work. No sound comes out.

He leaned across the table to cradle my cheek, slip his clever fingers through my hair. Try to raise my chin. "No, you have to tell me. This is it. Come on."

"Fourteen."

"Oh, God!"

He looked perfectly wasted, like he was going to cry. In fact, his eyes were swimming. I want to shake him, punch him, anything to make him stop.

"Wait! I'll be fifteen on August 9th! That's only next week—" (No better, laughing and crying at the same time.) "—In a year I'll be sixteen; I'll have my driver's license, and never need a friend again to take me anywhere, and in three years' time I'll be eighteen—" He just groaned. "Well how old did you think I was?"

"I don't know; guess I didn't think. Sixteen maybe."

"Please."

"Please what?"

"That's only one year's difference."

"What do you know? You're a kid."

"Kid yourself!" I cried. "You're a bigger kid than I am!"

"Do you have any idea how well paid I am to stay a kid?"

"Keep talking."

"No! You don't know me. You don't know what I'm like, or what I've been."

"Funny. Bill Graham said exactly the same thing."

"Graham?" he said suspiciously. "What about Graham?"

"We met him at the concert. We wanted him, when he went backstage, to tell you—well, how much we liked you. He said we couldn't really, because we didn't know you, really. And you might snore, or have B.O. or something, we didn't know."

That made him laugh. "Graham said that, did he? Son of a bitch. Wait'll I get my hands on him. Still, he was right. He was being funny, but I'm not. And you don't know."

"Tell me."

"No."

"Come on."

"What d'y'want me to do, tell you dirt and run you off?"

"Sure. Go ahead. I dare you to!"

"Oh, God. How did I end up in this?"

"You fell down in the street by my car."

His silver eyes flashed. "That wasn't nice!"

"I didn't think so either."

"Oh, you are a one, you are! You deserve anything you hear."

"I haven't heard anything, yet."

"Okay! Vital statistics. Okay? Thomas Peter Rhymer. Born August 20, 1953. On a farm in the north. Place you never heard of."

"Try me."

"Eildon."

"Oh no!"

"What?"

"You're *not* named Thomas Rhymer from Eildon!"

"Yes I am!"

"True Thomas lay on Huntley Bank,
A ferlie he spied with his ee,
For there he spied a Lady bright
Come riding down by the Eildon Tree—"
"Shut up!"
"Harp and carp, true Thomas, she said,
Harp and carp alang with me—"
"Shut up!"
"For if you dare to kiss my lips
Sure of your body I shall be—"

"In a pig's arse! I'm sorry, but I don't expect anybody to know that shit outside of Britain. Must I come all the way to America to hear that?"

"I'm sorry."

"But my name *is* Thomas Rhymer from Eildon. There've been people named Rhymer about Eildon for a thousand years, and not a few of 'em have got the lack of forethought to name their children Thomas. My grandfather was another. Satisfied?

"All right. I'm twenty-nine years old. Twice as old as you, plus one."

"The books all say you're thirty."

"They lie. Won't be thirty for two weeks yet. Oh, and my papers say I'm thirty, too. But I'm not. I changed it. Forged it on my baptismal records. Long time ago."

"Nobody adds to their age! Actors take years off."

He shrugged.

"Why?"

"You don't want to know that."

"Yes I do."

"No."

"Try me."

He looked away. "Let's just say, there are some people in some situations, feel a whole lot less guilty if somebody's fifteen instead of fourteen, like you yourself found out with me just now. Now it's years too late to change it back. I don't think you know what I'm talking about."

"Is that how old you were?"

"None of your fucking business how old I was."

"Lucky you didn't draw someone who wanted you twelve instead of thirteen."

"Tell me about it."

"I just read the papers."

"Well I don't, if I can help it."

"You're still bitter."

"No I'm not. Learned a lot from that. Went into it with both eyes open. Then I got bitter. I was walking around with all this self-pity, like I was ruined. Like I was some kind of victim. I thought this..." He cast around for words. "...this person knew it all, and had me, and was set to use me up, like a raft of others. One night I got real brave and looked him in the eyes. I was amazed at what I saw reflected there."

"What?"

"My own fine face. I was the one and only. I'd had that poor clown in a slow fire all the time, and never knew. He was the victim. I was something else. I never been anybody's victim since. Except maybe my own."

"Who was he?"

"Agent. In London."

"Still your agent?"

He looked perfectly aghast. "God, no. Wrong kind of agent, anyway. I did some, well, modeling when I started out." His eyes fell, the smallest perceptible gesture of sadness. "I was really pretty once." He raised them to mine again. "You still like me?"

I nodded.

"Afraid of that. So, where was I? Twenty-nine years old. White male. British citizen. Education, almost none. Occupation, professional musician. I'm a damn good one, too. Give me an hour with an instrument, I can entertain you on it. A week or two, and I can play it well."

The whistling kettle squealed. I delivered Tom his second round of instant coffee.

"Assets. I'm a millionaire. I guess you don't care. A hundred times over, if my taxmen don't lie. That much again in contracts, maybe. Other assets. One country house. You should know all about that. One London flat, which ain't bad, really. Two big Mercedes which run, as a rule. One Ferrari which don't."

"Painted desert camouflage."

"I bet you got that poster of me in it on your wall."

"You bet."

"I loathe it. It's a piece of shit. Never been married. Never been arrested, strange enough. No diseases. Pretty strange too, I guess. Been taken to court twice."

"What for?"

"What kind of fan are you? Come on."

"The kind who'd rather hear from you, than from some scuzzy magazine."

"I bet I got you this time. All right. A pair of society ladies, rich as the devil, shared a London town house for recreational purposes when the husbands weren't around. The husbands weren't fools. They hired an agency to document the dirty on their wives. So the detectives posed as a security outfit and approached the ladies directly, offering to burglar-proof their fancy place. They ate it up. Plenty about that house to tempt a thief all right; but what scared them was their husbands might come spying.

"Long and short of it was, they paid their own husbands' men to hang a camera in each room, like a bank."

"Sounds more like Watergate."

"No lie. They got footage of half-a-dozen parties. Some titled men. Some foreign VIPs. But the one they showed in court had a very exclusive guest and entertainer list. Me."

"Alone?"

He shrugged. "*Retrofit* was the new release. The ladies were partial to musicians. Besides, I was nobody. Damn lawyers felt free to make a sideshow of me. I was hauled up for 'corrupting morals.' Witness and correspondent and exhibit A through Z."

"What did you say you were doing?

"Seeing how the other half lives. I said what I thought. I was neither the first nor the last to play their games. They should show the court those other films, and see what kind of reputations fell. Those women were my elders. The younger of 'em had ten years on me, no matter how sleek she looked. I was barely twenty-two. What's more, they were my betters. Should have been. Anyone's morals were in danger of corruption, it was mine.

"Then the ladies counter-sued with adultery charges of their own, and one of 'em had pictures of her husband kissing up to a pretty school-chum of his son's. In the middle of all that public circus, a reel of the evidence got ripped off from the court and peddled to a skin-flick magnate by 'men he didn't see and couldn't identify'.

"There were party-films of me doing an act I never did on stage for sale in every porno shop in Soho."

His hands slammed into the table. "It was the detectives themselves that ripped it off, who else? They'd got paid twice as it was for the same bit of spying; first by the husbands, and one of those chappies was rich enough to have bought Harlan's and my new little contract off of EMI and shredded it, if he so chose. The other was an MP."

"Military Police?"

He gave me a withering glare, and muttered something under his breath. "*Member of Parliament*, ya twit!

"The ladies paid 'em the second time, and they were richer. The one that wasn't titled was heiress to half the loot in Denmark. D'y'think men like that'd be above making a third pile selling a peep at my goods to an admiring public? If ever I can prove it was them, I'll take the last penny that they made for damages."

"Did you see the pictures?"

"I own a full set."

"Do you think it damaged your career?"

"When I was the infamous Redhead in the Sauna? The Toast of Swinging London? Sales on our album tripled in one week. Not that kind of damages. But. Harlan and me'd just made it on our own fair and proper, as musicians. Now here I was, back on the street naked and for sale. I'll let myself be fucked to get ahead up to a point. But fuck me and make money off it, I'll have my royalties.

"Like I've had about enough of this discussion. Was that what you read in your magazines?"

"Not exactly."

"Not exactly, no. You don't get the *News of the World*. Well, you'll not have *heard* of the second suit. It was from a man, the singer of a punk band we toured Britain with. He didn't like my style at all. He called me a faggot, which I don't care for, then he tried to horsewhip me with a mike on the end of a cord."

Without warning, this is it. The word I never could have said. He's brought it up himself. "What did you do?"

"Took it away from him. Took a couple of his teeth out in the process. I thought I'd left his face more suited to his music, but he didn't agree. I got sued for battery. I pled self-defense. There was never any doubt about it, I had witnesses." A great hole opened in the conversation.

"And are you?"

He studied me with calm pale eyes. "What?"

"Gay."

I nearly choked. His calm expression never wavered.

"Now I am pretty sure," he said, twisting his empty coffee cup around this way and then that, "I understood what my punk friend meant by the word he used. But. I am not at all as sure I know what you might mean by yours."

"I guess, that you like to..." I couldn't force it out. "That... well, that you sleep with men instead of women."

He shook his head. "Anybody who has been around me for as much as twenty-four hours knows, I got no objection whatever to balling women. And I've got 'em lined up at my door for the privilege. Any man in my position does. All I have to do is call out 'Next!' That's honest. I'm not putting on. That should take care of your question."

It didn't, of course. Because the question wasn't "Gay"; I don't know what that means either. It was Harlan and Harlan and Harlan, with his glorious thicket of black hair like a midnight forest a person could get lost in, and his twenty-four-carat eyes.

"But you've slept with men and women both."

I've touched something; the eyes aren't calm anymore. "What's all this 'slept with'? You think I do it in my *sleep?* Use the right words! What you're talking about gets done in loos and doorways and people's offices and the backs of cars! The foot of the Nelson Monument!"

"You haven't done it there!"

"Yes I have. It's been a while."

"How was it?"

"Just wild. If you like pigeon shit. But where I sleep is private! The people of either sex that I still want to find around my bed when I wake up next day, I could count on the thumbs of one hand!" He jumped up and stalked off in a fury. Made his circuit of the front room. I'd about given up and gotten tired of listening to him kick the furniture, when he stuck his head back in the door. "I've slept with you, as a matter of fact. What do you make of that?"

No chance to tell him. He raised his voice and rode straight over me. "The truth, maybe the pity of it, is that most people will lavish almost any kind of obscene privilege on the person who knows how to turn them on."

"Will you?"

"What?"

"Lavish stuff on people who turn you on."

"Me?" Another laugh. "I was never that hard up." He flopped back into the chair. "You're still trying to find out what I am. What turns me on. What I am is pretty obvious, really: not very nice. Like it says in the song, I'll be anything it takes to wind you up. I knew what cards were in my deck when I was still at school. Sex is power. I get off on having my own way."

"With men and women both."

"Will you not give up until you hear me say it? Sure with both! Why not? Bit of fun either way, actually. Assuming the person's reasonably attractive. See, I'm not the one to write off half my audience before the show. Now what have you learned, tell me, that you didn't know? That you haven't read in *Rolling Stone*? At least between the lines? Or in *Creem*, for Chrissake?"

"That I'm not reasonably attractive."

"I never said that! For one thing, its not true."

"You said you get your way with sex. You've wanted to get out of here like anything."

"Whoa! I think I'm being seduced! Don't try that bit on me! You're way out of your league. I'm a very accurate judge of what situations I can fuck my way out of, and this is not one of 'em. You've gone and got yourself into some kind of different place with me—"

"What place?"

"I don't know. I'm trying to find out. I just know I'll have to see you home."

"You poor silly charmer! You couldn't see your own sweet self home without my help!"

He pointed a furious finger. "Don't you call me names! I didn't say I was able. I said I was responsible. And if virgin was how you came up here with me, then that's the way you'll go."

"Whether I want it or not?"

"I don't know what you want."

"Yes you do."

"No I don't! I don't think you do either. Is it fifteen minutes worth of a good time? I don't believe so. An hour or two if I'm hot, does that sound better? How about a whole fucking weekend? Would you be satisfied with that?"

Tears slid down my face in two slow steady files. "Is that all there is?"

"Ah, come on, girl! Look at me! You've had the best I've got to offer: a solid two-hour show. And all it cost you was the price of a seventeen-dollar ticket. Please, please be satisfied! I haven't meant to play hob with your dreams. You've gotten in too near, and seen what you shouldn't, and you're all turned off, admit it. It's your own doing. You didn't have to stick so close to me."

My tears are like his words, pouring out faster and faster. "You don't know what turns me off!"

"I can guess."

"Don't bother! I'll tell you what it is! One lousy thing: you think it's smart to talk so Goddamn hard! You'd tell any nasty, filthy story you could dream up on yourself—"

"That's untrue! There's many things I wouldn't tell on myself, 'cause they're not true. I never was a whore. Strict sense of the word. And I never had sex with anyone against their will. Never. You think I'm dreaming up stories, girl, you think again."

"How about against yours?"

"Mine? Against my will?"

"Uh-huh."

A long, guarded, thoughtful look, then, "No."

"I think you're too proud to admit it."

He gave a funny little lift to his chin: "Pride does have its uses."

And I screamed at him, "Not when you can't bear to admit that you might even love somebody!"

His eyes went very wide and round. "I didn't say a *thing* about love!"

"I noticed."

"*That* is a different matter. *That* is *very private.* I don't tell my private business! If I did, it wouldn't be private—just some more shit and tinsel to plaster on my 'public persona,' and titillate people like *you* into thinking you'd seen something *intimate.* And I won't do that."

"Then you shouldn't leave your bedroom door open where there are mirrors on the walls, and people like me are still standing in the bathroom!"

Outside, a slow wind combed the meadow. Fir needles sifted down across the roof. A squirrel found something worth scolding. The pot of water on the stove was nearly at the boil.

Tommi sat bolt upright in his chair like a man who'd been gut-shot and had not yet fallen over. "You what?"

"You know what I mean."

"If I did I wouldn't ask."

"Back in San Francisco."

"What?"

The kettle whistled a disaster signal.

"How much did you see?"

I couldn't answer him.

"You are going to tell, or I will shake it out of you!"

"I saw the way you kissed him."

"Oh Christ." He put his head down on the table.

"He's your lover, isn't he."

I got up to quiet the kettle, make two more cups (the last) of instant coffee. I put one close beside his hand so he could feel the warmth. It didn't move him. His cheek was glued to the Formica. If only I could stroke his hair.

"It's a bit like asking me if I'm a virgin. You don't have to answer."

The head came up. "You let me be the judge of that. I've got this damn little accountant in my mind, y'see, saying I owe you one pound of flesh. So you've set me up, and sent me up; let me go on, when it was only one thing you were after. My memory is wasted! That's the truth. I've bits and pieces of that concert. Nothing after. You could be lying all the way, because I *don't know* what I did. I have to guess. Which means you get to spy inside my head and not my bedroom this time. When the brains were passed out, girl, you surely didn't miss your share. Why is it, can you tell me why, that anybody who's got a pound of flesh coming will inevitably choose to cut it closest to the heart?"

"You don't have to answer my fool question!"

"I'm thinking maybe I do. And how about your friend? How much did she see?"

"She was asleep. I'm the only one."

Again, no warning, the blush of mischief danced across his face. There was only one word for that color. Rose. It made me think how other parts of him are also rose. I couldn't afford the memory. "Course, if it turns out the person I kissed was the boy from room service, I'm going to feel an awful fool."

"There wasn't any boy from room service."

"Didn't think there was." He's looking at me steadily. "Are you ready?"

"No."

"'Cause this is *my* answer, the way it is. Either you understand it or you don't; you hear me out.

"Well, I was nineteen by this time, been my own man for five years. That should answer another of your questions."

"Your count or theirs?"

"Mine." He gathered himself, studying his fingers on the table. "I was working at a place called Manny's, off Portobello road. Hardly quite a club: somewhere between a club and a coffee house. A lot of kids were hanging out there. Guy that owned it's name was Manfred Gilhooley."

I laughed in spite of myself.

"It's true! Manny Gilhooley, so help me, and—"

"Was he a terrorist?"

"Not at all. That's just the most Irish name I could think of when I wrote that song. But it's worse than you imagine, 'cause he's half Chinese."

"Oh no!"

"Oh yes. His old man was a China hand before the war, and when the Commies ran him out he got to Hong Kong with his Chinese woman, and the kid grew up on a back street in Kowloon. A very decent chap, Manny; he's still my friend.

"Anyway. There was an upstairs on this place with rooms in it. He lived in some, and let the others. When anyone would take 'em. There was nothing like soundproofing, and you got the whole fucking show through the floor at night. Manny had me playing for him at one in the morning after his last real gig had packed it in, in trade for my room.

"Well, I still played the streets for a living. And the noise didn't matter to me; it was done when I was. It was a steady clean bed for once. I could depend on it. Even gather a few possessions. Manny'd taken a bit of interest in me, I believe, and he didn't think too much of my living arrangements." He shrugged.

"Anyway. I was doing my act there one night. When I felt somebody studying me."

"Studying?"

"What I call it. Giving me their whole mind and *seeing* me, not just facing the stage with their eyelids up. You know? Well don't look so impressed; I can sense these things, you know. People have all kinds of senses they don't use. I have a few of those developed; that's why I'm good at what I do. It's like standing in the sun. You don't need eyes to tell you where the heat comes from."

"There must be half of every audience like that."

"Not so. I feel one or two in a small house, maybe none."

"What's it feel like in a stadium?"

He laughed and flushed. "Ah, I could tell you now, but you'd be shocked at the language. There's a few out of twenty thousand, that's the truth. Talk about what turns me on. But it's not so much fun in a way. I can't find each one eye to eye.

"But you know that business in the show where we put Harlan out on top of the crowd, and he keeps playing? Seems to me almost inhuman while he's doing that, for anyone to look at me instead of him. So if I can keep from ogling him myself, and I can't always—I like to check the front rows then, and find out who's still mine."

"I saw you do it."

His face lit up. "That was you, was it? Under my feet at Oakland? Nothing too wrong with my memory. That was you! Figures, don't it? You still think I can't sense where I'm wanted?"

"I never said you couldn't."

"You thought it, though. But the time I was speaking of. I could feel somebody's eyes like that now. Really hot on me. I looked where I felt it coming from. In back there was this young man. My own age. Black hair. And a face like an ivory angel. I didn't believe a living soul could have a face like that: I must be doing it to myself somehow, seeing him wrong. Or else he was something uncanny that had come for me. There wasn't a girl there didn't look like a dog beside him.

"I kept expecting him to vanish, or turn another way and look like everybody else. He just stood and desired me. When I finished, he slipped out with the rest. That hurt, you know: to have seen a face for the first time, and feel all shriveled and deprived the moment it was gone.

"I could have pinched myself. Next day wasn't any better. I thought 'Come on, Rhymer, can you be so lonely as all that? Y'really gone over the top when you start hallucinating lovers. Stay off the pills, is what you should do. Stay off the brandy. Get more sleep.'

"So I tried that. Friends came to hear me; brought some chicks they'd met. Everything looked normal. But two nights later he was back. I felt him, exactly like before. And after, it was every night. Each time closer to the front. I didn't need to see him. I could feel right where he was. I could have warmed myself in front of him.

"Then one night, when people went away and I came back out for my gear, my apparition was waiting for me. He'd set himself down at a table. I could see he was quite real. His hair was not like it is now. Just this expensive young dude. Tailored suit, pretty Italian shoes—and a guitar case stuck between his knees.

"I tried to pay no attention, but he got too much for me. So I turned around and said, 'You wanta talk about it?' He opened his case on the table, took out this Stratocaster—"

"The same one?"

"Come on, he's only got half-a-hundred—came up, and stuck his cord in my amp. Just like that. Never a word."

"Some introduction."

"Symbolic, don't you think? And do you know what he played? It was my own little song. My silly dumbshit song. Only when he played it, it had ornaments on it, and it had variations on it, such as I never dreamed of, like it was something rich and really fine."

"Which song?"

"Never forget that. It was 'Glass Hammer.' When I could get my jaw shut, I took my old acoustic and started to play with him, as well as I could. Some kids were still hanging out; we got a little crowd. Manny came back to check the noise, and ended playing bass on the piano.

"I was dying to see how much of my act this wonder knew, so I shifted into 'Flying Eyes,' and he came right along with me. He had fancy business all thought out for that one too. He'd done the lot by ear. We must have jammed through half my stuff. I was on a table top, dancing with the tambourine.

"And Manny said 'Look, you boys are young, but this old man needs sleep. What say we break until tomorrow? I take it, this is the nucleus of a band? You haven't introduced your friend with the axe.'

"How could I? I didn't know his name.

"But he covered. Shook hands with Manny. Big smiles. 'Oh, pardon my manners, or the lack thereof.' Wonderful head-boy accent. 'Harlan Parr. I'm a student of Early Music at the University of London.' You know how proper he can be.

" 'Pretty early music,' said Manny. 'I don't want to sound previous, nor do I kid myself that you'd be playing here for long.' Something like that. 'But when you have that act shined to suit you, I will pay the two of you twice what I am giving you, Tom.' He named a figure that was more like three. Then he turned the lights out on us.

"We stood around on the sidewalk. I didn't want to say goodbye. He said he had a flat on the other side of town. I could crash on his couch if I wanted. I said I had a room upstairs.

" 'You mean here?' he said.

"I made the bed up clean for him; spread my old sleeping-bag on the floor. It was nothing but a short break too. Next afternoon we played guitar at each other until supper, had a fine one, and talked music right down to my gig. I got to sleeping bag on my floor again. A few days of that and even I could figure out he wasn't going home.

"I couldn't believe what was happening to me. Me in my torn-up Levi's and boots, and my Levi jacket with nothing under it."

"Cheap radical chic."

He rolled his eyes. "Specially when you've ripped 'em off from the donation bin at the Oxfam shop.

"He would sit cross-legged on my bed, and me on the floor opposite, with my back against the wall in more ways than one. And we'd talk. You might think we came from different planets, but it seemed we had the world to talk about. Music. Art. How I come up with the things I write. How he learned to play. Things I'd do, if I got rich and famous. Things I'd thought, or read of, and never knew a one that I could tell it to, until him.

"We had such a time. Harlan likes to live well; he wined and dined me all over London. Places where they would have thrown me out on sight if I'd tried to go by myself. He was paying. I didn't like that. But he *had* put me out of my bed. And the pleasures of his company left me little time to go hustle the street. That was my livelihood; there was not much slack in it. I wasn't sure he understood. I wasn't even sure I cared. I could have starved to death smiling at him. And I would have been ashamed to touch his hand."

"What about his studies?"

"Down the drain. I don't think he heard another lecture. He kept up his master's lessons for a while, lute and classical guitar. I went to one or two of those with him. He'd play, and this half-blind old Spaniard would offer his criticisms. I couldn't see as there was much to criticize.

"One afternoon, I was trying a new piece I'd made for Harlan. He wanted to show me a chord of some kind, and I was being more than usually dense about it; so he put his left hand over mine, like so, and his right around to reach me on the strings. Thing about that was, it put his cheek against mine, and his arms around me.

"And that just took my breath away. I was so stuck on him, it wasn't fair. I couldn't think what he was saying. I turned and looked at him, right up close, nose to nose, as it were. And he kissed me."

"*He* kissed *you?*"

"He did. Didn't know how, very well. But it was terribly sweet."

"What did you do?"

"I kissed him back. Well, I put the guitar up first, I couldn't afford another. And he quite took to it for a bit. Then he got terrified, and cried 'I don't want that! I want to go home.'

"'Friend,' I said, 'you are already there. You can't fool me, I know when I'm wanted; and I've been watching you move in for two weeks now.'

"So he got all hysterical, and called me names. Then he tried to punch me out."

"You're bigger than he is!"

"Be that as it may. Subduing Harlan without hurting him or getting your face broke is not that easy. He's built like a wildcat, and he can be dangerous.

"By the time I got him pinned, the subduing was kind of hands-on intimate, and oh, well."

"The reason for the fight had kind of vanished?"

"Right."

He grinned shyly. "Hey, you're not dumb, are ya?"

I shook my head. "You two sure go at each other."

The grin faded. "Not all the time."

"Do you always win?"

There were signs of it reappearing. "Well that wouldn't be much fun, now would it?"

We sat and listened to the fir needles on the roof.

"That night he wouldn't go down to watch me play. I couldn't argue with him. I was all strung out. I was still so high on loving him. I played somehow. A little scared that he'd be gone when I got back. I don't know what I played, new words to old tunes. Things I made up then, or had only kept inside my head, and never spoke to anyone. Oh, what that crowd must have made of me.

"When I went back up, the room was black; thought sure he'd gone. But he was asleep in my bed. The moon shone in at the window. He was naked. I thought about him lying there, and listening to me playing down below.

"Didn't seem much point to my sleeping on the floor after that. I undressed and got in beside him. Pulled his covers up. I couldn't bear to wake him. And the next night we played Manny's, the two of us together."

"How did you live?" I wasn't ready for his tale to end.

"Oh, so well, I've got no words. We played all night. Slept the morning. Taught each other how to love all afternoon. Sorry. You wanted me honest.

"But Harlan taught me music. Just a thousand and one things about real classical music that I'd got no way to learn. And I taught him how to make the most of all he has. How to work a crowd. Took him out on the streets. We played the tube-stations and the parks."

"Was he happy?"

"Oh, God, was he. Like a kid run away with the circus. Well, you know. With that father of his. He'd had a pretty locked-down youth. I guess you don't know. Got me again, haven't ya? You want to know about Harlan.

"Harlan's father is ordained, C. of E. That's what he does now. He is also some kind of scholar or international authority on Middle Eastern history. Islamic Studies. He taught that, up at Cambridge. Whitfield Parr. You'd have no trouble finding all his books.

"Harlan's mother is an Arab lady, Christian Arab out of Lebanon. Some kind of nobs her people were, too, as near as I can tell. Most beautiful woman I ever met in all my life. I'm not joking. Enough to set you back. Well, look at *him.*

"He was their only one, and he was brought up like a prince, believe me. Harlan is a gentleman in every way. Oh, he's made himself over, to match with me. But his old man. All the most terrible things that might come to mind at the word 'gentleman' are what he is. Maybe nothing bad comes to your mind. But I couldn't spend one hour in a room with that man. I couldn't.

"Only had to meet him once. When we were first together, Harlan and me. It got obvious to his parents, I guess, that he was not going to school where they thought he was.

"Harlan drove me up to Cambridge; never been there earlier nor since. Harlan had his own car. Kids I knew didn't have cars; it was pretty much like paradise. And we were going to be honest. Make a clean breast of it. He'd settled his mind: he wanted to be a musician, not a scholar, and he was set to tell 'em so. I tried to look good; I was going to be with him. Bought me a suit. Cut my hair. We fought about that, he was letting his grow.

"Harlan's parents kept this big house, with maids and all. And they served us tea.

"Oh God, that man. His students must have dreaded him. He has these little gold-rim glasses which he takes out of a case, and a gold watch on a chain. He sets the two of 'em before him on the table.

"And he and the mother both went at Harlan from either side, on the one hand this argument in Moslem theology, and on the other your latest update on the music scene at Cambridge and the lives of the society people they all knew. Never a word of what we came to tell. But from time to time the old man glanced at me. He didn't need to say. I was everything wrong beside his son. I was the wrong class and the wrong religion. I'd come from the wrong place, and by the wrong roads, too. I'd got no culture and no education. Never mind the rest. Although he saw, believe me.

"And you know the worst of it? He has Harlan's eyes. The very same. Harlan's eyes, looking right through me, like I hadn't any clothes on. Or even any hide over my bones. And my bones were trash.

"I excused myself to the loo, and found a kitchen door I could slip out. Just walked away. I hitchhiked some; rode a bus or two. When I got back to London, to my room, I had this big new bottle of cheap brandy. I must have drunk the lot. I got shit-faced sick falling-down drunk. I wished I'd die. I didn't think I'd ever see Harlan again, not after he'd had his talking-to. I doubted he'd even come back for his clothes.

"So I don't know what time it was when he let himself in. But he found me like that. He got me up. Made me take a wash. Fed me broth. Put clean linen on the bed. And you know what? He'd left that nice little car up at Cambridge. He'd gotten home poor, the same as me.

"You say you're all turned off because I won't admit to loving anyone. Is it my pride that offends you? Let me ask. Suppose you had one truly fine thing in your life, just one. And you were living in my situation, with pressmen clinging to your trouser legs and crawling up your shirt. How would you behave? Would you hand it over to the fuckers, and let 'em kick it down the street?"

"I guess not."

He laughed and mimicked, "I guess not." When he spoke again, his voice was heavy with tears. "Well they didn't live happily ever after, did they? I have some things very terribly wrong with me. Don't ask me what they are, for I don't know. I've every reason to be good to him. I want so to be good to him. But I get high, and I get drunk, and I—well, let's just be frank. The first thing that I do is look for somebody to fuck. Probably the second as well. I find 'em too, with dismal regularity. Usually underage and female. Though I'd be a liar if I said there weren't exceptions.

"You fit the profile pretty well, in case you didn't realize, back at that hotel room. And I was right on schedule. I would have banged you in about five minutes, if Harlan hadn't got me first. No regrets."

"You said you didn't remember."

"Another of Rhymer's educated guesses. Am I wrong?"

"Harlan's estimate was fifteen."

"He leaves time for the niceties."

"It still made him flaming mad."

He almost laughed. "If he'd been really mad, I'd not have made it from that room still in your company. When he goes up in flames, the world knows. It's his Arab side. Those people have hot blood. I've nothing at all to match it.

"But I just make him sick. Physically sick. The way we've come to live is no damn good. He's tried to kill himself a couple of times. Tried to kill me, once."

"What'd you do?"

"Took him to emergency. Got his stomach pumped. Took the knife away and broke it. Whatever was required."

"Seems like you've put up with plenty from him, too."

"Well, look who's talking! You don't even know me, and you put up with me through all of this! Do I have to ask you why? What's love for, anyway? If I can't bear his pain? God knows, I've been the cause of most of it. It's all so senseless, that's what hurts. I could do without the fame. I could do without most all the money. I could do without every damn thing I've got, except the music and him."

"You told me you weren't gay."

"So I'm not. Strict sense of the word. Matter of semantics, ain't it."

"Would you say he was?"

"Who?"

"Harlan."

"I never asked."

"You've lived ten years with him! What d'ya mean you never asked?"

He raised his voice. "Because I know for sure he's one thing so unnatural, which I'm not."

"Which is?"

"Faithful."

Oh oh oh. I fell for that one.

"He'd had chicks before I met him. Pretty sure from the way he acted."

I'm thinking about ten years, about the look on Harlan's face when Tommi kissed him, ten whole years of that. I was five years old ten years ago. Most of my friends' parents' lousy marriages were shorter than ten years. I think about my parents' twentieth anniversary.

"What's the matter," he said, "I got straws in my hair?"

"No more than me."

"Well, how about it? Y'heard enough to ruin your afternoon?"

"Tom."

He looked up.

"Have you ever really loved a girl?"

"No." He's studying his hands again. The grains of salt on the tabletop. "Doesn't mean I couldn't, though."

"You never could get married."

"Why do you say that?"

"Harlan."

"He says I should, maybe. Says if I ever saw a real girl, I could stop fucking the mirror."

"What?"

"His words. I try not to think too much about 'em."

"You've talked about *that?"*

"Look, we talk about all kinds of things."

"Ever had someone in mind?"

"No," he said simply. "We were just talking."

"He'd let you leave him?"

"He didn't say that! I never would. My share of the world walks around in his shoes. Any chick that married me would have to be a very understanding girl, that's all."

It was almost sweet. Pathetic. All I could do to keep from laughing. And crying. It *was* sweet.

He giggled. "I got these fantasies about getting married in Westminster Abbey. I'd like that. A real cosmic rock production right in there with the kings and queens. Couldn't ever do it, though."

"The church wouldn't approve?"

"Wrong religion. I'm not C.of E."

"What does that mean?" (I was smart enough *not* to suggest Corps of Engineers.)

"Church of England. I'm Roman. The family up north was never anything else as far as I know. Not that they were very religious; drove fifty miles for weddings and funerals was about it. Chap Mother married afterward was Irish. They went to Mass until the changes. Once the Latin faded, they got the balls to take up birth control. But not to confess it, y'see. Or to go without confessing. We never went back. And I was an altar boy for a bit; can you picture that?"

I could, in fact. "Do you believe in God?"

"Is it that laughable? Don't you think I should?"

"I wasn't laughing."

"Got nothing to do with any church." He looked away. "It's just that, I can tell I'm loved. And I *know* when I'm loved. Everything I need has always come. The looks and skills I've got, to do what I've wanted. The people and breaks I needed to get by. The love to keep me sane.

"And some awful nice kicks in the chops, too, which I needed, every one. Never any pain, even the worst, which wasn't meant to leave me with some lesson of good. That's what I think. Sometimes, I could stand in the street and laugh and sing and dance, and weep like a loon for gratitude. Y'know? I don't see any sense to me at all, if there's nobody to be grateful to. I'd say I'm very well acquainted with the love of God. We each one do our acts in front of it, after all. There's no place else to go."

His silence grew so long, I thought he'd finished. He sighed at last, and turned back toward me with the quietest face. "What would you really want from me? Supposing you could get it?"

"A house full of redheaded kids, I guess."

He got up abruptly, and went his circuit of the front room. Not angrily this time, striding and knocking things about. When I could see him through the door he moved slowly, looked at old family photos on the wall, and out through windows. Scuffed his bare toes along the rug. He came back in and stood beside the table. "I had my tubes tied off when I was twenty-one. I never did like accidents."

It's the end of the world.

I won't stand for it! I know every turn of his head and rise of his voice. I know the smoothness and scent of his shoulder, and the taste of his mouth. I *can't* let go of him without a fight; I've chased him close enough in spirit to lock my fingers on the tail of his shirt. He'll have to pry them off now, one by one. And bust my knuckles.

"Doctors can repair that sometimes," was what I said.

"The odds on it ain't good, though. Not that I haven't thought about it. Still, I could try to have that done. I guess I might do that."

Aching silence. He didn't say it. I haven't coped yet with Tommi Rhymer sterilized: he *didn't* say the words I heard just now to me. I heard him wrong. Maybe he heard *me* wrong.

He's giving me a long hard look through narrowed eyes. "Huh," he says.

"What do you mean by that?"

"Yer crazy." He keeps on looking, so I might as well look back. "Maybe it's me should be checking out your vital statistics, now you've heard the lot of mine."

"You still left something out."

"Such as?"

"One drug habit."

He howls, "You're not supposed to say that! That's too unfair; when you're the one that's got me all cleaned out!"

I howl right back at him, "How do you plan to *stay* cleaned out? Well, it has to take longer than two weeks! From what I've heard, the odds on that are lousy too."

"Fuck the odds! I've thought of some tricks. Soon as I get back to England, I'll enlist a bit of help from Nick and Rollo and friends, and give sweet unsuspecting little Harlan a nice ride to the country. Put that big house to a decent use for once. I'm going to lock myself in with him, and watch him perish for two weeks, same as you've done with me."

"I didn't mean to watch you perish."

"Ah, you don't understand! That's the finest birthday present anybody ever handed me!"

Talk about unfair.

"You've given me my life back!"

All the love I have, I've brought him open-handed, only to watch him now, turn and pass it on rewrapped, a sweetheart's gift for Harlan Parr.

"Hey, look at me. You've given me my life back. And Harlan's too, I do believe. Once both of us have got that pain invested, we'll watchdog each other like the hounds of hell, believe me. Oh, come on! What else can I say?"

My head wags dumbly. "I don't know."

He walked off toward the window by the stove. "I could love you for it."

What? I gaped at his slim stubborn back. *What?* All this time I've strained so hard never to let that same word out. "*You* said that!"

"Sure I said it. I said a lot of other things, too. You haven't been listening."

"I was listening!"

"Why didn't you say something?"

"I was afraid you'd stop."

"I might, too." He swung toward me. "Y'know that? I might stop. But I'm not stopping yet. You have pen and paper?"

I opened the drawer in the kitchen table and took out a pencil stub and a pad.

"About that country house. It's an awful place really. I loathe it. Nothing goes on there but parties."

"You make it sound like the house in *Rocky Horror.*"

"It looks like the house in *Rocky Horror,* believe me. So..." He hands me back the paper. A funny English address. The house has a proper name, not a street number; the village is double-hyphenated and the county unpronounceable.

"Nobody lives at this address. It's not my agent's or my fan club's or my road manager's. And if anybody picks up mail there, I do. I'm giving this to you. If you give it to your girl friend or it circulates around your school, I'll find out soon enough, and you'll never hear from me again. Y'understand? Okay. Now you, for your part, are going to rent yourself a post office box. And send me the number of it, at this address."

"I'd be glad to give you my home address."

"Not now, that's not what I want. If you're going to have a lover, y'need some privacy. You don't want t'have to beat your mum to the mailbox every day. It's not dignified. Doesn't work well, either. You rent the box, okay?"

"Okay."

"You'll hear from me. And three years from now, I'll be back. Between August ninth and August twentieth. You'll be eighteen.

I'll still be thirty-two for a bit. I'll put a free week in our schedule; that's at my discretion. After that concert, you come get me."

"I'll have my driver's license."

"I'd like to ride back up here when I'm conscious. And I promise, any question y'might have to ask me, I'll have a proper answer for you." He was sitting at the table across from me again. He let his pale eyes fall away from mine. "Trouble is, in three years' time, you'll be all grown up. I'll just be three years older. It's then we may not like each other much."

I said, "I'd give that one the poorest odds I've heard all day." I remember jumping up and slamming around the table into his lap, and wrapping both arms hard around him. I guess I couldn't stand to look him in the face.

He didn't complain. After a while he began to rock the kitchen chair backward and forward. From the front legs, to the back legs, to the front legs, to the back we rocked. "You may think," he said, much muffled by my shoulder, "I got no raising. But that's not exactly true. I was well taught early to speak the truth and pay my debts. If I'm still here in three years, you could be the devil to repay."

"Tom."

"Mmm."

"How long have you done drugs."

He took his face out of my shirt. "You call that love-talk? Come throw your body in my lap and murmur 'How long were you on drugs?' Y'gotta get better than that! Depends on what you mean by drugs," he said.

"Just drugs-drugs."

"Pills since I was twelve, like everybody else. Liquor since I could afford it. I'm no drunk, though."

"You don't look like a drunk."

I get the little silent laugh. "I don't look like a junkie either. Money helps. Pardon me, but it's not anything I want to talk about. Not like pressing me to talk about—well, about those other things. You can sit down at the public library when you're home. Nice sharp head you've got, shouldn't take you half an afternoon to figure me all out, and just how slim they'd say my chances are. Never expected to make thirty anyway."

"I was thinking about Harlan."

"So was I. You wouldn't understand. God, I hope you wouldn't. But it started out as something very intimate between us."

"You could say the same for a suicide pact."

"Oh la!" he crowed, "Y'got a way with words! You're as big a cat as he is, and you're half as old. Will you put that address in your pocket? You're gonna drop it, and not know where it went."

"I'm not asking what you took, back in San Francisco."

He looked up warily.

"But what went wrong? Was it bad stuff? Or did you get mixed up and take too much?"

He had this funny frozen expression.

"Or don't you know?"

"I'm very careful with those things. I don't like accidents."

"How about Harlan."

"I take care of both of us. Him first, then me."

I imagine the elegant little bathroom in their hotel suite, the soft fluorescent bulbs around the mirror. And Harlan standing there, the same slow terror on his face as Tom's wore when he passed out in the alley. His mind like a computer fed some fatal error; crashing, dumping memory, going, going down. The only eyes to see him go, his own reflected in the mirror.

"What are you trying to say?"

"Where do you think he went, after we left him?"

His voice took an exasperated edge. "I don't remember leaving; how could I answer that?"

Maybe there was water on the bathroom floor. Maybe he's fallen in it. I see his black hair clinging damply to his cheek, to the smeared tiles of the floor.

"Would anyone else have keys to your room? I mean, beside the ones he had?"

Slowly, Tom's face rose into my view, the terrible pleading face of a scared child.

"How long would it be before they looked for him?"

"They wouldn't ever look," he whispered. "They'd know he was with me."

Nothing could prepare me for the cries that came tearing out of him. He opened his mouth, sucked as much breath as his lungs would hold, and screamed. His body turned rigid, paralyzed under mine except for a heave of ribs as he drew a second monster breath and went on screaming; all his nervous networks were shut down and reassigned the only task that mattered: pumping out his awful hemorrhage of grief.

He had no words but wordless sound, and I had no defense. It's cling to him or blow away. I clung to him. Then the screams metamorphosed into wails of *"No!"* And the *No's* into terrible words.

"What are you? Oh, no! What are y'trying to do to me? I won't believe that! I said I believe in a God of love, and I do! My God wouldn't take him off by my fool hand and leave me here behind! There wouldn't even be any justice in that! I'd be in hell! Before I'd even died, and I haven't ever done what could deserve that! All I ask, when it comes his time to die, would be to take him in my arms and go out with him! I wouldn't live one day after I knew he was gone; I'll do it to myself, I swear I will! You couldn't stop me!"

I clung to him. I knew it was true. No matter how close and hard I held him, I couldn't keep his wretched death away; it was coming from inside. Still the rush was slowly passing.

"But that's not the way it is!"

Another great shuddering breath.

"I've learned from this! I say, I always learn. It'll turn all to his good, you'll see. I'll make it up to him. I *have* to make it up to him, and I don't mean a bigger slice of a rotten pie—"

Gasp.

"I can prove it to you; just you wait! I know what—reality—what it feels like; not like this. I know why I cried like this. You should too, 'cause you were right."

Gasp.

"I'm not clean yet. I'm a long way from it. It's the horrors come on me again, that's all."

Gasp.

"But I *will* be clean."

Another gasp. No more words.

I said, "I believe you."

"Do ya now."

"Tom Rhymer, I really do like you."

A giggle crept in between one gasp and another.

"God knows why."

I said, "I bet he does."

Chapter 8

OUTSIDE, THERE SLOWLY GREW the noise of a Volkswagen van bashing past brush and falling into chuckholes.

"That's Skye!"

"Who?"

"My friend, come back to get us!"

I fell out of his lap; he made a quick round-trip to the windows. "Right. Now listen fast. If you want anything to do with me, you have to show me you can keep a secret. As far as she's concerned, we didn't get along. Y'got me? I was sick, I screamed at you, I ran off. I still might sue. It was a real shit scene."

"Okay."

He caught my arm. "One more thing. Someplace on the way, please, let me use the phone. Call Harlan. I have to know. If he's alive, he'll still be where I left him. Y'know what I mean? But I can't go walking in there and not know."

"Okay."

By the time Skye knocked he was in the bedroom, safe behind a locked door.

How many contradictory passions can cram onto a human face? Skye's belongs in the *Guinness Book of Records.* Fear, suspicion, envy, contempt, awe, desire, curiosity. She jumped a mile when she saw me. And I checked myself in the bathroom mirror before I let her in.

"How was it?" she whispers.

"Oh, just wild, if you like stale Bisquick. And instant coffee. And canned beef stew. Here's your old sleeping bag, did anybody miss it?"

She's leaning closer, still peering avidly into corners for any stray signs of the action. "I mean, *how was he?"*

"Put it like this. He says he might not sue."

"Oh."

And now look at her. She thinks she understands it all. Whereas all she really knows are her own expectations: that I'd be in "such deep shit she didn't want to know me." As for the truth, well, I'm not about to hand that over to Skye and let her kick it down the street.

I got her safely occupied turning the van. I climbed the pole and killed the power. When I came back for Tom, he'd disguised himself in every scrap of Falconer-family outer clothing he could find, hat, shades, jacket, and scarf. He didn't look quite like Tommi Rhymer the rock idol, but the effect was uncommonly peculiar. We didn't talk. I'd fastened the shutters from inside. Now I locked up.

Skye's head hit the roof of the van when she saw him.

The drive out was no problem. Skye had calmed down considerably. She'd been out and back on her own after all, no one to impress if she put on a scene. So I made faces at the sun, and pulled the visor down on my side. Actually so I could ogle Tom in the mirror on its back.

We passed the Summer Home Tract. Rustic cabins, some pretty close to the road. Cars and pickups parked between the trees. I saw Tom's pale face turn, his black glass eyes take note of how near he'd been to freedom all along, by what a slim margin of trickery I'd kept him in.

Down the ridge to the reservoir we jolted and across the dam with its motor homes and polyester retirement couples on their campstools, fishing. Up the long forested ridge to the highway and real traffic: campers chugging up the grade to Kirkwood and Tahoe. Nevada hay trucks barreling down toward the high prices and suburban sprawl of California. The trip back home from Pardee always makes me sad as anything.

Going up I see the wilderness arrive. Coming down, the woods are acrawl with tacky eateries: Kountry Krisp Chicken, burgers, seafood! And realty signs every hundred yards, Wild West Realty, Murrieta Realty, OK Corral Realty. For Sale, mini-ranches, woodland estates, 1–2 acre view lots w/water and power, financing available. Easy terms.

There's even a shopping center at Pine Grove.

Jackson from this side is crowded and squalid and hot. And beyond the hills, the valley freeways roar under a pall of smog. Miles and hours of nothing to look forward to. Just where vegging out is usually a mercy, I wasn't even drowsy. I was losing Tom.

Lockeford. Clemens. Long straight country roads and farm traffic. Nobody ever stops at fruit-stands on the way back home. I watch Tom's shades turn this way and that, and wonder if he's looking for America. We've ridden in grim silence, but there's still his last wish to be granted. "Skye," I whisper, "he has to use the phone."

"Where do I go?"

"Gas station, I guess. You'll need gas." We came to Highway 99. A sudden hustle of gas stations, fast food, freeway motels, coffee shops, all with forty-foot signs. "Go to the el cheapo place; I've still got cash."

"I don't see a phone booth."

"Phone booth is next door. So's the restroom. Look, it's the same as last time; you can't use your mom's gas card or she'll see where you've been. Here, money. They've got munchies inside. Buy some."

She's third in line to the regular. I get out, work the sliding door for Tommi. Tom. Whatever. Side by side we walk across the asphalt. I like him so much. He's barefoot, and the fancy gold slacks are grayish now. He has grandfather's field jacket over those, and his hair stuffed up inside my father's camo hat. My sister's mod cat-eye sunglasses, too. Pretty strange. But he looks like one of the family. We climbed between the parked cars, across the divider into the Texaco station where the restrooms are. The phone booth's on the other side.

"Come in with me?" he said. "I want you to hear this."

We both got in and shut the door. It was a very tight phone booth. The dark glasses fell off him. I was plastered up hot against his front, and neither of us could bend down to get them.

"Oh," he said in that gasping sexy whisper he uses on his records, "I *want* this phone booth!" We both started to laugh, just like the party-game where everybody lies on the floor, and you put your head on somebody else's stomach, and somebody laughs, and then everybody laughs, and you can't stop laughing and you can't breathe and it goes on and on. I swung my hips hard into him and he gave this smothered yelp of terminal anguish.

"C'mon, be kind," he whispered. "I gotta make this call. Your friend'll come looking in a moment." He got the receiver in between his ear and mine; I dug for change.

"Information: what city please?"

"San Francisco."

"Please hang up and dial again, Area Code 415, 555-1212."

I dialed it for him.

"What city please?"

He said, "San Francisco."

"Go ahead."

"Number for the Hotel Montor, please."

She gave it to him and I dialed it. We had to put more money in.

"I'd like the room number for a Mr. Harlan Parr."

A terrible long silence. What if he's gone. And all the laughter and horseplay were nothing but the one last cigarette for a condemned man. Tom said he'd die. Where can he even go to do it, without his Harlan waiting? Will we have to drive him to a lonely death and put him out? He can't even show his grief in front of Skye.

I never prayed for anybody's health as I did now for Harlan Parr's. I prayed as if he were my own lover, and my share of the world walked around in his shoes.

"Here we are. Sorry to keep you waiting; it seems Mr. Parr changed rooms yesterday."

I felt a wave of ease course down his entire body.

"I'll ring it for you."

"Right." It must have rung a dozen times. "Answer the fucking phone, Harlan."

There was a click at the other end, and a very quiet "Hello?"

"Harlan."

Dead silence now.

"Where are you?"

"Phone booth."

"Where?"

He covered the mouthpiece. "Where am I?"

"Stockton."

"Where's that?"

"Never mind!"

He uncovered the mouthpiece. "Never mind."

"Who's with you?"

"Never mind."

"Are you in some hospital?"

"You got a tracer on this phone?"

"Christ, no. What do you take me for?"

"Everything I can, as a rule. You know that. Are the cops looking for me?"

"We never told 'em you were gone."

"In two weeks? I could be dead!"

"You're not."

"True enough. But, I meant, about the night I left."

"Tom."

"What?"

"I lied, love. I never phoned anyone."

"Well. I think we might discuss that one in full." He lowered the phone. Covered it. "He should have, though," he breathed against my mouth. "He was right, y'know that?"

We began to kiss. I got his jacket zipper down, and wriggled in against his shirt.

"Better not do that," he said. "I might get aroused." Another stage voice, the low soft very male one. *"You want a guided tour of the Mecca of Love?"* He already was aroused. Like our two nervous systems were hot-wired together.

A little tinny voice said, "Your three minutes are up: deposit one dollar and seventy-five cents, please." I have to laugh. This is the full red-hot fantasy trip at last, with all our clothes on, in broad daylight, standing up in a dusty country phone booth outside Stockton.

I paid. He got the phone back.

"Hey. Harlan."

"You're with somebody. I can tell."

"No lie. Look. I want you to tell me you didn't ship my clothes."

"Not all of 'em."

"I need, like an ordinary coat, and something to put my head in. Okay?"

"Is that enough to do you for the next two weeks?"

Tom giggled in spite of himself. "It's enough to do me up the back stairs to your room, y'silly fart! You know that door in the alley? Have the stuff down there in..." He covered the phone. "How far are we from him?"

"Two hours, maybe."

"Harlan, what time have you got?"

"Two thirty-five and—twenty-seven seconds."

"Be out there at five o'clock. Straight up."

"With pleasure."

"I bet you didn't even miss me."

A dry laugh from the far end: "Com'ere and say that."

"See ya."

Tom hung up the phone. He embraced me tightly. I still got a glimpse of his face; it was split into a grin from ear to ear. Though his eyes were screwed hard shut, a tear leaked out from under the wet red lashes of each one. I bet no Renaissance master ever pictured ecstasy that way. Shows all they knew. I saw a man experiencing proof positive of the existence of a loving God.

After a time, he dried his eyes on my hair. "What I've been trying to tell you, after my own fashion," he said quietly, "is goodbye. That's my life on the other end of that phone. And I'm going back to it now. I have to, no choice, just like you've got your family and your school.

"It's not such a bad life either. I won't have you thinking that. It's a lot more normal every day than you'd suppose. Belshangles doesn't have a manager; I pay myself to do that job. I'm a good businessman, believe it or not, when I'm sober. Like my grandfather in that respect: no schooling, but I drive a hard bargain.

"He was a famous man: old-time fiddler in the north, my grandfather. It was the coming of the radio finished him. Took his audience. People all went to American jazz. Fewer and fewer cared to hear the stuff he played. He had to farm to keep himself. But I've gotten even for him, haven't I? Every time my music makes the charts I think, I've turned the tables, haven't I? I've got a desk in an office with secretaries—"

"Male or female?"

"Female. All right? And half a dozen telephones—"

"I bet you wear a gray flannel suit."

"I do. And I go to business lunches."

"What do you do about your hair?"

"Tie a black satin ribbon in it. Have you still got that address?"

"In my jeans."

"Promise me you'll take it out before they're in the wash? Then make a copy, and hide the two in different places. Come on, I'm serious; I don't even know your last name."

"It's Falconer."

"Shut up! I've got a very selective memory, and I won't remember that. Don't you understand? I'm only trying to have confidence you'll do as you were told. I don't want to know who you are, or where you come from, or what your dad does, or even if you have one!"

"He's a Stanford professor."

He stared at me incredulously. "Well. That ain't half bad, is it? Huh. For Chrissake, girl, haven't you taken a clear look at me yet? I'm a vain, ignorant, posturing cock-rocker! Tom Belshangles Rhymer! Aside from the obvious, what ever would a professor's daughter stand to gain from associating with me?"

"About the same things as a professor's son, I'd guess."

He looked absolutely dumbfounded. He tried to speak a number of times, thought better of it, and finally said, "I suppose you play guitar?"

"A shit-lousy electric bass."

"Well you can't have Nicky's job."

"I don't want Nicky's job."

He sighed and hung his head. "Lemme try again. What I don't want, what, with my ego, I couldn't stand, is to be a tired old queen still looking for you in three years' time, if, having come to your senses, y'don't want to be found!"

"Don't call yourself that!"

"Well, it made you listen. Now if y'get off me, I could open this door."

"Sorry."

"Sorrow not required. There. I've said it all. Won't be any more 'goodbyes' in the car. Try to talk to me, I won't answer. When you put me out that door, don't call my name. 'Cause I can't look back. Do you understand?"

"I think so."

"Can y'go on liking me?"

Back in the car, Skye had finished the Hawaiian Potato Chips and was working on the Hot-n-Spicy Pork Rinds. Nobody spoke. She looked as curious as hell. Ten miles of valley freeway later, Tom's face disappeared from my mirror. He slept like a child for the rest of the ride.

Altamont Pass: west out of the Valley. The heat begins to give way, and the wind to rise. On the slopes a spindly host of power company windmills raise long arms to greet it. Livermore Valley is five degrees cooler, and the last steep pass beyond it breathes the cold salt-breath of San Francisco Bay.

On the Bay Bridge Plaza we parked the van and waited. Tom was awake and watchful in the back. I pointed to the dashboard clock; he nodded slightly. We sat till a quarter to five, then began our final run. I paid the bridge toll. Evening fog was piling up behind the hills and pouring through the Golden Gate, but on the Bay the sun still glittered. I saw whitecaps, anchored freighters, the hundred white-and-colored triangles of a sail regatta.

Here was the Broadway exit, first one in S.F. I even remembered how to find the Hotel Montor. He hadn't wanted us to drive him all the way; Skye circled toward our alley entrance. We pulled in at a fireplug down the block.

I let him out. He'd taken off all the things that didn't belong to him: hat, field-jacket, sun glasses. He looked approximately as he had when he ran off into the dark two weeks before—silk shirt, silk slacks, no shoes. Only much dirtier. And healthier. Not many people on the sidewalk. Fortunate. Oh, but he was shocking with that fiery mane all down his back. One young man in earrings stood at ravished attention as he passed.

Like he said, there were no more goodbyes.

Tom walked to the corner. As he rounded it into the alley, he began to trot. The car rolled forward, and for a moment I could see. Halfway down the alley a trim little figure lounged against the wall. He had a black coat folded on his arm, a cap pulled far down on his cloud of dark hair. Like the photo on the back of *Holy War*, he was studying his watch.

Tom's trot became a run. Harlan saw him coming now. Sweet God of Mercy, what a look. Even with his shades on it could count for arson. The two were together. Harlan swept the coat around his lover's shoulders in one swift practiced gesture. The cap went over his bright hair. They vanished into the building as if they'd never been.

All the Pardee things he shed went onto me still warm.

I am going to be a black-belt equivocator by the time this all blows over. In just the next few days, I bet, I'll have a lifetime's practice in the art of stonewalling. Starting with Skye. All the way home.

Lord Jesus Christ, have mercy on Tom
Lord Jesus Christ, have mercy on me.
Lord Jesus Christ, have mercy on Tom.
Lord Jesus Christ, have mercy on me.
Lord Jesus Christ, have mercy on Tom.
Lord Jesus Christ, have mercy on Harlan.
Lord Jesus Christ, have mercy on me.

Skye dropped me at the Stanford Student Union, I gave her all the rest of the money, only kept enough for the phone. Papa answered.

"Hey."

It was the phone booth scene on instant replay.

"Where the hell are you?"

"Phone booth."

"Where?"

"Tresidder."

"Stay right there, we'll come and get you."

"C'mon, it's all of four blocks."

"You might disappear on the way."

"Don't be sarcastic."

"Where have you been?"

"Pardee."

"What?"

"Pardee Camp. You can go up there and look. I ate a lot of food. I accidentally broke your bedside lamp by mistake. I've got on clothes that come from there."

"Why?"

"I was cold."

"No! *Why were you there?* How did you *get* there? How did you get *back?*"

"There was a lot I needed to think through." (True.) "I guess I needed privacy." (*Really* true.)

"That's no excuse!"

"Right. It's a reason. Are the police out after me?"

"Police, sheriffs in four counties, descriptions of you nationwide, you name it."

"Papa, look. I love you. I'm not lying. I love everybody, and I'm very, very tired. Please call the search off while I'm walking home." That's basically all I had to say. To anybody. They couldn't read my mind.

The next ordeal to face was my own room.

Childish, shabby, claustrophobic. All that glitter stuff. Tommi's face and Harlan's. Fragments without meaning, scissored up for sale. The really real was what went just before the shot or after it, when they stopped holding their collective breath. The talking, jiving, scuffling. Making music. Making love.

It wasn't the kiss that ruined things. I'd thought it might. It was only an image among many, one with Harlan's wicked witty eyes appearing slowly over the rim of his dark glasses, or Tommi cradling a plastic coffee cup across the table, the freckles coming out across his nose. No, what really trashed those sleek commercial session shots like a floodlight shone on all their undeveloped film, blasting, leveling every sexy image down to gray, was Tom poised naked above Bright's Creek Falls.

Every time I went to enjoy them, he glimmered up in memory, brighter and brighter, till nothing else remained. An Icon of Desire all right, not tacked on anybody's wall. Not rolled up in cellophane at Tower Posters. Not for sale at any price. Inside my head, the only place.

· — ·

MAMA: You're taking down all your pictures.

ME: You can tell.

MAMA: I'm sorry.

I pull the glass-headed pins from another poster. Bring it down. Roll it carefully around the rest. "Why? Why should you be sorry? They're my pictures."

"Oh, you took a lot of joy in them. And there was always something simple I could buy you, that I knew you'd like."

"Well that was then, I guess. This is now."

Whoa. Cliché City.

Silence lasts while a couple more come down. Tommi in dreadlocks. Tommi and Harlan looking like secret-sharers.

"Was he such a disappointment to you?"

So that's what she thinks. Touching, kind of. I see quite suddenly, the fact I can't tell her the whole truth doesn't mean I can't still be kind. I wouldn't have known it two weeks earlier. I learned that one from Tom. Inside my head, the only place.

"No, not at all! I can't tell you how wrong that is. He was wonderful. But this isn't. I'm growing up. I can't buy reality. I'm sorry too; I loved every one of them. I still do, in a way. Its just time to take them down now."

"I guess you did need privacy," she says.

"Uh-huh."

· — ·

THEN there was the little chorus of whispers among my friends as one or another slept over at my house and saw her first bare walls: *"Oh my God!* Have you seen her *room?* She's taken it *all down!"* I could think about Tom's quiet mouth and level gaze under pressure, and bear up through that time in relative good cheer. My withdrawal symptoms came on later.

He was right. I could go to the library and look up everything they had on drugs. And bisexual guys. Then I could begin a long, slow slide into the Slough of Despond. He only jollied me along to get away. If he felt free to laugh and cuddle with me at the end, it only meant that he'd been getting closer to the door. Closer to safety and Harlan, and a shared needle, probably.

But do I really think that? No.

Essential now is understanding. I *do* have his number. Literally. Copied on two slips of paper, one under the felt that lines my jewelry box, one at the bottom of my track-ribbons. It did *not* go through the wash. But do I have a real message for him? The same question Bill Graham asked us, and I still don't know the answer.

· — ·

THREE months later, almost to the day: the phone rang. It was poor old Sandy Malmquist (whom I've known since kindergarten), long distance (big fifty miles) from Santa Cruz. Her mother has invested heavily in rental beach houses, which they fix up, paint up, whatever, two weeks of the year. She was in one now, and Sandy wanted peer-group company.

Another four-parent Kalifornia Kid with more loose money than the law allows. Dead giveaway: her name is Malmquist and her mother's name is Nelson. Her father lives on Maui. I never get invited there.

I said "yes" before I asked Mama if she trusted me. She said, "No!" but put me on the Greyhound with my homework anyway.

I must have made one lousy fun companion. Practically catatonic. On a misty-bright and balmy flat-calm California winter weekend at the beach, with the Boardwalk amusements in full swing. On the Twister twenty-seven times. On top of the Ferris wheel, where you can watch the young wet-suited dudes look macho surfing ripples. On the carousel in its glass pavilion, where kids laugh and whoop with the calliope, catch the brass rings and pitch 'em at the painted clown's mouth whirling by. Some go in, some don't, same as it ever was.

While I go through the motions on full auto, wholly absorbed in puzzling over Tom. I need to send him something all expressive. We ate the hot dogs and the cotton candy de rigueur. Turned up our collective nose at the crummy beach clothes, and read our way through the whole bumper-sticker shop.

Just my mood, I guess. Some of those things I normally find funny. Now all I can see is this litany of nastiness and tears:

"Fuck you very much." "Ass, grass or gas; nobody rides free." "Have a nice day, asshole." Etc., etc. All the "I heart this" and "I heart that's" looked so inane, the inevitable "I don't give a shit what you heart" seemed a breath of good stale air.

About the only one which made me smile (always has) was *"Damn, I'm Good!"* Bald-faced, innocent self-satisfaction. It didn't set out to discomfort anybody. It reminded me of Tom. *"See, I am a born musician. Give me two hours on any instrument, and I can entertain you with it; two weeks and I can play it well."* That wasn't pride; it was almost humility. I don't think even the Desert Fathers could have objected. The only thing about himself which never gave him any pain was his gift of music.

The Sin of Pride acknowledges no gifts. Pride is always lying. It says, "I'm so good, I need no help."

Tom was screaming to be helped.

What on earth does he need to hear me say? Not "Take me, I'm yours!" The walls of the maze he wanders in are built up of the bodies of young girls just waiting the word to lie down and roll over. Getting younger every year, in relation to him. Part of him is still fourteen and growing old. If one more flying fuck had been the remedy, he wouldn't need to send to California for it. What an awful, sad reward for being beautiful! Worse for a child-man with a loving heart than all the heroin, cocaine, amphetamines, cheap brandy, expensive brandy, and whatever the hell else he could find to be on.

Of course, the very worst kind of industrial-strength pride says, "I'm so bad, no help can save me."

The man I remembered might loathe himself for a fool and a prat, so mired down in destruction he saw no way of pulling free. But he still went on gamely doing his act before the love of God. It was the only stage he knew. I longed for him not just to *feel* good, but to feel *good,* to have hope in some gentle future, if only growing old in peace beside an aging lover.

I bought the *"Damn, I'm Good!"* sticker, and carried it around all the rest of that day rolled up inside a small brown paper bag.

· —— ·

THE homework got done all right, and left behind in Santa Cruz. So Monday I cut school to do it over. That meant a free afternoon.

About a mile south of Campus on El Camino is a private mailing-address place. To tell the truth, I was a little scared of the regular Stanford Post Office. Scared if I rented a box there, everyone would know. Scared they wouldn't rent to me at all, because I was underage. Scared they'd know what I wanted it for, and laugh and point. General all-purpose scared. I figured a private mail drop is the place for clandestine love affairs. So that is where I went.

They rented me the box, in the middle of a wall of others: about as big as a lunch-box, with a number and a keyhole and a little see-through glass in front. They didn't ask how old I was, but I still felt embarrassed. I said I was a fan club. Rent was less than I expected.

Then I biked back, not to Stanford, but to the South Palo Alto Post Office. It is more anonymous to send than to receive. From a separate location especially. I had the address from under the felt on the bottom of my jewelry box. In there with it was the apology he wrote when he took off on me the third time, spindled and wrapped with a little treasury of long red hairs salvaged from his sheets.

I'd typed it on an opaque airmail envelope, my handwriting not to be trusted. Inside went the folded bumper sticker. Now my new mail-drop address got printed on the back, and again, with fanatical care on *two* cards inside. I checked it all multiple times, and sealed the envelope.

Maybe I licked it too wet. Or not enough. Maybe it wouldn't stick. The envelope was quite opaque, privacy assured. Held up against the sun to see if everything was in there, nothing showed. I resisted the urge to tear it open. It disappeared inside a canvas hamper at the post office. Airmail to England is only forty cents.

Then began the Agonies of the Damned. The moment that cheap tacky bumper-sticker from the Santa Cruz Boardwalk lay in the mail beyond recall, it seemed so obvious how inappropriate it was. Unfortunate and dumb in every way. Inexplicable. He'd probably take it for a brag about my own good qualities and be completely turned off cold. Twenty-twenty hindsight.

I'd never hear from him.

Why couldn't I have waited on him? Found out what it was he had in mind? Bugger what I had in mind. *He's* the important one. Maybe he'd be vaguely perplexed, and pitch it, and make whatever use of the address he first intended. That's hoping for the best. One week to England, say, and one week back. No sense to check the post box for at least two weeks.

Two weeks and one day, the little glass showed empty darkness. Two weeks and two days, three days, four days. Three weeks. One month. You know the greatest act of blind faith ever made? A second month's rental on that empty box.

One month and a half, maybe. Close to that. The glass is filled up, gray, from top-to-bottom and side-to-side. Oh God, tell me *it's the wrong box!* No it isn't. Tell me I've left the key at home. Nope.

It's a good-sized mailing envelope, heavy, not manila, but a gray slick-sleazy foreign paper, utterly, entrancingly un-American. Pasted with a raft of canceled British stamps, and addressed to me in a hand I recognize. You know my whole life's greatest act of conspicuous luxury? Biking home with that envelope unopened.

And nobody's home but me.

Inside is a pulpy gaudy English magazine like a foreign *Us*, or *People*, only a little worse, with a picture of some punk chick on the front. Careful now. If my bumper sticker was obscure, his magazine might be the same.

Start at the front, and study every page. The index. No mention there of Belshangles or Tommi Rhymer. Ads for funny products. Titled socialites. Incomprehensible politics. Lots of that. TV shows I've never heard of. Unfamiliar busty starlets and badmouthed comics. A long string of jokes I can't get. One joke I am afraid I *can* get: the whole magazine. There's nothing in it of interest to me whatsoever. It's a return shot for that wretched sticker.

So it came down to the very last page but one; and what looked like a standard feature, a "funny picture of the week" sort of thing. A concert photo, Belshangles on stage. It was an indoor club-type venue, a low wide stage with a ramp projecting from it, a place for Tom to dance.

"The English," said the caption, "have always loved their entertainers."

Two little fan club chicks have come over the edges of the ramp at him. One's nailed him just below the knees, and the other just above. The upper one has her cheek against his thigh, and a face of pure bliss. And there he is, arms flung out for balance, wide-eyed and open mouthed in (as near as I can tell) a screech of appreciation at getting grabbed.

Underneath, it said "For the gentleman's own assessment of his talents, turn the page."

On the last page of the magazine another photo, the continued story. The girls are still half-on the ramp, but they've let Tom go. He's headed back toward stage: a quick teasing look over his shoulder, red hair, arms, legs, hips all going. Beyond him I can make out Harlan crouched into his Strat, playing for dear life.

And across the butt of Tom's black sequins, pinned very ostentatiously below the belt, is a white bumper sticker, reading very legibly in big block letters *"Damn, I'm Good!"* like a lady's favor on her true knight's sleeve.

First I laughed until it hurt, and then I cried. I rolled around on the rug and yelled. I was never so glad to be alone in a house. I pulled the staples and took the pages out. Then I got a folder, wrote T.R. II on the front, put the pictures inside and positioned it on the corner of my desk where the former T.R. folder had lived for years.

It was a genuine game we were both playing: not me playing, say, field hockey, and him playing strip poker. We were both playing *Ping-Pong*: pinging and ponging away, co-operative as anything. And the ball was back on my side of the net. So I thought. Turned out, it wasn't. Wishful thinking checks the post box every day. Scarcely a week's passed, I haven't hit on anything to send him, when a second envelope appears behind the glass. A small, thin, slick gray envelope.

Inside is a sheaf of papers: bills from a gym, a bodybuilding place in London. Several months of someone's private workouts. Name and address of the person billed are neatly scissored out.

I get what it's all about. He wants me to know that he's still clean. His health means much now, like Harlan's chastity, and he's working hard to keep it. I get a sudden laughable picture of Tom all bulging and muscle-bound from pumping iron. I know just what to send him.

Next day I biked to Movie Memories and bought the illustrated script of *Rocky Horror Picture Show.* I found the place where Dr. Frankenfurter first shows off his "artificial man with muscles and a tan" to Janet, who says, "I don't *like* men with *too* many muscles" (my sentiments exactly), and he replies in campy outrage, "*Well!* I didn't *make* him for *you!*" That page got cut and posted off to England. Beautiful. My hero, T.P. Rhymer, staying clean against the odds. Fuck the odds! I wondered what close calls he'd had, what triumphs and what disappointments.

Had he driven Harlan to the country, like he said, and "cleaned him out?" Of course. And how had he survived it? Did Harlan swear and fight and try to run away like Tom had done? Had he wept and puked and starved, and gone to crash in the bathtub? Did Tom leave him his all-important privacy to suffer in? Or did he hold him fast regardless until his anger was worn out, then kiss and wrap his sickness in a lover's comforts? I liked to hope it was possible.

But it's not my business.

Semester grades come in at school, and mine are good; not quite straight A's, but good. So I mail 'em to him. I wonder what he'll make of that. Stuff I read about the English school system sounds so foreign, I can't decode the basic terms. Tom walked off from that school system like everything else belonging to childhood when he was fourteen.

The reply was remarkably prompt, one page torn cleanly from a pretty book of English nursery rhymes. On side 1:

When land is gone
And money spent,
Then learning is
Most excellent.

Now he *would* think of that: him with his millions and his back-street education and his funky country house. I turned it over to side two:

Tom, Tom, the piper's son,
He learned to play when he was young,
But all the tune that he could play
Was "Over the Hills and Far Away,"
Over the hills and a great way off,
And the wind shall blow my topknot off.

Tom and his pipe made such a noise,
That he pleased both the girls and boys.
And they all stopped to hear him play
"Over the Hills and Far Away,"
Over the hills and a great way off
And the wind will blow my topknot off!

I know that wind! I'd say we're very well acquainted: none other than the hard, cold one which blasts more growing space around the heart. Not even an unwholesome feeling, once the shock wears off. *And*, I know what I need now (Mama's sewing is a pile and a tangle; in the end I have to ask her for them): eight glass-headed pins, *all* different colors.

Quick, back to my room: get out the *"Damn, I'm Good!"* photo, and pin it meticulously to the wall above my bed, with

"Tom, Tom, the Piper's Son" beside it. Only then I notice, Mama's standing behind me.

"You're in my room."

"Tommi again," is what she said.

"Oh, Tommi still."

"I thought you couldn't buy reality."

"Can't. Somebody gave him to me."

"Somebody important?"

"To me, for sure."

She sighed. "All right. I won't ask any questions."

"Good."

"It's just that, well, I liked Tommi."

"Uh-huh."

"He looked like he'd seen the bottom of the barrel and knew the way back up." (If only she knew the half of it.) "I wish you could have held on to Tommi, until you were older, and the fantasies could turn into a real man for you."

I have this wave, this regular tsunami of elation crashing on my head, like I've won an Oscar, the Kentucky Derby, a Fulbright, and the Irish Sweepstakes all in one. Two really splendid words which no kid ever gets to use, all grownups gain immediate rights to with the territory. My time has come to say them.

I say them.

"We'll see."

Acknowledgments

The author gratefully acknowledges the sources listed below for permission to reprint song lyrics and prose passages used in this novel.

"Behind Blue Eyes"
Words and Music by Peter Townshend
Copyright © 1971 (renewed) Fabulous Music Ltd.
Published by FABULOUS MUSIC LTD.
Administered in the USA and Canada by Spirit One Music (BMI)
All Rights Reserved.
Reprinted by permission of Alfred Music

"It's Only Rock and Roll (But I Like It)"
Words and Music by Mick Jagger and Keith Richards 1974
Lyrics Copyright Sony/ATV Publishing, LLC
Reprinted by Permission of Sony/ATV Music Publishing

"Nothing to Fear"
Words and Music by Danny Elfman
Copyright © 1985 LITTLE MAESTRO MUSIC
All Rights Administered by SONGS OF UNIVERSAL, INC.
All Rights Reserved. Used by Permission.
Reprinted by Permission of Hal Leonard Corporation

"Pictures Of Lily"
Words and Music by Peter Townshend
Copyright © 1967 (Renewed) Fabulous Music Ltd., London England
All publication rights for US and Canada controlled by TRO-Essex Music, Inc., New York
Reprinted by permission

"One Way or Another"
Words and Music by Deborah Harry and Nigel Harrison
Copyright © 1978 Chrysalis Music and Monster Island Music Publishing
All Rights Administered by Chrysalis Music Group Inc., A BMG Chrysalis company
All Rights Reserved. Used by Permission.
Reprinted by Permission of Hal Leonard Corporation

"The Black Stallion"
Walter Farley
Copyright © 1941 Walter Farley
Reprinted by permission of Random House LLC, New York

"Tarzan of the Apes"
Edgar Rice Burroughs
Copyright 1914 A.C. McClurg & Co.
Reprinted by permission of Edgar Rice Burroughs Inc.

"The Island Stallion"
Walter Farley
Copyright © 1948 Walter Farley renewed 1976
Reprinted by permission of Random House LLC, New York

"Tarzan the Invincible"
Edgar Rice Burroughs
Copyright 1931 Edgar Rice Burroughs
Reprinted by Permission of Edgar Rice Burroughs Inc.